VILLAIN

By

D. W. WILSON

ISBN-13: 978-1539393450

ISBN-10: 1539393453

I dedicate this book to George William Wilson (Jingler), 1931-1998.

CONTENTS

The characters within this book are fictional, the storyline is fictional – the author expresses this. However, there are some true stories incorporated within in this book. This is to give insight into a world that many people have only heard or dreamed about. Whilst I have taken a back seat for many years, a story and its characters, their plots and their scandals unfolded in front of me, and what I have tried to achieve is to climb into the mind of the villain. The villain portrayed within this book becomes the best at his chosen criminal path, from start to finish. I hope this book opens up your eyes and your mind.

PROLOGUE

A town stands on the banks of the River Tyne. In its heyday, North Shields was one of the most notorious towns in the world – its clubs, pubs, its people, were all part of its signature known throughout the Commonwealth. The cosmopolitan peoples of North Shields put this small seaman's town on the map, notorious but loved by those who dwelled there.

I would like to introduce myself. My name is David Wilson, I am a British merchant seaman and an offshore crane operator. I have worked all my life at sea. I have been a doorman and a taxi driver whilst home on leave throughout my life, and I have also worked on construction sites, so I bet this leaves you wondering why I wrote a book called *Villain*. Well, I was brought up in a town full of them as a young child and I also had dealings with them as a man. I remember the bars, the clubs, and the nightclubs my town was once in abundance of, and the characters who also lived and drank there and most fitted the description of this book. They were criminals like my father and his friends; their wheeling and dealing, their scams, their robberies, believe it or not taught me and my brother the life I describe within these pages, because the people who were in my life from a very early age were the real-deal Goodfellas on my doorstep.

I recall a conversation I once had in my taxi. The woman I picked up was once a prominent policewoman in North Shields; she mentioned my father's pub and many others. Her hatred towards the men of that era was apparent, she clearly disliked and still bore deep resentment towards them. Her words – North Shields was full of villains. I thought about this. There are them and there is us (the police and villains). The book's inspiration came from us and their teachings throughout me and my brother's lives. It taught us one very valuable thing – it's far better to know the dance than to participate in the dance, because some wolves work alone whilst others need a pack.

The unknown villain is far more dangerous than the known. I should know, my teachers were Goodfellas.

Welcome to my world. Welcome to *Villain*.

1

Them and Us

Davy and Jimmy ran past the Havelock; two scruffy kids. The year was 1981, a warm summer's evening. The noises of drinkers echoed from the pubs that once dominated their town. It was going to be a busy Saturday night. The jukebox from the Alnwick played Billy Ocean (*red light spells danger, can't hold on much longer because red light*). The boys walked quickly along the road, scanning the area for the police cars that were trying to catch them, listening for the distinctive diesel rev and screeching. The breaking crews of North Shields born to become villains, expected to be indoctrinated into the world of villainy. Welcome to Shields, where being a villain was a way of life, the police were the enemy, and kids followed in their father's footsteps.

2

The Beginning – Clive Street

⸎⸎⸎

The bottom road of North Shields once bore host to the Commonwealth, predominantly Commonwealth seamen from all over the globe, of all colours and all religions. North and South Shields, at one time was the most cosmopolitan area in the whole of Great Britain, the Arabs on the south side (sand dancers), to the cod heads on the north and the Irish in Jarrow and Hebburn – a very rich variety of people. The first ever riots took place in North Shields between the Maltese and Yemeni communities. The Maltese chased the Arabs to South Shields and the turf war was settled. Lines were drawn, hence the nicknames were given for each town.

The author's father was brought up in Clive Street along with his uncle Jimmy. They were known as the Vellas. Their stepfather, a Maltese gangster known as Manny Vella, ran most of the prostitution that was rife within the Clive Street quarters during the 1930s and 40s. The author's grandmother worked as the Mama San, providing for and keeping the girls that worked her bar in check, so to speak. The area was notorious worldwide, and many criminal activities took place in the once-slums of the bottom road, from loan sharking to murder. The place had its history and its vagabonds. Joe Block – a book was written about him, and a film by Thomas Hadaway. His involvement with the Maltese Falcon (Mafiosi of Malta) and the twenty-six murders (alleged) that took place there. Also, his involvement in three murders in Clive Street (also alleged), and that's what we know of his loan sharking with Manny and other Maltese Mafiosi that resided in Shields. This was all relayed back to the author as a kid growing up, along with the referral to Joe Block as Uncle Joe. The author would like to add that this was always referred to as a mark of respect. To call this man Uncle was the way it was in the days of his father, a whore's son, who had many aunts and uncles as the communities back then all looked out for one another.

The author recalls one story about a woman they called Auntie Dolly, a blonde lady with a scar right across her face who worked Clive Street back in their father's childhood. She was working for a vicious pimp, a Maltese gangster – his name was never told to the author. One day she said she was leaving; she was going to settle down with a customer she had met and they basically fell in love. The pimp was furious; he couldn't lose a money maker like Dolly, so he resorted to getting a knife. He slashed her face and cut her breasts, cutting her nipples off. The author's father saw what happened and was comforted by the lady. The author's grandmother was furious about what had happened and told her husband, Manny. The pimp shortly disappeared. Rumour has it he was taken care of. Only the circle of whores and gangsters of North Shields know how and where and what happened to him, and they are all dead now, but one thing the author can say because of that event, the blonde millionaire with the London accent and the scar on her face who came to visit and stay in their home in the 1970s, the author grew up to call her Auntie Dolly.

Pictured, the Golden Fleece. Joe Block is standing in the doorway behind the three ladies with the children.

An old man chased a purse being pulled along the pavement outside the Mariners. The two little boys played the trick – as the old man approached they pulled the cat gut some more. The old man looked at the purse with a puzzled look. "What the hell?" he said, as the German barber Rudy Seiber came out of his barber shop on Borough Road and shouted at the two boys behind the police box that once stood on the corner next to the Mariners pub. Old Joe Block waved his fist, cursing both the boys. "You wait till I tell your father, you little shits."

Jimmy and Davy ran towards Stanley Street West.

Villain Land – Clive Street, the slums.

To give a villain a badge as a taxi driver, the villain will always be the villain. Not many people know how to work a system but with old-school values and a strong code of ethics, the villain portrayed within this book becomes the best at his business, and money and wheeling and dealing come naturally. The unknown villain is far more dangerous than the known. A loner, a shark among the shoal, has been unleashed on the Tyneside streets.

3

Debt Collector

Davy Walker sat on the outskirts of Whitley – a drop-off. Another eight-pound fare, another happy customer.

"Thanks. The banter was great, hinny," said the woman as she received her change, exiting the car.

Davy was halfway through his shift, waiting for a phone call to take a break and go do business. It was all part of his day-to-day life, the knuckle dusters in the glove compartment of his car ready to earn their keep. The job, a smack-head, a bad gambler who hadn't paid their bill and needed to be given a reminder. When they do not pay they get dealt with, and the enforcer was none other than a humble taxi driver who came at them with a cheerful smile. A phone call, and an address would be given and instruction on what the mark owed. A simple transaction dealt with violence, and this twenty-stone enforcer knew exactly how to make a withdrawal using brute force and cunning. The unknown face, unknown to the crowd, the most dangerous individual. Unknown in the world of drugs and extortion by the abusers and misfits that have become victims of their own habits.

The phone rings.

"Hello," said Davy as he set the car in park at the Royal Quays. "Yeah, yeah. The west end."

The address was given – one of the many typical terraced houses that make up the west end of the town in the Newcastle suburbs. His name was given, and his description.

"And he thinks he is getting a deal. Just knock twice on the door, pause, then one more knock. He thinks it's a coke deal. Smash him up, Davy. There are no kids there so it should be pretty straight forward. He owes two hundred and fifty quid as well."

Davy knew he had to do this quick and clean. As he put the plotter into brake, he headed towards the mark. His adrenalin pumped as he proceeded to the address given.

Davy reached the destination. A Ford Fiesta sat outside the house the mark was in. Davy parked the taxi around the corner as he walked slowly around to the address given. Two knocks and a pause, then the third, all as planned. Davy had both hands in his cardigan pockets as the door was acknowledged.

"Hello, mate. Hi," said Davy.

"Come in, come in."

The music was playing in the background (*ahh, ahh, ahh, ahh, staying alive*) as he guided Davy into the living room, unaware of the hit that was about to take place. A blonde bird (woman) sat on the settee, drunk as a skunk, wearing a flowery dress with her cleavage on display.

"We have been partying all night," said the mark.

She looked at Davy as the mark said that with a disgusted look. "No, I have been waiting for a taxi. You said you were going to phone. That was an hour ago. You lied to me. There's only me and you here. You said a party with loads here, you sack of shit," said the woman, directed at the mark.

"So how much you wanting, a Henry?" said Davy.

"I still want my taxi, I told you a bloody hour ago. I am not interested."

The mark started sniggering as he started counting out cash on the table. "Well, more like a two fifty," said the mark.

"You like your sniff (cocaine)," said Davy as he quickly pulled his hands out of his pockets, putting his arms around the mark's neck in a sleeper. "Only trouble is," said Davy as the mark went limp, "you should have paid your bill."

Davy gloved his hand with the brass knuckle duster and quickly got to work on the mark, beating and smashing his fists into the mark's face and body. The blonde watched in total amusement, a sinister smirk across her lips, and it looked like she was getting turned on by the events unfolding.

"Sorry about this," said Davy, picking the money off the coffee table and his mobile phone. "He won't be partying anymore," said Davy, directing his conversation at the blonde woman.

"No problem, he's an idiot anyway," the woman responded. "He's been trying to bed me all night, giving it the big fella (man)," said the blonde, spitting at the mark and cursing him.

"Well, I am leaving now. Nice to meet you," said Davy.

The blonde stood up and kicked the mark in between the legs. "Well I am not staying with that," said the blonde.

A bloodied mess lay on the floor, unconscious. Davy put him in the recovery position. "I don't want him choking to death," explained Davy.

Davy walked out; the blonde followed. He wiped his fingerprints off the door handle before he slammed it shut.

"Can you give me a lift?" asked the blonde, after Davy dot punched the mark's windscreen on the Fiesta with his tungsten.

"Can't follow me now, fool!" muttered Davy. "See you around," said Davy.

The woman looked at Davy. "Please, I need a lift. You obviously have a car."

As she walked with him, trying to keep up, Davy just stated, "I don't know you and you don't know me," as he walked around the corner in the street where his car was parked.

"Look, please," she said. "I do not want to be around here if he wakes up. Please give me a lift if you can."

Davy never breaks protocol for anyone but he agreed to her demand eventually, and the best solution to get a witness out of the area was important, as it was wise. "Just this once. Don't ask questions, understood?" said Davy, jumping into his car.

The blonde agreed. "Ok, thank you," said the blonde as she climbed in the front passenger's side.

With that, Davy and the blonde calmly drove away, using the side street as their getaway. When Davy eventually got out of the area he took the woman to her address. She leaned over and kissed him on the cheek, saying she wouldn't mind taking him to bed. Davy looked back and said, "Not today, love. That idiot might know where you live."

She replied, "No, no. I just met him," explaining he was trying to bed her all night. They only had coke (cocaine). "But that was all, he doesn't even know my name," she explained. "He met me in Newcastle on the drink, said he was having a party. I stupidly accepted. Look, please come in, I just need a good shag," said the blonde.

Davy said, "Perhaps I could come in. After all, you did kick him in the balls."

He put the plotter in the glove box and finished his shift, sending a text stating, "Done."

4

Making Bread

Sitting in his cab on a Friday evening, Dave was counting his money. *The fares will start coming fast*, he thought, holding his throwaway untraceable mobile he kept in his cowboy boot. The gear was stashed in a magnetic box in his wheel arch, a perfect set-up. The punters he picked up, especially the young ones, would ask, "Do you know anyone for a bit of carry-on, mate?"

Davy just nodded. "How much, fella? A Henry £250 pure, a gram £100. He doesn't do halves so the choice is yours." The lads would hand the money as a fare and the gear would be in their change, hands always kept low.

Davy only carried three wraps at any one time so the transactions were simple. Green was never carried; it stinks and is a pure giveaway – a mistake like that attracted the wrong attention but it could be obtained. Sometimes gear would be buried in locations all over Tyneside, a drop, so whilst working that particular area Davy could easily get access to it. His cunning and his careful planning was always important to him whenever he started a late shift, especially the weekends. E and acid, the party drugs, were always on demand, especially for the gay scene. Davy often dropped homos off in this area and their appetite for the party drugs was in constant demand.

It was business to Davy. He personally found the homosexuals disgusting; he had no hatred towards them, he just didn't like the way they flaunted their sexuality. As a heterosexual he found it unnatural. Being raised on the streets of Tyneside made him like that. His money was also weight in his eyes; he always made sure he had only £100 on him including his float, so money would be bagged in waterproof jiffies and also buried in numerous drops, carefully surveying the area at all times, making sure he wasn't being watched, his locations always changing to avoid routine as in his eyes this led to displacement.

Davy was far too wise for any mistakes, especially in the world he was working. Far too many rats, far too many untrustworthy characters were within the Newcastle underworld. Their code of honour, the old-school values, were lost since the murder of a hard man in Wallsend. Not many carry the code of ethics in this day and age; the twelve-year-old on the BMX in his black hoody is the new idea of gangsta. Their Valium addictions make them perfect recruits for any firm operating within Britain. Now they obey their drug lords, kill at will if instructed, carry the gear and distribute the gear, all on a Halfords BMX. Not many gentlemen villains operate but Davy, he considered himself the gent. A smile, a hello, a greeting – it all helps in the world, the criminal underworld.

He still clenched on to the values instilled during the 1970s, when villains used pubs to discuss their next job, where disputes were settled in a back lane. Tyneside's Goodfellas, their code never broken. So a good teacher would provide good advice and Davy was the student all those years ago.

Sitting in his car listening to Smooth Radio, the Motown classics, the Diana Ross, Sam Cook and many more, made Davy drift off in memory of his childhood on a bottom road. He could hear the revellers, the bars, the taxi doors, the hustle and bustle of his once-vibrant town. A job comes through – Alexandra pub to Tynemouth. Davy acknowledges the job and proceeds to start his evening. Time to make money honestly and dishonestly, either way. In Davy's eyes money is money. Doesn't matter how he earned it – his motto: make fast cash.

After his fifth job he started receiving his punters for the goods. They required a Henry, a gram, twelve Es. It was business as usual, money in his hand, then a drop or pick-up to his secret stash. More money to be hidden, a grand here, five hundred there, placed in secret locations which were many. A plant pot or a garage were the preferred locations; the cash was rolling in like the waves that lashed the north pier whilst Davy dropped in Tyneside.

His woman was texting. "You going to be long tonight?"

When's this shift going to end? thought Davy. "Hurry up," he said to himself, waiting for a customer with all the time in the world. Davy always set his goal at £100 pounds legitimate and anything above that was easy money. He was up to £86 pounds for the day; two or three more jobs and he would be going home for his dinner then back out for a few hours to start his villainy. In the circumstances that this woman met Davy, there was an instant attraction. Her dark hair, her sassy look, her entire aura, how she presented herself, and above all she was on the same wavelength – a criminally minded chick with a hot body and fast-thinking brain, and she knew how to make the money. Bashing up the coke in the distribution chain, her knowledge as a businesswoman was invaluable to Davy. He called her a criminal bombshell; she could hustle and charm the Archbishop of Durham if she put her mind to it. Fate brought Davy and her together. It had been a full six months since they both met in the west end of the town; she was a twenty-five year old, Davy was twenty-seven, and their lives were more similar than they could have ever imagined. This relationship truly was fate; they bonded like Bonnie and Clyde.

5

The Loan Shark

—⸙•• ———————————— ••⸙·

Luke Stanmore stood in the living room of the first-floor flat. Jack Thompson had run his last hand at poker; he was already credited £500. He, in gambling terms, was shit out of luck. *One last hand*, he thought to himself, gesturing to one of the organisers of the makeshift casino that was situated in Percy main.

"Can I borrow a grand? I swear I am good for it."

Luke looked over to Ken. "Look mate," said Luke, "you are in five hundred already. If I lend you this it's two thousand you stand in owing me. I expect it paid back in full, you understand? No messing about this time. You owe me." Jack agreed to the loan shark's terms, his car taken on as a deposit. "You turn me over, Jack, I swear!" Luke pointed out again. "Ok, make payment."

Jack went back to the table and started playing again, watched carefully by the sharks that organised the game.

"Have you heard from the big fella?" said Luke as he lifted his hand, drinking his bottle of rosé wine.

"Nah, not this week," said Ken, gesturing to the croupier to change his deck of cards.

Jack wasn't faring well and it started to show; he was down two hundred quid and was still trying to bet high.

"At this rate he's going to be skint in half an hour," said Ken, looking at Jack sweating buckets at the table.

"All the more for me to lend. His house, his car, will be mine tonight. The fucking degenerate. When will the stupid learn?" said Luke.

Taking a long draw on his Cuban, "See the big fella's got himself a bird. Pretty thing," said Ken.

"Yeah, a real beauty," said Luke. "His work is something else. Barbed wire wrapped around the fool from Whitley's head, he lost his eye. Ken, the man's an absolute psychopath," said Luke.

"Yeah, he sure is," said Ken, "but he gets the job done, I think you would agree on that," waving his hand and pointing to the table, gesturing for another drink.

"Now it's time to call the big fella. I have some work put his way."

"What this time?" said Ken.

"This time I want the man's nose cut off," said Luke as he started to phone Lanty.

"Poor twat," said Ken, sparking up his cigarette.

Lanty Atkins was just finishing his evening meal when the phone rang.

"Hello," said Lanty as he answered. "Yeah, yeah." The address was given.

"He thinks you're interested in his car, wants to meet up. He should be carrying goods as well – if not, check his flat. A reliable source has guaranteed that it's there." Lanty was told, "There's four grand in it for you. He still owes more so take his fucking nose as a deposit, let him know he has twenty-four hours to obtain the rest or his nose gets blended."

Lanty agreed, "Yeah, ok," and hung up.

Luke put his phone in his pocket, looking over at Jack now sweating profusely. He was down £700 and still betting large; the pile was like a mountain in the middle of the table. Jack looked at his hand carefully and went all in – £300 – the last of the grand he just loaned, his throat dry and his nerves starting to show. The two other players sat at the table, suspicious of each other when the Chinese guy shouted, "Call!"

Jack really was trying to keep his nerve. This light-heavyweight boxer had been running low on luck all night and looking at the pile of cash on the table and the rings, necklaces, and car keys that also made the bounty, it really was worth the gamble. The Chinese guy went first. His hand was a flush, then the ginger gay with the 'tache just threw his hand at the table; his prize possession, a Mark 2 Golf, now the proud owner was one of these two.

The Chinese guy started to put his hands on the table as if to scoop up the riches, when Jack said, "Not so fast." He produced a royal flush. He had won one hundred and forty grand cash plus all the cars and jewellery. The Chinese guy went white; he loaned fifty from Luke and now he had to pay the loan shark.

Cheki Wong approached Luke humbly, like a quivering degenerate. "Luke, my friend, I lost big time. If you can lend me more I can win it back; I promise I can make good. You know me, I can make money. I am good, Luke. You give me money, I can win in Newcastle. Please."

Luke looked at this excuse of a human and simply said one word, "Pay. I get my money, your restaurant, I get to become a partner now. So as of tomorrow you work for me, understand? No ticket, no laundry, you understand me, Cheki?"

The Chinese man looked back at Luke and started to cry. The gay ginger guy stood talking to Ken; he was also in debt to Luke. His Nissan wages were to be handed over every month until he paid off his debt. Also, other little jobs were being put into place – a trip down to Manchester and Liverpool was his way of clearing debt. His boyfriend stood at the corner of the room stroking his beard, furious that his man lost all and still owed the loan sharks money. They both bitch-fought with each other as they left the flat.

Jack was over the moon; a win like this had set him up. He walked over to Luke. "Here, two grand, as the loan stated." Luke took the money. "Cheers," Jack said. "Luke, I presume you're going home now," Jack said. "Ken, give me a Henry (three grams of cocaine). I feel like a celebration," said Jack, putting the keeper ring on his finger. Everything else was placed in a hold-all. The car keys in his hand, he exited the flat with slaps of achievement on his back. Jumping into his minted VW Golf, he saw the two homosexuals standing on the corner, arguing like females do. "You need a lift?" Jack said to the ginger guy with the 'tache. His boyfriend with the beard just stared in disgust.

"Nah, I'm getting a bus," said the ginger guy.

With that, Jack drove off with a burst of power.

6

The Wedding Present

Saturday, Gillian Albertson's big day. She always wanted a white wedding. Malcolm Smithy (Mal), the love of her life, was to marry that morning and make her his wife; this good-looking woman with sable-black hair and sultry blue eyes had been with her man for two years. Beforehand, she worked as a stripper in Sexy Chics in Aberdeen, making money taking her clothes off for people to ogle and gaze at. Her lesbian shows, her one-on-one sex shows, all part of her act to extract as much money out of the punter as possible. Then Gillian met Mal, a fire proofer from Howdon, Tyne and Wear. Life was good for her; Mal provided her with the security she needed and today was her special day. It was her wedding day and nothing was going to stop her from marrying the man she'd grown to love.

As the time approached, Gillian anxiously waited for the car to arrive. Her bridesmaids all stood watching as the wedding car approached her home in Elgin Avenue. Perfect – the sun was shining and Gillian bloomed. Her chief bridesmaid, an old work colleague from her days as a stripper, stood next to her. "Ooooh, here it comes," she stated as the car pulled up alongside the door. She climbed in and headed to Christ Church in North Shields for the ceremony.

Mal stood at the church freshly shaven, not his usual hobo-looking self. "Have you got the rings, JJ?" said Mal as he fidgeted with his flower lapel.

"Yeah, I have them," said JJ. Blackwood was a close friend of Mal's. He was over the moon Mal asked him to be best man at his wedding. "Don't worry, I won't let you down," said JJ.

A stiff drink was handed to Mal – a vodka and lemonade. "The car's approaching, best get inside." The guys swigged their drinks and went to the altar.

The church was packed; everyone was there. This was the wedding of the year and many were there for that reason. Tom McNeil sat at the back of the church; the vows were being read and both were getting on with the ceremony. The organ played, the usual wedding banter, everyone was smiling, everyone cheerful.

The procession exited the church ready for the photos. The bouquet was thrown; a member of the groom's family caught it. A blistering sunny day in North Shields, the daytime do was being held in the Park Hotel, Tynemouth. However, Tom never obeyed rules; his attitude towards people, his whole approach to life was that of arrogance. An individual who could be described as a dirty, drug-dealing lowlife, a scumbag; he would sell to children, he would force his victims to put their wives and daughters on the game or work their debts off in strip clubs. The man, in drug-dealing terms, was the lowest of the low; a smack and crack dealer, even crystal meth, nothing phased him. Mal didn't notice Tom sitting in the back of the church; he didn't know him, nobody did apart from Gillian, a west-end lass who had a dark past she hid from everybody. Tom's intentions were certainly not for the benefit of Gillian or Mal; he had a sinister agenda at hand.

Two of his lowlife friends were sitting either side of him; a protection clause. As a fighter he was useless; he couldn't fight his way out of a paper bag. Just a dirty lowlife coward who wanted to create problems. Poor Mal had no idea that this piece of excrement was going to destroy Gillian's day.

Many years back Gillian performed in a strip club owned by Tom. She participated in a certain movie produced in the back of his sleazy club; her performance with three men and a woman was kept secret for many years. Tom had the DVDs and the pictures that would eventually lead to the poor girl's demise, his wedding present to the woman he once controlled. She eventually escaped his sick, perverted world of drugs and sex with sixteen grand of his money. Tom wanted revenge and he wasn't leaving until he got it.

The evening time, people danced and congratulated the bride; her day was looking like a dream. Her family and friends made toasts, speeches, the whole thing was just perfect. To Gillian, it was the best day of her life. "I am going to my room to get my normal clothes on," said Gillian. Making her excuses to the guests, she exited the function room and made her way to her room accompanied by her chief bridesmaid.

As she went to her room at the other side of the hotel she heard a voice, the recognisable voice of Tom in the other room across the corridor. The door was ajar. Gillian went white. "Hello, Gillian. How are you?" he said in his Aberdonian accent. "So you got hitched?"

The two men bundled her and the chief bridesmaid into the room.

"Well if it's none other than little Sarah. You ripped me off as well," Tom said sarcastically, directed towards the chief bridesmaid.

"We can scream, you bastard," said Gillian. "You disgusting, horrible bastard. My man will beat seven bells out of you. Who the hell do you think you are?" Gillian said, starting to burst out in tears.

"Go ahead," said Tom, "but I think he will be interested in this."

Switching on the TV, the DVD played.

"Remember this scene, Gillian? Three guys, darling, now that's some fucking movie," said Tom, sniggering.

"What do you want? What do you want?" said Gillian.

Tom looked at her. "Just to wish you luck and give you your present, Gillian. And you, Sarah. You can join. Remember, I know your wee (little) sister."

Pulling out his cock, he instructed the two women to suck now. He said, "You should have invited me, Gillian, you dirty slut. You stole from me, now suck."

Crying and having to perform, Gillian nodded her head. She absolutely hated this man now.

"Gillian, you must be taken on your wedding day," said Tom, lifting her bride's dress then telling one of his goons to penetrate her from behind. The whole thing took twenty minutes and Tom zipped up his trousers and proceeded to leave. "I must congratulate the groom. Don't worry, I won't tell, it's our little secret," said Tom with a sinister smile.

Gillian lay on the bed, sobbing. Sarah curled up terrified beside her.

"Open your dirty mouth, Sarah, and your sister goes on the game. Remember, you little thieving slut, I own Aberdeen."

Tom left the room, swaggering. He walked downstairs. Mal was in full flight when Tom approached him, saying, "Congratulations, pal. You married a good woman there!!" He then left the hotel. Mal, unaware of what happened, continued to celebrate.

7

A Nice Pint of John Smith's

Drinking in the bar on a Sunday evening, Jimmy Walker sat with Kerry, commenting on the John Smith's he was drinking, stating, "It's a fine pint, that is, Kez. They must have a good cellar man." Kerry sipped her half in agreement with Jimmy. The two socialites enjoyed a night out at the pub. Jimmy, a sea captain, loved his beer, his wife, and his family. "You know, Kerry," said Jimmy, "I think I might retire and buy my own pub in the next few years. I reckon I could do it, you know. I think this sailor needs to pack his kit bag for the last time and come ashore."

Kerry frowned, knowing he came out with this story every time he got pissed, then in the morning he forgot what he said and wanted to go back to sea. Time was getting on when Kerry said, "I think we should be going home now." Jimmy agreed and started to finish his pint.

Over at the pool table, young lads were carrying on when one of them started to get a bit aggressive. "It's my fucking turn. I was fucking next." The youngster stood, chest puffed out. "I am fucking telling you I am next," said the young, aggressive male.

Then all of a sudden, it erupted. A pool stick was snapped over the lad's head, a bottle was smashed and rammed into another's face. The barmaid shouted, "I am calling the police!"

When this was heard pool balls were thrown behind the bar, smashing optics and glasses. "Ohhhh," said one of the youths. "You're going to grass us up, are you?" He aimed his fury towards the barmaid.

"Right, nobody in here leaves," said the main instigator. "Nobody. Understand?"

As he screened the bar with his eyes, Jimmy, a big man and not afraid of anyone, kept silent. Kerry sat next to Jimmy, emotionless. She learned many years ago that keeping shtum was the best policy whilst in a situation like this. One of the young lads walked towards their table. "Well," he said, "you got anything to say?"

Jimmy, emotionless, stared into the youth's eyes and said, soft and low, "Why are you coming to me, sunshine? I haven't said nothing but you are coming to me, involving me, so why the hell are you coming over doing just that?" Jimmy stared into the youth's eyes, not flinching, not showing any kind of fear. The youth blinked. *Ahh*, thought Jimmy, *you are a sneaky little coward.*

The youth turned and looked at his friend as if for reassurance. Jimmy got ready, poised, waiting. The table was getting ready to be hinged and smashed into this little runt. One false move, one signal and all hell was going to break loose. Jimmy knew his power and strength and it frightened him. He once punched a man in Tynemouth and because of that the man in question became retarded. He almost killed him, so Jimmy, violence, and drink were not a good combination, and the youth standing before him had absolutely no idea what would happen if violence did erupt.

The youth turned back, facing Jimmy. Quick as a flash, the table was flipped, smashing the youth across the room. A punch landed squarely on his mate's head, knocking him clean out. Now Jimmy's adrenalin was primed; a primal instinct kicked in, everything was clear, focused. Now his predator mode was fully kicked in.

The main instigator ran towards Jimmy with a bottle. Jimmy side-stepped and grabbed his arm, almost breaking it. He grabbed him by the neck and lifted him up in the air; before the youth knew anything, Jimmy body-smashed him into a table, breaking the table in half. The youth was screaming. Jimmy quickly smashed a stool across the youth's back and punched him in the side of the temple. The youth was out cold, lying on the floor with a broken jaw.

The others started to try and run away, trying to get out of the pool area to no avail. Jimmy walked over slowly. "So you like to fight. do you?" said Jimmy.

The youths begged, "Please, please."

Jimmy just grabbed the first, pile driving his head into the pool table and flicking him away effortlessly. The other started to try running past Jimmy. Dodging him, Jimmy tripped him up, making the youth fall against the bar. The youth held the bar counter, screaming for help to the barmaid he had just threatened moments before. "Call the police! Call the police!" shouted the youth as Jimmy rammed both fingers into his eye sockets, the blood streaming from the youth's eyes and his screams of mercy as Jimmy raised his big fist and clubbed the youth on the top of the head.

Four guys lay in that pub, pulverised by a man who simply wanted to enjoy a pint. Jimmy walked back over to Kerry and said, "Perhaps I might stay at sea, this bar racket is too athletic for me." Apologising to the bar staff, Jimmy left with Kerry. "Still," said Jimmy, "it was a nice pint of John Smith's."

8

An Ear to Talk To

Gillian sat in the house checking the pregnancy gauge. It was clear. She had stressed out for weeks about the event that took place in the Park Hotel. She wanted to tell Mal but she didn't know how to. This was the man she loved, this was her husband. It would kill him and she didn't want to cause him that stress. She detested Tom; her hatred grew daily. Her whole life had been turned upside-down by her former boss, and what really made her hate the man more was the fact he had films of her in her past life. She wished she had never performed such movies. She often contemplated suicide but since Mal came into her life she was happy once again. She had found true love; a man who treated her like a woman, not an object that could be discarded once finished with.

Gillian knew of Luke; she also knew of Luke's connections. She met Luke through Mal on a few occasions. He was at the wedding. Luke told her, "Don't ever break Mal's heart." Gillian contemplated approaching Luke, but she feared Luke would tell Mal. Her head was spinning; she must tell Luke. She couldn't go to the police; she feared all her past would be exposed in a court. She needed to tell someone and she eventually decided she was going to break her silence to Luke. If anyone could help her, she was sure of one thing, it had to be someone of a reputation and a good understanding. Her whole life, and any chance of being happy, was hanging by a thread. Her decision was final and she had to confide with a known gangster.

Luke sat in his five-bedroom house in the outskirts of Gosforth. Success had brought him great riches, not bad for a lad who was brought up in the Ridges. He became a street thug loan shark from an early age, watching the old-school ways being played out in his neighbourhood. He remembered the time as a child when a police van, known on the street in 1970s Britain as a meat wagon, lay parked in his street. Swaying back and forth, and boots and crunches, thuds and slaps were heard coming from the back of the vehicle. The doors sprang open and a bloodied man was dragged from the van by the police officers who administered the beating.

"Now," said the burly sergeant as he wiped his fists, "you fucking keep out of my territory. If I catch you here again you will get more than a beating."

The man lay on the street, a bloodied mess, coughing blood. The sergeant lit a cigarette, and with a sinister tone in his voice, directed, "Now fuck off," to the mess lying at the side of the pavement. Luke watched as the police climbed into the van and drove off. One beat policeman walked away, swinging his baton, and whistled as he strolled down the street.

Looking into his half-empty wine glass, Luke blew smoke from his Cuban into the empty half. He was just about to go to bed when his phone rang. "How's married life, then?" said Luke. "You looking after Mr Smithy, Missus Smithy?"

Cheerfully, "It's fine," said Gillian with a nervous tone.

"Well what can I do you for, sweetheart?" said Luke, as Gillian was plucking up the courage to break silence.

"Can-n-n I see you? I need to talk to you. It's very important and I can't speak over the phone," said Gillian.

Luke sat upright, concerned. "You alright, pet?" he said.

Gillian said, "Please can we talk?"

"Yer, well, what about? Mal?" said Luke. "He is your fella."

Gillian pleaded, "No, Mal must not know anything about our conversation. Please, Luke, I beg you."

Luke paused awhile and said, "Ok, ok. All I am saying is Mal should be informed. My wife, Maria, she will be with me and we can talk. Is that ok, Gillian?" said Luke.

"Yeah," said Gillian. welling up a little.

"Alright Gillian, come to my home tomorrow morning at about ten." He gave Gillian his address. "Come up, sweetheart, but I still think Mal should be informed. Just saying, that's all."

Gillian said, "Thank you, I really need to talk to you. Please keep my husband out of this conversation. Please." She made Luke swear.

On that, Luke agreed and said, "Goodnight, I will talk tomorrow."

Putting down the phone, Gillian knew she had to tell someone; she had to open up her heart. The events that took place were tearing her apart inside. Revenge was what she wanted and her hatred toward Tom McNeil was growing every day. She wanted him dead and was determined to see that done.

9

The Nightclub with the Caves (The Jungle)

Sitting downstairs in the nightclub only fitting for the Tyneside criminal fraternity, Davy sat drinking his pint of heavy. The cocaine lines on the table and the smell of cannabis lingered in the air. Patric Hernandez played at a deafening volume. This was Shields; this was the Jungle, a night spot notorious and infamous worldwide – a hideout for all who were involved in Tyneside's criminal activities. A fight in the Jungle often erupted and its victims often walked away with real scars; from knife merchants, to a glass in the face. If you wanted a fight in this place, you got one; no ifs, no buts about it. A tough club, a worldwide reputation carried by the Commonwealth seamen that drank in this place.

The prostitution girls wore their price on the sole of their footwear. It was a widely known place where a sailor could pay for the services of a Shields woman for that night. Growing up around this and seeing the faces, the trouble, the vicious fights, and the business of drug-dealing, theft was engraved into every kid's mind who was brought up in the vicinity of the clubs and bars of 1970s North Shields. It was the Geordie equivalent of Goodfellas; you either joined them or you became prey to them. At one point the Ridges Mafia exceeded 100 men. You walked in their domain with intentions to create trouble, you got literally done in (beaten up).

Many a time Davy's eyes had seen victims laid out at the side waste ground, beaten to a pulp, their bloody, drunken faces, teeth knocked clean out, gashes from being slashed or glassed, from broken arms to jaws, the likes of which he could never truly explain. For a young lad to see this brutality, he knew the script on most of what life growing up in Shields was about.

Jimmy walked over with Toma. "We got some," the youths explained. "Twenty-four hour trips." LSD, acid, best ones on the market at the time. Davy took his, a full one. Toma was already tripping and Jimmy was just going into the cycle of the trip, a term used by LSD abusers to mean 'ready to party'. It took about half an hour for the effects to take place.

Davy sat looking at the floor of this dingy nightclub; the swirling colours, the acid was kicking in. A woman sat on Davy's knee and started to kiss him, grabbing his member and allowing him to play with her vagina. She was not very old and the dark lighting of the nightclub hid her. Nobody could see what was going on, nobody really cared. This was the Jungle, 1980s, and it was alive. Davy rubbed that shaved vagina most of the night. The woman asked if he would like to sit in the darkest corners, to which he agreed. Slipping out his member, she started to suck, until he exploded in her mouth. Eagerly, she drank every drop. Still playing with her inviting vagina, she leaned over and kissed him on the cheek, saying, "My husband's in bed, otherwise you and me would be doing it tonight."

Davy looked at her, off his head on the acid he had taken three hours before and said, "That was amazing."

She kissed him on the cheek again and said, "Same time next week then?"

This seventeen-year-old lad received a blow job in the Jungle and was off his head on acid, possibly one of the best nights out he ever had in his entire life. He didn't realise, but he was actually baptised into the notorious Jungle and was being ear winked into the crime crew by certain individuals that headhunted the up and coming villains in order to join their ranks. This kind of behaviour wasn't the first or the last Davy would experience. The shoreline in South Shields; the venue in Spennymoor when he worked as a floorwalker (unofficial bouncer) checking the dealers and their activities in selling E and acid on the vibrant rave generation scene; his taxation of dealers and the acts of violence which enforced his authority attracted the molls exited by a bad boy's reputation and his lavish way of giving money. Fast cars, cocaine, parties, and the lifestyle he led were very thrilling to the ordinary checkout girl, secretary, or hairdresser. To them they were given a free pass; they were treated differently. A villain and a plain Jane was a common sight in Tyneside. These girls thrived on the limelight so being an accessory to a thug was commonplace.

Davy stood at six feet and weighed in naturally at fifteen stone. His muscles bulged and his fast temper earned him the reputation of a dangerous enforcer. However, his life wasn't always like that; he was a victim of violence himself on two occasions, jumped on by two known villains in the Jungle at seventeen years of age, his eye cut open and his lip burst, covered in blood. This seventeen-year-old stood and took everything these two muppets could give and was still standing. He thought to himself as he sat waiting for a fare years later, how he waited and the calf became a bull, of his unexpected encounter with the two muppets that dared try it on in his youth. The chip shop in Shire when the main culprit stood there, his eyes filled with fear at the heavy standing waiting to get served.

Davy remembers the day well, how he rubbed the tip of his tongue against the scar he received on his top lip. He remembers how he said, "Hold the chips, darling," to the muppet's wife working behind the counter. "How's you, fella?" said Davy.

The guy took off out of the shop as kids entered. Davy didn't show violence in front of children. Dave turned to the woman serving; paying for his chips, he walked out of the shop. Seeing the guy up the street, he told the woman, "I don't need to run, sweetheart, but he better keep running." With that, Davy went to his car and drove off.

The other was even more memorable. The guy in question was out looking for opium. When he walked into a flat where the dealer proprietor lived, he took one look at Davy sitting on the settee and you couldn't even imagine what was going through his head, fear being the main factor. Davy remembered sensing this, he could smell it. It was as potent as shit; the guy knew he had to get out fast. His cheap shot in the Jungle a few years earlier was his stupidity; he wasn't prepared for the initial outcome and certainly wasn't equipped to deal with any kind of altercation. Davy stood up; the guy went white with fear and couldn't get out of that flat fast enough.

Apart from that, Davy remembered the Jungle, the funny side of that era, how he and his mate sold two girls to Filipino seamen. Their ship was in for repairs in Smith's docks. The two girls in question were virgin Jungleites – clueless of the reputation, pretty, and naive about the tough club they entered. Easy bait for two seasoned Jungle patriots at that time. Dave, with his good looks and Toma with his blue eyes and blond hair, were typical young lads from Shields. Picking up two easy birds from the then-packed bars of Whitley Bay was easy; bringing them to the Jungle was even easier. Their timid and obvious signals were an easy spot to the seasoned lads and lasses who drank in this bar frequently.

"We are just going to the toilet," said the two girls as Toma and Davy sat down in one of the many caves downstairs. The deal was done unknowingly, with the equally naive Filipino sailors. They all pooled together fifty quid; with that, Toma and Davy left, leaving the girls to unknowingly sit down and wonder where the two of them went. Davy laughed as he remembered how he and his mate sat behind the Golden Fleece pub wall across the road from the Jungle and watched the fireworks fly once the girls realised what their two suitors had done.

The year was 1986, a year when two lads from Shields sold two Whitley Bay birds to sailors. The primal instinct of making money the Shields way was taught to them; the school of life was certainly apparent with these two characters. Both lads went to the key pub,

Jinglers. After that, Davy explained the thing they did to his father, the owner. With laughter and pats on the back, the two got pissed throughout the rest of that morning.

10

The Seaside Town Known as Whitley Bay

The Olive Grove Compass club, Easy Street, Idols, Silvestor's, and the Sands, to name but a few of the bars and clubs of Whitley, a vibrant, very busy seaside town. Hen parties to stag parties, wall-to-wall fanny, this place catered for many people from all over the country. The guest houses, hotels, and the fun park known as the Spanish City, the town of Whitley Bay catered for all ages.

Every year a two-week holiday known as the Glasgow Fortnight over Easter saw many a family, young couple, or social group visit. This was ended in the mid-90s by a group of Londoners that moved into the town and couldn't stand the noise, and most importantly they didn't respect the fact that Whitley was a noisy seaside town. Before they came, complaining about noise and the North East's drinking culture could have been investigated before these people moved in – would have been the first step. Also, a smoking ban nationwide didn't help the pub trade very much either, but the early years of Whitley was an era when money could be made. Drugs and extortion were rife during this period; owners paid for the door. The protection provided was organised by the criminal entrepreneurs of that day. You paid the door, stayed safe. Drugs were distributed on the first point of contact – the door. Generally a nod or a show of how to obtain came from the door supervisors that worked the clubs and pubs of South Parade.

Davy made money, lots of money, during this period. He would often park his car, a punter would jump in, buy the goods and walk out after a drive around the block. It looked like a taxi fare, simple and easy without arousing suspicion. Business was always being made in Whitley. Tynemouth was another little goldmine; the plaza stood looking over the long sands, its roller rink, amusement arcade, and not forgetting its nightclub, Surfers, a place where the gentle goth would hang out. Before the introduction of rave party revellers, Tyneside ticked over as a place that catered for all kinds of people and many enjoyed the mind-bending drugs offered by the dealers eager to peddle their product.

Davy sat in his car listening to Diana Ross on his radio; his polished boots shone like mirrors, his feet out the door reading his paper, ogling the woman on page three. *Another fare, another customer,* he thought. Always suspicious of a new face, Davy had a sixth sense in spotting a plant. Their body movement, the eager way in which they would ask for product. The game trained many and many fell prey to the simple tell-tale signs. Generally, if someone wanted something it was a familiar face. The familiar face was given and moneys were given by the familiar face, who would then go back and give to the person making a purchase. Davy was well aware of the penalties that would be administered if he let his guard down, and fifteen years was a very real possibility if he ever did slip up, as they say, so Davy adopted a policy of ultra-suspicion. His music played loud during a transaction and hand gestures were to be made to identify how much product they wanted. A touch of the nose twice gestured a gram; ear touch, acid; nose stroke, ecstasy; touching the meter with a double-fingered gesture or single was the quantity that was needed. Davy had this enforced, visors always pulled down to give some coverage of the dealing that took place. Far better than any kind of street deal whilst doing business from inside a cab, especially with surveillance teams on constant watch throughout Tyneside during this era.

He never dropped the person at the place of pick-up – this attracted too much attention. He always chose where the drop would be, often within walking distance of the deal's final destination. Clockwork and efficiency were the key in the dog-eat-dog world of Tyneside, and being street smart was always primed in Davy's world.

The buzz of a job came through. Mariners, return trip; a deal was being made. Davy drove off to the next customer.

11

The Three Mugs

A fare pick-up from the office, Davy was en route. A busy Saturday night as usual. He hated picking up from the office at that time; it was eleven thirty in the evening, all the idiots were churning out of the bars. Fights often broke out at the rank and generally you were picking up and taking straight to A&E Rake Lane as a result.

Pulling up outside Railway Terrace, his fare, a fat-looking twat with a tattoo on his neck, climbed in. "Newcastle but pick up in Walker," said the fare with a scowl.

Putting the meter on, Davy started to drive. "Whereabouts in Newcastle?" said Davy.

"Foundation nightclub." A busy, up-market club situated off City Road on the Quayside.

"Ok."

Davy drove the Walker route. The County Hotel, a rough, cesspit bar, lay at the bottom road of Walker, a place where idiots watered. Not the kind of place you would choose for a night out and certainly not the kind of place you would want to take a fare from two skinny, dirty-looking rats stood on the corner.

"That's them," said the fat twat, gesturing towards them.

Davy pulled up. The two rats jumped in.

"How's it gan, Keith?" said one of the rats.

Davy started to drive off.

"So how's it gan?" said the rat in the back, directed towards Davy.

"Fine," said Davy.

As they approached City Road, the fork in the road turned into an orbital in order to get to Foundation.

"So you made much?" said the fat twat in the front.

Davy's adrenalin kicked in, holding his money sack. "Nah, mate!" said Davy.

The two idiots in the back started sniggering.

"You sure?" said the fat guy.

"Yeah, I am sure," said Davy.

Before Davy knew it the fat twat turned his wheel – a one-way street – almost causing the car to crash. Davy, quick as a flash, smashed the money bag off the fat idiot's head, knocking him clean out in the passenger's seat. His adrenalin through the roof, Davy spun like a cat, directed to the back, grabbing, gouging, punching, biting. The pair in the back started to scream, trying to get out of the car. Kicks in the head of the fat fuck made him slump into the corner well of the passenger's seat. Davy's elbows found their marks on the faces of the other two. A big man like that moving like an alley cat in the back of a VW Vento was unreal, but he smashed and punched the two clowns in the back effortlessly.

The door opened and the pair managed to get out, running to the corner of the street. Davy, now in red-mist rage, turned and looked at the fat piece of excrement in the passenger seat. Climbing out of his car, he slowly walked around his car. Blood dripped from his eye and with bite marks on his fists, he was like the devil himself. The pair looked in absolute terror as Davy looked at them. "I will get you, you stupid little wankers. I will find yer, you watch."

Davy approached the passenger door, opening it, and grabbed the fat guy, breathing heavily. "Come here, twat. Try rob me, you scumbag," said Davy. The fat twat's foot got jammed as Davy ripped him from the car. In a rage, Davy stamped and beat the fat guy to a pulp, smashing the door many times off the idiot's leg. Bloodied and beaten, the fat twat was ripped out of the passenger seat using his eye sockets as leverage. Dave smacked him in the face a few more times and went through his pockets.

"Now, arsehole," as Davy ripped the ring and necklace from his neck, "now I rob you, you piece of shit."

Davy jumped in his car; still primed, still dangerous. He proceeded up the one-way street with his hazards on. Davy knew he needed the car cleaned; he drove up to Shieldfield garage and wiped down his car, jet washing the blood. Davy phoned the police; he needed an alibi. If he was seen he would try and talk his story over. He was more concerned about the one-way street as he knew he could explain his story to the police, hoping nobody saw or heard what happened. He knew that the fight wasn't taped but to make sure he needed to know. In the back seat Davy found fifteen wraps, cocaine, and a mobile phone. It must have come out of the jacket of one of the rats he'd beaten up. *Class*, thought Dave as the police van entered the court, a response van equipped with tea, coffee, and a (bloody) head shrink. A cup of tea was given; the officer stated, "No, nothing has been reported. They are gone."

Dave gave complete opposite descriptions of the would-be robbers and after, thanked the policewoman. When the phone started to ring, Davy looked at the policewoman and said, "It's the wife."

A smile on her face, she said, "I will give you some privacy."

Davy answered the phone. One of the smack-heads was on the other end. "Well, well," said Davy. "Looks like you boys are missing some weight," as he thumbed up to the response officer with a smile. "Well it's all mine now, you stupid little cunt. Looks like you get fucked either way. If I see you, you get it, or your dealer takes care of you, you stupid fucking mug."

"Fuck. Look, mate, we don't want no trouble," said the voice on the other end.

Dave could hear the other ranting, "Fuck, fuck," in the background.

"Well," Davy said, "looks like you and yer fucking boyfriend crossed the wrong one this time, now fuck off." With that, Davy closed the phone.

Smiling at the police officer, he drove off. Driving past the policewoman, Davy said, "Thank you for the support, I am going home now."

She said, "No probs," and said, "see you," as Davy drove off to Shields.

12

A Party in the West End of Newcastle

Tiger Tiger, a brand new nightclub, opened in Newcastle. Wall-to-wall fanny (females), the disco music played at full belt. Davy was out with his brother Jimmy and a couple of his mates. These men, all in their late twenties, were all up for a party and a supply of cocaine ensured that they could get just that. The lap dancers to the barmaids all wanted a piece of that action, and Davy, Jimmy, and the two friends knew a little flash of cash and a line of coke ensured a cock was getting sucked that night. Jimmy, a big man, liked to survey the area; he especially enjoyed a fight, his power and strength unmatched, and only the stupid found out the hard way.

Davy stood talking to a lap dancer on the dancefloor. She was interested in a few grams and Davy was interested in a threesome with her and her mate.

"So you lick pussy?" said Davy.

"Love it," said the lap dancer. "I love it up the arse as well, and my mate, she is just as bad," she said, rubbing her hand on Davy's member.

"Well we can see what we can provide," said Davy, watching his brothers approach towards the crew (west end gang) sitting in the far corner. "Excuse me, darlin'," said Davy. He knew all hell was going to kick off and was preparing to wade in, win or lose. Davy was a primal fighter and he never left any soldier behind enemy lines. He could switch on adrenalin like a lightbulb. You could feel the tension in the air; it was going to get very nasty very soon.

Anth walked over. "Davy, are you feeling that?" Anth, also, could sense the trouble brewing. Jimmy moved closer to the biggest one, and waited to get just within striking distance. A muppet came up dancing in front of Jimmy and Davy was now on the podium ready, until Davy noticed the guy Jimmy was gunning for. It was calmed as fast as it was ignited. Davy knew the big fella, a head doorman from Newcastle, a very hard man and very much like Davy and Jimmy. He was just about to strike. Also the doormen of the club were all on edge up to that point.

The next thing, drinks were being bought and everyone relaxed; the strippers came back asking for sniff, and the whole place came alive.

"You coming back to a party?" Davy asked Larry.

"Yeah, why not?"

After the club the taxis all went to the west end, a council house outside Roman Villa. Inside, pussy everywhere. The strippers started to perform a lesbian show. On the table, a mountain of sniff was placed Davy and Jimmy were doing lines inches from a pierced vagina being dildo probed. The kitchen lay in the back; granite tops, American fridges filled with vodka, rum, Bacardi, gin; the place was a crib, money paid on tables by numerous villains. This was the Newcastle fraternity and Davy and Jimmy were right among the whole shebang.

"So mate, how you doing?" A friendly voice was directed towards Davy.

"I am fine, fella. Lovely place you got here. Being in the life really has rewarded you," said Davy.

"Yeah, well it has, but I still don't trust many around here," BFG said. "There are far too many little rats wanting a piece of my action, and far too many think this is for the taking. Once in a while they get a reminder, randomly," said the BFG. "Keeping the flock in check, we wolves have to."

"So," Larry said, "You're a Goodfella."

"And if Larry Towns says that, then that's good enough for me." BFG chopped a line up on the granite top. "You want one?" he directed to Davy, a Hollywood he had just made.

"Yeah, why not?" said Davy. "So you get much of this, then?"

asked Davy.

"Yeah," said BFG. "We tick by. You can shift, I hear," said BFG.

"Yeah I can, the gays love the smell of this shit. Saturday, I make a fortune on fares up to Village People land," indicating the gay scene of Newcastle. "Little homos love their party Smarties (pills) as well," said Davy, swigging a gin and tonic.

"So you want do business?" asked the BFG. "I get the best on the market."

Davy looked at him square in the eyes. "What's my end?" he said.

"I sell to you at a good price, pure. You – you get to do your thing," said BFG.

"We can do business," replied Davy. "Good salute!! (Cheers)"

The two men clashed glasses; a new business deal was born.

"I am just using the toilet," said the BFG.

Davy said, "It's your house," with a laugh. BFG laughed as well. Davy started chopping up a few more lines.

13

The Idiot and the Smack-head Girlfriend

In walked the Albert Reece. A big lump joined the party. Known throughout the west end's criminal community, he, with his skinny, drug-addicted girlfriend behind him, approached the kitchen. He stood next to Davy, still standing at the bench. This guy was as intelligent as an earth worm. Davy remembered his attitude towards the others in the party; it was as blatant as it was comical. People feared his reputation, or it should be rephrased, feared his family name – a bunch of bullies that have only stayed within the vicinity of the west end since their father's day in the 1960s, and because Davy and Jimmy didn't jump to his entry he considered this a threat to his little kingdom of villaindom.

"Who are you?" he directed towards Davy.

Davy looked at him. "More to the question, who are fucking you?" said Davy.

"My name is Albert, everyone knows me," said the idiot.

"Really?" said Davy, looking at the comical excuse, thinking, *This idiot's out of his depth, he feels threatened.* "Ohh, well I don't know your celebrity status, mate, but I do now!" said Davy.

Albert looked at Davy, his intelligence level no match for this man that stood before him. "You ever been to jail?" said Albert.

"Nah," said Davy. "I prefer Tenerife or Mallorca," Davy responded. This conversation required brains to baffle stupidity.

"Do you fancy my lass?" said Albert, waiting for any show of weakness.

Davy responded, "Not really, but if you want me to shag her, mate, you could just come out and ask me. I mean she does look a bit rough but if you are offering me your woman, fella, I could facilitate her. But please, if I have to, do you have any condoms? I mean, I ain't going anywhere near that without proper protection, and if I could request a bag for her head as well, as she looks a bit of a pig, mate."

Albert looked at his friends, his eyes wild. He had just been humiliated in front of half the west end. You could smell the fear in the lot of them. Al boy had just chosen the wrong man to try and intimidate.

A voice in the background shouted, "Hoy!!!" It was the BFG's main man. Words were said as he gestured Al boy over. Albert went white and quickly buggered off (left) with his Baghead girlfriend, leaving the party. The guy approached Davy in a friendly manner. "Whoa, big fella. You are the man," were his first words. "My Name's Dave, pleased to meet you.

Davy introduced himself and Jimmy. "With all that testosterone I feel like a pirate. All I need is a patch on my eye," said Davy, laughing.

Dave laughed. "Yeah, he was certainly out of his depth on that one. Arrrrr." He mimicked a salty sea dog. Laughing, the men struck up a friendship that morning.

Jimmy and Davy enjoyed the party for the rest of the morning without incident. Davy and Jimmy clearly made their mark as two guys that nobody fucked with in the west end, and they made a very powerful friend in the process.

14

Glasgow's Narnia

Some people handle situations and some people can't. A trip to Glasgow one summer was one situation that needed to be handled very carefully.

"Do you know where we can get some carry (cocaine)?" said Bob.

"Yeah. I can get you some carry on. How much do you need?" said Sam. "A Henry? (three grams) But it will be a taxi ride out a wee bit," said Sam.

Bob agreed and after a phone call the two guys ended up getting a taxi to Easter House on the suburbs of Glasgow, rough as fuck and rife with crime. Bob was a Shields lad; he knew the dance and was a player back within Newcastle criminal ranks.

"Ok," said Sam, "we have to go up to the flat. It's ok, I have known these guys all my life. You're vetted by me." To be vetted in Glasgow meant you were ok. If you were not vetted you didn't get seen to. Also, the person introducing someone within this world was held responsible for the person he vouched for. In other words, if he brought the Old Bill or a grass, he was also put in the line of fire, and punishment in a place like Glasgow was death. One in the head, two up the arse. A Glasgow send-off was its common name, done by a kid on a BMX or a dispatch rider wearing a motor cycle helmet.

Sam pressed the button, number 5. The graffitied lift started to move. "I phone once I get on that flair (floor) and they send someone to meet us," said Sam. They never gave him the number of the flat they were in, another trait used by criminals – don't say numbers.

At the lift, a young kid greeted them. Bob followed Sam and walked to a flat. Following the kid, they walked through a door, passing a lass and a lad smacked out of their heads in a filthy living room. They went upstairs into the squalid bedroom; the kid opened a wardrobe door and walked in, and through a hole in the wall leading to the next flat, he directed both the men to the living room.

"How's it going, Sam?" said the dealer.

"Fine, fella. This is ma friend, Bob Chatten. He's a Newcastle lad; I work with him," Sam said in his Scottish accent.

The laddy sat down and started making wraps of cocaine.

"So a Henry, you say?" he said, pulling out a rock. "Two hundred and fifty pounds. That's pure, by the way," said the dealer.

Bob paid.

"Do you fancy a line?" said the dealer, chopping up some straight off the rock.

"Yeah, why not?" said Bob.

Bob and Sam sat down.

"Fancy a wee swally? (drink)" he asked, tossing both men a can of lager.

Agreeing, they opened them. The fellas started talking. Bob was a bit more relaxed; the people he had just met were more on his wavelength.

"Where's your toilet?" asked Bob.

"Just upstairs," said the dealer.

Bob excused himself to go and take a piss. Going upstairs, Bob went to the toilet. Lifting the seat, Bob had the feeling something wasn't right here as he took a piss. A bath with a curtain also shared the toilet. Bob, being curious, pulled the curtain back. "What the fuck?" he muttered.

A man lay in the bath. His throat had been cut from ear to ear. Bob quickly finished his piss. Using paper, he wiped his fingerprints and his DNA off the toilet's handle, the curtain, and the seat. He washed his hands in the sink, wiping the handle. He walked down the stairs.

"How's it going, Geordie boy?" said the dealer, a sinister grin on his face.

"Fine," said Bob. "I see someone cut himself shaving," indicating the corpse upstairs.

"Ohh, aye," said the dealer, laughing. "He's not going to be here long."

Bob sat back down, steadying his nerves. It didn't bother him, the corpse, just the fact that he wasn't expecting that sight. Drinking his can, Bob said to Sam, "Get a taxi, we are going to a party," not making it obvious he wanted to get out of there as quickly as possible. Saying their goodbyes, the two guys exited the flat.

Bob pulled Sam. "Listen, mate, there was a stiff (dead body) back there. I am not bothered about how, who, or fucking why he was there, what I am more bothered about is my fucking DNA and the fact that if we had been, say, raided and caught in your mate's house, we would be accessories to a fucking murder. You understand me, mate? In future, we deal with them coming to us."

Sam looked at Bob. "I never knew, Bob, mate," he said. "If I had of known I wouldn't have went. Fuckin' hell, man."

"Never mind," said Bob. "In future we get delivered," said Bob.

"Ok," said Sam. "Now let's go get wired (stoned)."

Jumping in the taxi, the men told the driver, "Take us to the lap dancing bars."

The next day, Bob travelled back to Newcastle. Business deal sorted, he called Davy, who took him to Luke.

"How was Glasgow?" said Davy.

"Adventurous," said Bob. "Funeral baths in that place."

Davy smiled. "Yeah, it's certainly an eye-opener up there," he said, sniggering.

15

Not Wired Correctly

─────◦◦◦─────

Davy Walker sat in the house, looking out of the window. His two prize peacocks paraded on full display in the back garden, the courtship dance. Taking a sip of his cup of tea, Davy picked up his paper; a lazy day to lounge around and watch TV, the night before still vivid in his mind. *What a fucking nut job*, thought Davy as he flicked through the channels of his TV, reminiscing on the night before's events.

Dean Larson had just got out of jail; he spent most of his life in jail, institutionalised. Dean was too far gone; his crack addiction and his lack of morality and respect had turned him into a very disliked, untrustworthy individual. His attitude to feed his addiction was getting worse and increasingly violent, taxing drug dealers and young lads of their money and most importantly, taxi drivers of their takings. His arrogant swagger was not going unnoticed. His days were being numbered and he didn't even know it. His seventeen-stone frame diminished through years of drug abuse, he no longer was that man. Pushing fifty, he still thought in his head he was a twenty-year-old. Stupidity at its highest level.

The phone rang. Davy knew what it was all about before he answered it. Jimmy was on the other end.

"That dirty parasite," he said on the basher phone, indicating the events last night. "He took five large, something has to be done. I want his head on a served on a platter."

Davy said softly, "It's in hand. We need a meet, a sit-down to discuss this problem," indicating the phone.

"Talk needs to be minimal and spoken only in codes."

"I know, I know, it's all in hand," said Davy as he finally found the channel to watch.

"Meet me in the morning at the usual place, the park scots," said Jimmy. This was always code – it was to be Preston Cemetery. Davy used codes, places that had meaning of exactly the opposite. This prevented surveillance from the Old Bill; a secretive arrangement, always alert of eavesdropping.

Davy put the phone down and sat down in his conservatory, and began watching his TV. *Looks like I have to dig something up*, thought Davy. *Looks like I have to go to work again.*

*

Saturday night, the bars were packed. Davy sat in his car waiting for the phone call; usual business, usual customers, nothing much changed his daily business of making money. The problem with Dean was still very much a reality. Davy was well prepared if a situation was to take place.

Davy was in Wallsend when the phone rang. "It's set up." Two simple words. Davy knew what this was. "He's on one."

Good, thought Davy. "Where?"

"Wallsend, the Queen's. Time to offload the shit."

Davy agreed.

Dean was looking for his next fix of heroin. Pushing it into his system on a daily basis, the hunger grew stronger; his voracious appetite was taking him into even more dangerous territory. It was just a matter of time now. Sitting in the back room of the Queen's, Dean took a draw of his tab (cigarette). He waited for the dealer with no intention of paying.

Everyone was terrified of Dean; his wiring was very wrong, unfixable (crazy). Dean sat drinking his pint. Davy waited for the dealer in Warwick Road, listening to his radio. The figure approached, the car the door opened. "How's you?" said Davy.

"I am fine," said the dealer. "Is it ok to smoke?"

Davy agreed, cracking the window. "Right, you got weight?"

"Yeah," said the dealer.

"Give it to me. You take this," said Davy, giving the dealer the small package containing the brown powder. "I keep this safe until this gets given. You're meeting that dick in the Queen's?"

"Yeah," said the dealer. "He's wanting a fix of heroin."

"Good," said Davy, putting the small bag of shit into his magnetic box. "Make sure he gets this," a sinister grin upon his face.

The dealer sniggered. "He won't be doing the Great North Run this year."

Dean was getting fidgety. *Where the fuck is he?* he thought.

His basher phone rang.

"I am around the back."

Dean quickly finished his pint and proceeded out the back door. Davy sat in his car, lights out, and watched as the deal went down. Dean searched the dealer, threatening him to hand over everything. "Is this it? You little shit," he said, smacking the dealer in the face. "You bring me one ten bag? You twat."

"It's all I had, and fifty quid," said the dealer.

Dean took it and his money, bumping the dealer, or so he thought. *Game, set, and match,* thought Davy, watching from a distance. The dealer ran off, bloodied from a burst nose and lips. Davy watched Dean walk back towards the bar. Once Dean was gone Davy started the engine and drove to the dealer, picking him up. Davy handed the bag and money back.

"Good job."

The dealer wiped his face. "Cheers."

Davy handed him a gram. "Make some up," said Davy, indicating the CD case. They both did a line and Davy dropped him off in Howdon.

Driving off, Davy used his basher phone, calling Jimmy. "Done."

16

Bars, Clubs, Pubs, Stealing – a 1970s Way of Life

Two young boys played outside the Cresta Club. The town of North Shields at that time lay bare; many waste grounds, many adventures. Kids of this era played games – bulldog, hopscotch – drunks fell out of bars. North Shields was a typical industrial town. Davy grew up during the 1970s along with Jimmy, playing down on the fish quay and old factories, climbing on board fishing boats or entering lofts of derelict buildings, which North Shields had an abundance of. And bars – North Shields had lots of bars. On Saville Street alone there were eight and they were always packed.

Growing up in this town, the boys learned fast the rules of survival, and learning their cunning from the villains and criminal minds of that era. Stealing and commercial burglary were all part of their indoctrination. The police were the enemy, villains were the good guys. The status quo of a hard upbringing. Grasses (snitches) were dealt with, with severe violence. North Shields truly was a town that if entered, you obeyed the rules. Fighting among the street gangs was commonplace; kids always fought to protect their territory. If a disagreement was not resolved you went up a back lane and fought. No weakness. If you showed weakness you became prey.

The boys would often watch this behaviour being played out among the adults. The police often turned a blind eye; it was the way of that era – dog-eat-dog. Some of the kids Davy and Jimmy played with were not as fortunate to enjoy a family life, mother and father. They were subjected to a life of uncles and Mammy's friend. Their mothers were working girls, whores who broke many a sailor's heart and bank account. The street smart would watch a sailor become victim, his wad of cash diminish in a week of partying with street whores who frequented the bars and the clubs of Shields. Sometimes the boys watched those very ladies trying to scale the fence of the docks in order to get on board the ships. The watchful eye of the ex-RSM who was head of security in Smith's docks often caught girls trying to enter the yard. Some days the boys would watch the same scenario unfold on the fish quay.

The era of money; everyone had it, from the fishermen to deep seamen. The prey of the Shields working girls almost always left fleeced of their wages or settling. Davy and Jimmy often watched events like this unfold and grew up fast in this environment. Their father, a drinker and old-school villain, was always in the bars of Shields. A well-known character, a cunning con-man, and a driver for the heists, robberies, and other criminal activity. His involvement with the Newcastle and Jarrow firms cemented his position as a blagger and rough. The boys witnessed the guns hanging in wrapping paper on the Christmas tree, to the money taped under floorboards. They witnessed the gold rings and chains, to the sides of beef, pork, lamb on meat hooks down the back stairs. The money on the table to the fine clothing, all stolen. The safes, known as peelers, the burning torches, opening them.

You can safely say these boys grew up fast and enriched within the Newcastle firms and the characters that named them Diamond Kid and Shwepsy Kid on account of one having his nappy stuffed with gold and diamond rings and the other for robbing the Jungle cellar aged twelve. It's hard to believe, however, but the boys were brought up tough. They wore second-hand clothes and hand-me-downs. Typical 1970s kids brought up on the streets of Tyneside; fighting, playing, witnessing. Their only chance of survival was to rob shops, getting their stay press pants, their bomber jackets, shoes, shirts – these boys literally clothed themselves through crime. They learned quickly how to scam money, loading metro machines with a rag then using their coat hangers to empty the stored change that built up in the change tube. Their stringing of slot machines, emptying them with 2,000 credits, a fifty pence piece with glued catgut just flicking the finger, adding up credit and emptying jackpots every time. These boys truly learned well from their villain teachers. The art of making money dishonestly was expected and followed throughout their lives. These boys made money.

Loan sharking in high school was the next step; the intimidation of getting that money back, the villainous way they pounced on the stupid who borrowed and couldn't pay, was beginning to become more violent, threatening their windows, the family car, their father's business, there was no limit to the lengths these boys would go to, and it was being watched intensively by the men who created them and introduced the boys to Tyneside's criminal family.

17

The Paper Baton

Sitting in the street cafe in a side street in Barcelona, Tommy Brand blended in as a tourist; just an ordinary Joe, t-shirt and shorts. No one knew him, no one would expect this guy was in hiding from the Newcastle firms.

Tommy had taken a parcel and didn't deliver; he instead buggered off to Spain and had been living in a trailer park for the past six months, but the six months had been expensive. His coke habit and his spending on living was starting to take its toll. Tommy had two grand left to his name and now he either had to get a job or face eviction. There wasn't a hope in hell he could go back to the UK; he was a marked man, a price on his head. He was going to get seriously battered, or worse, killed. Some very upset people lost money on his caper and they all wanted their pound of flesh. In other words, he was fucked. Smoking nervously, he sat waiting for Davy. He had contacted Davy the day before and wanted to straighten things out. Little did he know Davy was one of the people who wanted the pound of flesh.

Little fucking motherfucker, thought Davy as he sat in his hotel room. The noise of the car horns and the bustle of people could be heard from the open window; the net curtain blew with a cool breeze. Julie lay in the bed naked as Davy pulled on his trousers.

"You going for coffee?" said Julie as Davy slipped on his shoes.

"Yeah, darling. You just have a lie in, I will get some bread and coffee and the paper."

Kissing her on the head as he buttoned up his shirt, with that,

Davy left the room.

"How much for the sombrero?" said Davy to the seller outside the main entrance.

"Twenty euro," said the store keeper.

Davy bought it and proceeded to the meeting point, cursing under his breath, "The fucking little rat wants to meet me after what he had done. Fucking little idiot."

Walking to the street vendor selling British papers and rolling it up tight, Davy proceeded to where Tommy agreed to meet.

Tommy sat still, fidgeting, still nervous about the meeting that was going to take place. He knew he had ripped Davy off for three grand and he knew Davy would be pissed off, but he also knew Davy would listen and he knew he was fair.

Davy approached wearing the hat, his newspaper rolled up in his hand. He walked over to where Tommy was sitting. Without warning, Davy jammed the table where Tommy sat straight into the railings and proceeded to batter Tommy with the rolled-up paper. Screams began as Tommy's teeth and blood splattered the table. The low thuds slapping in Tommy's head were very distinct. Knocked clean out, Davy upped sticks and calmly walked out of the enclosure.

Heading down a back lane, Davy dumped the hat and the shades into a bin and the paper he threw in a skip. He could still hear the screams from the cafe as he walked into the ramblers and disappeared into the crowd, heading towards a cafe where he wanted bread and coffee and a crisp, new paper. He then headed back to the hotel. When he entered the room Julie still lay there.

"That was quick!" she exclaimed.

Davy put the coffee on the table and sat in the armchair, opening his paper, saying, "The early bird gets the worm," and crossing his legs. "It looks like it's going to turn out nice today, Julie," he said, sipping his coffee and breaking his bread roll. A short stay over the weekend in a romantic city like Barcelona really was what Davy needed. Tommy had no idea where Davy was staying so Davy relaxed a little bit. *Besides,* he thought, *if the little coke-head shit did go to the authorities, what's he going to explain? Plus, the motherfucker has to give his location and that wouldn't be wise with the amount of people after him. Stupid*

prick. He gazed out of the window at the hustle and bustle of a
Spanish street; a visit to the cathedral and a slow walk down the
ramblers was today's agenda, then an early morning flight back to
Newcastle via London. Davy was careful to cover his tracks. Always
suspicious and always alert.

18

Sniff Sniff

Some people have addiction, some people have real addiction, and when it gets so bad that your family savings, kids' education, everything, goes up your nose, some people blame the partner, their friends, the weather, anything instead of looking in the mirror and actually blaming themselves. Your best friends are dealers, you start lying to your family, the shit you put up your nose becomes a suppressant. Your plans never get fulfilled as you push that next line into your system. Welcome to the world of cocaine – a sick, twisted world where everything and everyone involved with its distribution and its purchasing are out for one thing, and that's money. Bugger your kids, bugger your mortgage, bugger your wife, car, grandmother, mother. Ohh, you have cancer? Bugger that as well. Money – if you don't have it, you get nothing. If you owe it, you pay or you deal with your newfound best friend coming at you with a baseball bat. Cocaine has no friends; it creates sharks, it destroys families, and has no morals.

Davy sat looking out the window; his thoughts drifted to a faraway island. He hated collections; he hated the looks on the faces of the kids of the drugged-up degenerate husbands, mothers, boyfriends, girlfriends. He hated collections, demanding money back, taking cars, televisions, to name but a few items. Chopping through his next line, Davy rolled up his twenty, snorting up the rest of a huge line he placed on his CD case. *Now it's time to collect off this twat.*

Starting the car, he proceeded to the home of one bad debtor. *Bugger it*, Davy thought, pulling into the street. Davy looked at the prize car sitting on the drive, the RS shining in the sunlight. Davy got out of the taxi, parking it up a good distance from the mark's house. *Well,* thought Davy, *time to introduce myself,* indicating to one of his lackeys (helpers) to proceed ahead. A knock on the door. Davy waited. A woman answered. "Yes? Can I help you?"

"Yeah," said Davy, "you can really help me. Is Craig in?"

"Craig!" shouted the lady.

"Yeah?" was his answer. Walking towards the door, Craig went white. He knew who this was, stuttering towards Davy, "I, I-I-I can-n-n pay! Mate, pl-l-lee-ease."

Davy wasn't having any of it. "Look, you friggin' degenerate, you owe twenty large. You fucking owe that! Now I am here to collect."

Craig Bell's wife looked at Craig. "What have you bloody done?"

Davy looked at her and pointed out, "It has nothing to do with you, darling. It has everything, however, to do with your man." As Davy ordered the lackeys to start stripping the house, taking TVs off walls, hi-fis, anything worth value, he barked at Craig, "The keys and log book to that car and the MOT and insurance certificates." Davy was thorough and precise.

Craig stood in shock after everything he owned was taken from his home. His wife and kids came to the door, bags packed and waiting for a taxi, totally blanking Craig. Bewildered and totally in shock, he fell to his knees as his RS roared and drove off, packed with his possessions.

Davy jumped into his car and drove off in the opposite direction. Phoning Luke, Davy stated, "All emptied, driving back." Davy started to get upset. "I absolutely hate collections. Visualising that stupid idiot's family, the look on the bairns' (kids') faces. Fuck! Fuck! Fuck!!!" cursed Davy as he drove home.

19

Re-mortgage and Repossession

Craig Bell sat in his home; it had been four weeks since the visit. His wife and kids were living at her mother's. Craig sat looking at the empty bottle of whisky; his crushed Pro Plus, which he mixed with his gram, sat on the table. The spaces on the walls showed up, bleached by the sun. Where once his prize plasma stood, a portable stood there now. The letters mounted up at the door, final demand, notice of court action. Craig well and truly messed up. No longer did any of his old mates come to his house; he no longer had fridges full of beer; he cried most nights. Exhausted, Craig stared at his hands. "What the fuck's the point?" he said to himself. "I fucking re-mortgaged seven months ago and now I have fucking nothing." *Repossession next*, thought Craig, making another line using the lotto ticket he bought. He started to snort.

So many things were going through his head. So many things. He couldn't think straight. Craig stared at the bottle, eyes welling up. He truly messed up big time. *The kids hate me, the wife wants a divorce, what the fuck can I do? There is no point anymore*, thought Craig. Destroyed mentally, the man was at a point beyond breaking. His whole life now looked back at him in half a gram of coke and an empty bottle of whisky.

The wire from the extension cable wrapped around the banister lay there with the open noose. Craig gulped down the remainder of his whisky. The bottle thrown to the floor, he scooped up the half gram, snorting the lot, and went to the stairs.

"Farewell," said Craig as the noose went around his neck. Rocking the stool back and forward, the stool fell. Craig's life ended. The end of a man who lost control and lost everything.

Craig hung there for two weeks. His daughter found him; he left one note saying sorry.

20

Biscuits and Tea

———————————————————

Davy and Jimmy often visited Luke's; the guys had a knack for turning up just as the kettle boiled. Biscuits would be sniffed out and the two vagabonds would sit enjoying tea and biscuits. Luke laughed. *The cheeky bastards*, he thought to himself. His French bulldog ran around the back garden chasing butterflies, bees, and shadows. *That thing is bleeding mad*, thought Luke, wearing his white boxers, vest, and night gown.

The door rang, Luke hiding his biscuits under the settee pillow. In walked the brothers.

"How's it gan then, big fella?" said Davy as he walked towards the kitchen.

Luke tossed Davy the envelope. "Ouch," said Jimmy. "You need a hand lifting that?"

Davy just laughed, finding Luke's biscuits and flicking one at Jimmy.

"Cheers," said Jimmy, eating one down.

W.T.F.? thought Luke. *How the fuck did he find them?*

Davy, flicking on the kettle in the kitchen now, pulled out of his pocket the rock of coke. "Anyone for breakfast?" said Davy as he crumpled a Henry on the marble bench, making big. thick lines. "Shame about that Craig," said Davy. Luke agreed.

"He was found by his lassie, wasn't he?" said Jimmy.

"Yeah, it's a crying shame but he did owe large and I have no sympathetic answer for that," said Luke.

"Shame about his family, like," said Davy. *Never mind,* Davy thought.

The men bantered on about cars and their wives for half an hour, enjoying lines. Davy always enjoyed company with Luke and Jimmy; it was the only real time these guys could actually talk, speaking in code.

"So you open for more work your way?" said Luke to Davy.

"Yeah, why not?"

The guys all agreed and shook hands on their arrangements.

"The usual fee," said Luke.

"Of course," said Davy. "I always aim to please."

Jimmy looked worried. Jokingly in the corner, "Yeah," he said. "Poor, poor souls. What the fuck?" said Jimmy, laughing.

Davy ground a couple of big lines and snorted one down his left then one down his right. "Whoa," said Davy, feeling the rush (cocaine effect).

"Now how would you like my next mark?" Luke looked over. "He needs a lesson taught. Ahh, primary school. A very naughty boy. Yeah, take some toys."

Davy gestured a slice to the nose.

"Yeah," said Luke, and waving his hand, Davy knew thumbs.

"No problem."

"The mark is a greasy jock. It's a trip," said Luke. "North."

"No probs," said Davy.

"Take a friend," said Luke. "I want this pig to squeal."

The men walked out into Luke's garden – a sprawling, well-kept garden.

"You still keep fish," said Jimmy, pointing at the pond.

Luke said, "Yeah, they're huge now."

Jimmy also kept fish. "Jap koi carp. Aye, canny."

Smoking his large Cuban, Luke laughed at Jimmy's face when he looked at Luke's fish. *It's so obvious,* thought Luke. *He wants my fish.* Luke looked over at Davy. *Jesus,* he thought. *He's getting bigger and more scarier than before. Poor bastards.*

Luke walked slowly around his acre of garden, thinking of the victims Davy was being unleashed onto; the machine needs to be driven and that machine was a nasty piece of work.

21

Time at the Bar, Please

Helen was just finishing off an early finish. Jinglers was a bar that very seldom closed early; it normally was open all night and the small hours of the morning. It was 3 a.m., the late 1980s. Geordie and Helen had enough time at the bar. "Ladies and gentlemen," was called.

Two brothers sat in the far side of the bar. "Fuck that old cunt," they whispered. One had been upstairs and pissed all over the floor, totally disrespecting the proprietors' hospitality.

"Fuck off!" shouted one, laughing at old George. "Make us leave, you stupid old bitch."

Davy sat there watching with Jimmy. The biggest one stood up, pint glass in hand, walking towards the toilet. Davy followed.

"Here, mate," said Davy, confronting him. "You can put that glass down, fella. You have been asked to leave."

The big guy positioned himself ready to ram the glass into Davy's face. It happened in seconds. Davy floored him. Lightning-fast hand speed knocked the big fella to the floor. The onslaught didn't stop at that; kicks and punches rained down on the big guy's face. He was systematically torn apart; kicks to his face, his jaw smashed, as Davy repeatedly stamped into his face.

As the big guy trundled down the stairs at the bottom of the stairs the onslaught continued, biting and gouging. Davy destroyed the guy – a machine fuelled by adrenalin. The doorman George employed stood looking terrified. This level of violence wasn't what he signed up for, he just opened doors and greeted people.

Faster and harder, Davy fought like an alley cat, giving no quarter.

The big lump's brother came tearing down the stairs, terrified. He had just been dismantled by Jimmy upstairs. The smell of shit lingered in the air as he darted past Davy, who was still smashing his brother up.

Two brothers versus two brothers; the competition was an even match. They eventually managed to escape into the street. The big fella received a smack off Jimmy which knocked him clean out, lying in the gutter, covered in bite marks and blood, his eye sockets gouged and face swollen. He was carried around the waste ground to sleep off his injuries.

George walked up to Davy, saying, "I never taught you to fight like that."

Davy looked squarely in his eyes. "No you didn't, but they fight like that. Don't ever question me again."

George looked stunned; his strict way of rearing the boys, introducing them to crime then taking it away from them, messed them up a little. If you fight in Shields, you fight like a villain; no ifs, no buts, and George playing the moral high ground after his escapades through life really was a bit rich. Biting, gouging, dirty, vicious, fighting was the way you won. The days of gentlemen and duelling were history.

Davy, at fourteen, was victim of a stabbing. He was attacked at twelve by a spanner-wielding twenty-four year old. He beat the shit out of the guy. Davy certainly believed in fighting fire with fire. All in, no prisoners, from the crowd in the Chinese to the doorman on the Metro, Davy fought hard and won through being vicious. The nastier you get, the nastier the fight. Word gets round; you don't play with this puppy as now it's a Pit Bull.

22

Memories of a 1970s Christmas, Photos,

and a Fly Runway

Sitting at Jimmy's table, Davy looked though the old photos.

"Some here of my grandma. Fucking hell," said Jimmy as he passed a beer, "Look at that tree.

"It was taken 1977," said Davy as he looked at the back. "Burt Avenue, remember?" Davy laughed. "That's the year we got kicked out on Christmas Eve."

Jimmy started to laugh. "That was you, you bastard. You started that."

Laughing out loud, "Yeah, I remember that well," said Davy.

Christmas Eve, 1977. Their father's mother, an ex-prostitute in her third marriage to a pisshead Scotsman. The boys and their younger sister visited the house. She wasn't the nicest grandmother and always compared her other son's family against her eldest, George's. The children were sat down in the middle of the floor and the presents were given like the kids should appreciate this old bitch's gifts – a tangerine and a shit pair of slippers.

Jimmy and Helen sat waiting, looking at Davy as the grandmother ranted. "I got wor Jimmy's boys this, watches, skateboards, you name it." The three siblings looked at this mockery of a woman then out came the presents. They knew what the present was when Davy sarcastically said, "Thank you, Grandma Rosey. You're the best." Picking up his present, he shook it with crocodile tears. He stated,

"Oooohhhhh, I wonder what it is this year."

Old Rosey went ballistic. She took the presents off the three of the kids and kicked them out. Helen and Jimmy laughed as they went down the path. Davy wasn't so fortunate; his father kicked his arse into next week. But still, in Davy's memories that was the best Christmas he ever had. Looking at the photo, the memories flooded back as if it were yesterday. Pictures of Lampton Lion Park, the memories of how they all piled in to the back of a car, the photos of the lot of them. long hair and flares from Lampton Lion Park to Edinburgh.

Davy and Jimmy sat down in that back kitchen going through the old photos of their childhood. The boys sat drinking their cold beer.

"So I hear you played a bit pool," said Davy.

Jimmy laughed. "Yeah, something like that."

"Sore losers," said Davy, flicking through the next album.

"Very," said Jimmy.

"So the notion of you gerrin' a pub is no longer," said Davy.

Jimmy laughed. "Yeah, something like that," he said.

"What's this one?" said Davy, picking up a picture of himself, Micky Stevens, and Jimmy standing outside the Colin Camble.

"Bloody hell," said Jimmy, "look at us there. It was the early 1990s if I remember correctly. Micky wiped his arse on a bird's (woman's) jeans."

"Yeah, I remember that. It was a Saturday afternoon. We were drinking in the Colin when a well-known Forest Hall villain used to frequent Shields at that time. This one day in particular he came with three others, including a woman. The woman, a blonde, pretty thing, also boasted a big mouth, talking to regulars like a piece of shit. She was asked numerous times to zip it, numerous times to check her attitude, even to the point where it almost came to blows."

Davy had already pre-warned them, letting them know he was going to have to be an unfriendly guy. He didn't hit women but he was prepared to beat the men in her company up and that would certainly have happened. Thankfully, Micky saved the day with a memorable act that still had Davy laughing his head off to this day.

He giggled, remembering how Micky walked up to her just after using the toilet and literally wiped his arse on her leg. A full-on brown runway was created on crisp white jeans. The woman turned all colours and spewed the high heavens, running out of the establishment screaming, embarrassed and humiliated. Her boyfriend, who was quickly advised and knocked to the floor, scrambled to his feet, burst lip and eye. He ran out after her. Micky, the main culprit, sat with a grin on his face, unfazed by events and activities that unfolded.

Davy laughed his head off thinking of that afternoon all those years ago. He remembered the Victoria pub on Borough Road, the escapades that were played out there; pool chalk, how he dipped his finger in blue chalk and smeared it on people's noses, unsuspected. Like his banter when he would call them Tonto, their faces painted blue. A true wind-up merchant.

Another photo appeared. Davy in the Stanley pub. Jimmy and Micky, Toma and Coatsey and more appeared. The Lindisfarne Club, the Dolphin, the Albion Grill, the Lampton Castle; the boys' father's era. The Fountain Head and Uncle Tom's, the Gardener's Arms; a rich collection of bars and clubs going way back to their father's era, the characters that drank in them gazing back at the boys in black and white or technicolour from the 1960s. Teddy boy, the 1970s skinhead, to the 1990s casual, the photos bore depth of the town's history and these boys were steeped in history and enriched by the characters photographed.

23

The XR3i Photo

The year was 1986. Dirty Dancing and the Dr Who song were widely played in all the bars nationwide. Davy, Jimmy, Toma, Mr Brown, and Coatsy were all going on a camping trip to Cumberland in Coatsy's pride and joy – a white XR3i. A white canvas tent was stuffed in the boot, sleeping bags, and two cases of Carlsberg Special Brew.

The boys set out on a Saturday night adventure to Brampton, Cumberland. Acid was taken to give the LSD effect. Once the boys arrived after the one-hour journey to the campsite of Talkin Tarn, a fire was lit and the boys cooked the sausages and bacon, not that it was eaten as the boys by this time were off their heads on chemically enhanced trips. The Lucy in the Sky with Diamonds effect.

The cases of Special Brew were cracked open and the boys decided a trip into Brampton was in order. Mr Brown was teetotal; he was designated driver as the boys all partied, going to the Scotch pub and the Leg of Mutton. It wasn't long before the local village idiots made their acquaintance, testing the boys on any weakness, of which there were none.

Now Coatsy met up with two of the most ugly girls the boys had ever laid eyes on – local bikes (easy meat) – inviting them back to the campsite that evening. With the Tilly lamp on the ambient setting, silhouetted were the shadows of Coatsy and this girl in the tent trying to give him fucking head. Davy, Jimmy, and Toma sat outside drinking cans, watching this unfold like a fucking movie. Davy threw a half can and by fluke it actually bounced off the tent with enough force it slapped Miss Piggy's head. She screamed, running out, pulling her dirty knickers up, calling us cunts. Coatsy followed quickly behind her, cursing us. The whole fucking campsite woke up; lights being switched on, dogs barked, the whole thing resembled a fucking scene from the Great Escape.

The owner of the campsite came out, furious, and kicked all the lads off. The tent was thrown in the boot and because Davy resembled a swamp creature as he was lifting from falling in mud and shit, he was thrown in the boot as well. Now the XR3i had a neat little centre rest on the back seat so it was easy to feed cans and fags through the hole to Davy, who was relegated to the boot. Jimmy and Toma sat in the back seat and Coatsy sat in the passenger seat.

Alan Brown was designated driver – a dopey, one-sentence kind of guy with very little savvy. Driving in the early dawn light, Alan Brown only went and hit a fucking crow. Its feathers went everywhere and blood splattered all over the bonnet and driver's side wing. Jimmy remembered this with a laugh as he looked at the photo of the car.

After about fifteen minutes, Brian asked, "What's that piece of meat on my windscreen?"

Alan said, "I hit a crow a few miles back."

The car was stopped.

"What the fuck?" said Brian, taking feathers off the grille and assessing the damage. A busted headlight and blood all over his shiny white XR3i. Brian calmed down, just ordering Alan to drive the rest of the way, calling him a stupid twat.

Now Jimmy and Toma and Davy were still partying like nothing happened, smoking green, tripping on acid, and drinking heavily. We entered Newcastle and a jam sandwich (police car) sat on the roundabout, flashing blue lights. The car was forced to stop.

"Name?" said the officer.

"Alan Brown," said the driver. "Fully comp and I have permission to drive."

"OK," said the policeman. Looking at the blood, he asked Alan to exit the vehicle to get a breathalyser, asking how the blood was on the car.

Alan said, "I hit a crow."

"May I look in your car?"

Looking at Toma, Jimmy, and Coatsy sitting stone-faced, he asked, "So may I look in the boot?"

Jimmy remembered, sniggering with Toma. Coatsy wasn't happy at all.

"Ok," said Alan, dopey as well as stupid.

Davy lay in the boot with the tent wrapped around his head, pretending to be dead.

"You're a wanker!" shouted Coatsy. "You bunch of fucking wankers!" He almost burst a blood vessel.

The policeman took one look and pinned Alan to the floor. A body, tent, shovels in the frigging boot. He called immediately for backup. Alan Brown lay on the ground with handcuffs, screaming, "No! No! No!"

Once the van arrived a team of coppers climbed out. The look on their faces when Davy climbed out of the back and said, "What's going on?"

The policeman's face was furious.

"You are supposed to be dead."

Davy went, "What? I fell asleep."

The other police were not amused. All five lads were arrested on drunken disorderly charges, driving a vehicle with a passenger not properly seated, and driving a vehicle with a front headlight out. They threw the law book at the boys; 80 pound fines and Coatsy's car was impounded.

Jimmy was laughing so much he almost fell over the chair. "That photo brings back fucking memories," said Jimmy, chuckling at the memory.

24

Manchester is Straight Down the A1

Gary turner looked worried. His boyfriend, Karl Pell, sat on the opposite sofa, stroking his beard. "I told you not to gamble. I told you not to lose that car."

"Ok!! Ok!!" said Gary as he looked in the bottom of his tea cup. "I have to go to Manchester, Karl," said Gary.

"No!! We have to go," said Karl. "My man goes to Manchester, I go with my man," with a gay kind of starry-eyed look.

"I don't want you getting hurt," said Gary in feminine concern.

"Don't worry about me, I can be a real bitch!" exclaimed Karl. "I will scratch their eyeballs out. Anyway, it's only Manchester, straight down the A1," said Karl.

"I hear there's a big gay scene in Manchester," said Gary, stroking his 'tache, licking his lips.

"We're there on business, you dirty slut," said Karl. "I know what you will do, you trollop," said Karl. "You can't help yourself, Gary."

"Ok, I have to go to this cafe and meet some people, then drive back. Once I get back I have to wait for instructions." Lifting the basher phone he was provided, "I am absolutely shitting myself," said Gary.

Karl crawled over. "You have me. Your own little Nissan worker."

Gary put his head in his hands and shook his head. "Fuck. What have I got myself into, Karl?"

Karl grabbed his hands, kissing them, saying softly, "Don't worry, we will be alright."

Davy was sitting in Billymill when the phone rang. "The gay man needs a taxi."

The package was there along with other envelopes, all in a wiped-down bag.

"I pick homo boy up, he takes the bag, leaves his bag in so it looks like he left nothing. I drive to the BFG after the job's done. Simple."

Davy pulled up in Ilford Road. Gary jumped in with Karl. Davy reset his meter. "Round the block trip. Silverlink, then back here. We understand each other?"

"Yesssss," said the pair nervously.

"Put your bag in the back," said Davy, watching the men through the rear view mirror, Davy checked they didn't switch the bag. "Now you take this one." The same-coloured bag. Davy had a tag just visible to make sure it was the right one.

"What shall I say?" said Gary in a gay voice.

"You say nothing," said Davy. "You will be contacted." As Davy drove down Churchill Street, "You say nothing, understand?" said Davy.

"Yesssss, I understand."

"Here. Here is the keys to the other car you will be driving."

Davy pulled up in Elgin Avenue.

"There's the car. Tank's full, now go to Manchester. You got the address?"

"Yesss," said Gary.

Karl looked at Gary, totally shocked, as if to say, "That was fast, holy shit."

"Reet (right), give me a fiver," said Davy, switching off his meter. Gary handed over the fiver, slotted on the back of Davy's seat. "Better to make payment than have surveillance teams watching. Remember, you keep shtum and it will work out well. Panic and ask questions and it won't. Now good luck, see you guys in seven hours. You phone for a taxi, ok? Ask for me when you get back."

"Yesssss," said Gary.

Both the men exited the car into the light blue Audi. Gary jumped into the driver's seat and Karl in the passenger's. They both drove off, indicating on Windsor Drive, heading for Manchester just down the A1.

25

Being Taught the Old-School Ways

Jack Thompson had it all. He paid for his flat and furnished it; the cars he owned, he sold all but one. The Mark 2 Golf, his fortune, served him well. Fanny (vagina) was available every night. He enjoyed the company of strippers; from Some Like it Hot, Maria, especially her pierced vagina and heavy tattoos, and her appetite to suck dick, really was appealing to Jack. After all, he had the green (money) and the car.

Maria often finished her shift and phoned Jack, her sex buddy. He provided her with protection for her other job as an escort, a prostitute to the high-flying gamblers that frequented the casinos. She was always discreet and never kissed her clients, as she told Jack, "Kissing's for you, they are just business." This girl, in every form, represented a porno star; her false tits, nose job, false eyelashes and blonde, full-bodied hair. To look at this woman was to gawp and drool. A bad girl and Maria knew it.

Jack was no novice to the world; his fast temper and his wide boy reputation allowed him to enter places and be respected by many villains; from the coke deals to the muscle hire, Jack had it all at a grasp. No more leftovers for this big fella; he was now becoming a major player. He already invested money on a little bit of carry on (cocaine) and his end was going to become very lucrative. Very soon the money would come pouring in. Shoe boxes stacked to the ceiling, floor boards packed to the brim, all of that money needed to be invested into other business interests.

Watching the television, Jack flicked through the channels. He heard the keys at the front door; it was Maria; she had just come back from the gym.

"Hi babe," she said as she walked into the living room. "You just get up? Lazy bones," she exclaimed.

Jack laughed. "Nah, been up a while," he said as he adjusted his pyjama bottoms.

"I am taking a shower," said Maria. "You coming in?" she asked, gesturing to Jack.

Jack could feel the swelling in his pants and agreed to her invitation. The shower was steaming as she immediately took him in her mouth, playing with herself frantically. Jack lifted her up with his powerful arms, putting his penis deep inside her. She moaned in ecstasy as Jack slowly pounded her.

The phone started ringing in the living room. Jack was just about to explode inside her as he drew himself out to get the phone when she drew him back, taking him inside her mouth once again. He exploded in Maria's mouth, pumping his load all over her face. She eagerly licked it up without hesitation, then kissing his tip, she said, "Well, you're clean now, you can go and answer your phone now." Sliding the shower cubicle closed, she began to shower.

Jack wrapped his towel around his waist as he went to his mobile. A missed call. Jack rang it back.

"Hello?" said the other voice on the opposite side of the phone.

"Hello, who's this?" said Jack.

The voice said, "Your package is ready. Phone this number." He gave the number to order a taxi. "Say, in half an hour."

"Yeah, sure," said Jack, still hearing Maria showering. "Got to go, Maria! Business!" said Jack, as he started to get ready.

"What was that?" said Maria, switching off the water.

"I have to go on an errand," said Jack. "Won't be long."

Maria acknowledged Jack, "Ok, get some milk on your way back," as she started to dry herself.

Jack phoned the number; the taxi was booked. The taxi number was given, requesting the specific driver. Jack just waited for the text back.

Davy pulled up in the street. Jack was waiting for Davy at his window.

Honk, honk!! Davy was outside.

Jack boarded in the passenger side.

"How's it gan, Davy lad?" said Jack as the car left the street.

"Fine, Jack. Did you like me dodgy voice?" said Davy, laughing out loud.

"I knew it was you, you twat," said Jack, talking about the phone call.

"Reet, the faggots (homosexuals) came through. See you still got the car you won," sniggered Davy.

"Yeah," laughed Jack. "So the girls were the mules?"

"Yep," said Davy. "Here is your end, Jack," as Davy passed him the paper McDonald's bag.

"Whoa, that's heavy," said Jack.

"Yeah," said Davy, laughing. "Almost as heavy as mine!"

A Diana Ross classic played on the radio as Davy drove up the A19. "Give it a twenty minute," said Davy, "I have a bit of that. You fancy a bit breakfast?" said Davy, indicating the CD case.

Davy pulled into a country road towards Seghill.

"So how's life in the fast lane? I hear you're all loved-up," said Davy.

"Yeah," said Jack.

"I heard about the card game, Jack. I was ready to pay your end if it went tits up. I pulled Luke about that," said Davy, "but it all came out in the end. It made you, in my book. You walked away with a lot of money, Jack, and in my book that straightened you out. So you own that place," said Davy. "Good, good. At least you ain't pissed it up against a wall. (wasted his money)"

Jack started to chop up the rock.

"Make 'em big, Jack," said Davy.

Two thick lines were made out of pure.

"Next shipment is going to be big," said Jack.

Davy looked at Jack. "Jack, listen to me. You just got 200 grand handed to you, don't get greedy, buddy. It attracts the wrong attention. Look, Jack, listen to me. You will be ok!!"

Jack agreed. "Yeah, yer reet," said Jack. He listened to Davy. To get advice from this fella you had to be in the circle of trust. Only a handful of people are friends in this world; the rest are acquaintances. Jack, in Davy's eyes, needed to be schooled correctly. Plus, Davy respected his family name and where he came from. Honour among the criminals was still deep within Davy's moral code.

"So! No more talk of deals until you run them by me," said Davy, rolling up the twenty note and handing it over to Jack.

"Yeah," said Jack, snorting the first Hollywood.

Davy took the case and snorted his line after Jack. "I am putting the word out. If they wish to make deals behind my back concerning you I will clip them in a heartbeat." Jack looked at Davy like the apprentice. "Knowledge is a big thing in my book, and loyalty, that comes with the territory we choose to play in."

Davy started the car and drove back to Wallsend. Jack shook his hand as he exited the car.

"Respect, Davy!!" said Jack before he closed the door and went up his path.

Davy drove off. He had made a small fortune on that deal as well. *Now it's time to give the news to the homos,* he thought, as he started to drive towards Ilford Road.

Both Gary and Karl were in the house when Davy knocked.

"Come in," said Gary.

Davy went upstairs.

"Would you like a cup of tea?" said Karl in a feminine voice.

"Nah," said Davy. "Reet, good news." The pair perked up, attentive and listening. "You have done a good job. Here is a grand. You took a serious risk handing them a brown envelope. The car, the Audi, it's yours."

Gary looked at Karl, totally confused. "Why are you doing this for us?" said Karl.

"I am doing this because you kept your cool and asked no questions. May I?" Davy pointed at the bench to make up some lines.

"Yeah, no problem," said Gary, still terrified of this man standing in his home.

Davy crushed a Henry then started to sort out three huge lines. "Reet," said Davy, rolling up a twenty. "We want you to do a few more jobs. We want you to do something for us. You will be paid for it, but you will do as we ask."

Gary looked at Karl.

"Look," said Davy, "I could have come here and not given you nothing. No car, no money, so let's not fucking bullshit here."

Gary asked, "What is it you want us to do?"

Davy looked into his eyes, offering him the rolled-up twenty. "Exactly what we tell you to do," said Davy. "Here is a basher phone. I will arrange another car for you to use. I do not like you using the same car twice. You're going back to Manchester, then a trip to Carlisle, and home. Your end will be five grand – simple."

The two gays stood looking at Davy, stunned.

"Well come on, get sniffing, I want my line," said Davy.

Gary went first, handing back to Davy. Davy handed to Karl, then he did his line after both gays did theirs. Davy took the twenty and placed it back in his wallet, leaving a pile of coke for Gary and Karl on the bench. "I will be in touch," he said, as he exited the house.

Back in the car, Davy lit his cigar whilst driving off. *Well, if I get this deal and the next, I will become a millionaire,* thought Davy. His biggest hurdle was those two guys. Using them as mules but making sure they were well-paid was the only way to secure their trust and loyalty, another rule Davy always stuck by. Davy phoned Luke. "The hand's been dealt." Luke knew exactly what he meant.

Once Davy had left, Gary looked at Karl. "The sooner I get this debt paid off, the better," he said.

Karl, stroking his beard, said, "At least we get to keep that Audi. You're taking me to Powerhouse tonight."

Gary looked at the money in his hand. "Well at least we were given something," he said to Karl. "At least they aren't just destroying us by taking everything," Gary agreed.

"I will come with you each time," said Karl in his feminine voice. "How much do we owe now?"

Gary looked at Karl, tears in his eyes. "Twenty-five grand. The last job paid back ten grand so by my calculations, I do a couple more jobs; on my calculator, right."

"At least we get a car, Gary," said Karl, mincing into the living room. "Let's forget about it and watch Graham Norton."

Both men sat on the sofa and began to watch TV.

"Ooooh, thank you, sir," said the salesman.

Davy clenched his fist and knocked the salesman clean out, stamping on his head as he went down. "Yeah, today's the day." Davy walked back to his car and quickly drove off.

The A19 was clear by then, as Davy sped up the motorway listening to his Motown hits, driving through the Tunnel, relatively satisfied that he managed to settle an old score. A celebration was in order. Driving to the BFG, Davy felt the rock in his jacket pocket. *A few lines; I feel I deserve it.* Plus, his adrenalin was through the roof. Calming down was his main priority. Thinking of what that stupid twat must have thought when he woke up, Davy laughed sinisterly. He had a sick sense of humour. *He certainly got a surprise. Banged out, thinking he was going to sell me a piece of shit car. What the fuck?* Laughing out loud, Davy thought, *The fella will think twice on ripping off people ever again.*

Davy entered the street. BFG was having a barbecue.

"How's it gan, Davy?" said BFG.

"Fine, big fella," Davy replied as he entered the garden.

"Grab a beer." Davy grabbed one. BFG noticed blood on Davy's hand, pointing out, "Been decorating, Davy?"

Davy wiped his hand. "Nah, just taking care of some shit. Is that lamb?" he asked as he looked at the rack smoking away, taking emphasis away from his injured hand.

27

The Thai Wife and the Chip Shop Owner

Serving the general public was a way of life for Helen and George back in the late 1980s and 1990s. Back then you could smoke in a bar, enjoy a social drink, and disputes were resolved one way or another, either over a pint or up a back lane. There were no Jeremy Kyle shows to argue like a fucking faggot in front of the nation; back then people were realists. You did wrong, you got slapped. A simple solution often solved a problem. You either accepted it or you retaliated.

Jimmy sat in his home, remembering the years in the pubs. It was 1987, just before Christmas. A guy walked in with a Thai wife; they lived in Cramlington, eight miles from Shields. The guy, in many people's opinion, was a loudmouth, flash with the cash, 'look at me, I have a Thai bride' status. His attitude towards young lads was also his downfall – an arrogant attitude, rather like the bully. It was apparent when the guy walked into Jinglers, the way he acted towards Davy and Jimmy as if they were shit. The 'I am the boy here' kind of image; that was soon to change.

The Jinglers, back in the 1980s bore host to the hard cases of the club and bar scenes. They would come to old Geordies to unwind and socialise without being on the alert mode, having to watch for troublemakers. Jinglers was a private members' club; occasionally the odd idiot did get in but that came as part and parcel of the territory. *Sometimes a pup strays from its pack and learns the hard way*, thought Jimmy.

That night in particular was one of those very nights. Big T stood at six foot four, weighing in at a natural twenty stone. His hand speed was phenomenal for his size; his hands themselves were like shovels and one thing Big T did possess, believe it or not, was good looks. A hard case who bore good looks like him was a very dangerous man indeed. In his company was another equally dangerous man – Big M. Not as aggressive as Big T but far more powerful. A heavyweight boxer in world rankings. These men loved Jimmy and Davy's mother and father and considered Jinglers as their private watering hole. Entry into this domain had to be vetted and approved and the guys certainly didn't take kindly to a stray coming to that bar uninvited, especially when that stray created problems.

The atmosphere changed as soon as Big T and Big M came into the bar; you could feel the tension drop. The guy in question had already been slapped on a previous encounter with the big fella and you could see it really affected him.

"You smashed me up, Tony! Left me with a broken jaw!" cried the chip shop owner.

His wife didn't want anything to do with him; she was more interested in Davy, who wasn't interested; but in her eyes she thought she was in for a chance with a nineteen-year-old, baby-faced Hanson kid. This was creating problems in the first place, as her possessive husband hated her flirting but was being a prick with the young lad. It wasn't his fault the woman didn't love her husband but this magnanimous prick couldn't see past that. He actually thought everyone was after his wife, and now with Big T in the picture, this person's insecure nature was blatant. In other words, he strayed back into the lion's pride; up the swanee without a paddle.

T looked at him and said softly, "You better check your manners, mate, or you are going to get knocked out again."

You could see the big fella losing it slowly. "But you beat me up, it was disgusting," said the mouthpiece. Looking at Davy, he scowled. "She's my fucking wife."

Davy kept his cool. "Here mate, you can have her."

Ready to strike at any moment, Davy prepared himself; his adrenalin started to kick in, the leg started shaking, a clear indication of going to war.

Jimmy recalls the next moment. Big T jumped up and put fat boy in a sleeper; in seconds the chip shop owner was dragged out of the bar and thrown down the stairs. His wife stayed and finished her drink, and went outside to find him, possibly crying his eyes out. Jimmy recalled that one night all those years ago and pictured the fat bully as a person who could give it but couldn't take it. He actually presumed he was untouchable until his second encounter with Big T. Many a fool presumed this kind of behaviour was immune from any kind of reprisal, and many found out the hard way.

Having Jingling Geordies marked as a doormans' retreat was more of a good thing, really. It prevented the idiots from coming in thinking they could behave like idiots, and it provided George and Helen with a stress-free trade. Only a couple of times were there any altercations in Jingling Geordies. The two brothers being one, the fat chip shop owner, to the Walker idiot coming in one night thinking he could impress people with his tattooed hand. If anything he stood out like a sore thumb. It was generally good people who drank in Jinglers.

His incisive attitude towards Chris Lorrimer on one occasion was his demise. All night he had taken liberties by insulting Chris over his disability. Chris had polio as a youngster and he wore a caliper on his leg. The man's top half, however, resembled that of a bull. He was huge, a very powerful fisherman. The idiot from Walker pushed Chris too far, insulting the man, calling him spastic and a retard. Jimmy recalled how Chris leapt out of his chair and literally drill-punched the Walker nutcase's head into the floor. His head literally smashed into the floorboards; knocked him clean out for almost half an hour.

Chris sat back down with his wife like a true gentleman until the Walker idiot woke up. He wasn't so keen on opening his mouth then.

Davy and Jimmy had the upmost respect for Chris; a very hard man who took no prisoners, yet a gentle, caring individual who kept himself to himself and would have sooner had a peaceful life without violence. But that didn't mean that Chris was incapable of fighting, far from it. This man was a very hard man; he worked as a fisherman. He might have had weak legs but his mind and his determination and his drive far exceeded anybody. That, most in North Shields knew, and those who knew Chris, knew that a foolish mistake from a Walker bully certainly put said bully into a very dangerous zone, and he paid the price for his stupidity.

28

Intimidation

Some people in this world are sore losers; they can give it but can't take it. Some of these people run to the authorities. They hide like little rats; sneaky, devious, and sly. There's only one way to deal with a rat like that; only one way to rectify the injustice they create. Make their life a living hell. A shiny car gets Nitromors, a family pet gets put in the cat and dog shelter, paint gets sprayed on a front wall, the windows get tungsten punched, the front door gets superglued, the locks as well. It might take one year, two years, even five years, but the effects are devastating. The grass, the informant, the eager to open mouths to authority in any form. The psychological effects cause most to recalibrate their actions, to actually think as they look out the window at their shiny black car with its distinct Nitromors finish.

Davy's retribution, his code – a vicious, nasty cunt who will simply not stop. You wrong this man, create a situation, and he can play very dirty games. Being sly to a man like Davy, phoning the police, informing the council, playing the coward's way, does the person no favours whatsoever. Davy played a very dirty game with people he considered to fit that profile.

The Royal nightclub, back in the 1990s, proved one such occasion. The guys from Wakefield had a fight and lost. Davy was minding his own business when the trouble erupted in the chip shop. One of the Wakefield guys ended up hospitalised and Davy was arrested as he was the only one standing there. The Wakefield guy accused Davy of this act, saying he knocked him out, effectively lying as the person who knocked the guy out ran away.

Davy was furious.

"Get that idiot told to drop these charges," he said to the owners of the chippy and the Royal. They agreed Davy had nothing to do with it; he wasn't involved. The guy, a sore loser, stood resolute. He was adamant Davy hit him; even with the evidence before him, he still was sticking to his story. It went on for weeks.

"Right, fuck it," said Davy. The van was hit, their addresses were approached, the cat and the dog went missing. These guys opened a can of worms. The final insult was the car clamp on the idiot's wife's car in Wakefield outside the school. Now this twat knew he was fucking playing a dangerous game; the others were all telling him to drop the charges.

A wheel bin outside one of their homes was set on fire, their cars were Nitromorsed; the game became relentless. There was divorce in the air, bags being thrown out on the street. The guy in question put his head in his hands and cried, begging Davy's friends for a solution. "Please tell 'im I am a stupid fool. Please ask 'im to stop."

The message was relayed back to Davy and when answering bail, NFA was read out by the custody sergeant. Once Davy sat in his car, reading the paper, a car pulled up alongside his. The ginger idiot sitting in the car scowled at Davy. "You blew up my van last night, you fucking arsehole."

Davy looked him squarely in the eyes, the street full of parents and children going to school. Davy kept his cool, blowing cigar smoke into the idiot's face. "Fuck off," said Davy, as he closed his electric window. The idiot sped off, furious. *Fire with fire,* thought Davy.

The numpty and the video, a clear case of stupidity. The gutless little cunt even thought he was untouchable; bags of rubbish emptied on his lawn, superglue on his doors, the car windows and tyres, the house peppered with creosote bombs. His wife was pulling her hair out. *Fight fire with fire,* thought Davy.

Davy remembered the words an arsehole once said: 'The power of the pen is mightier than the sword.' *True,* thought Davy, *but every action someone takes deserves a reaction. Fight fire with fire.*

29

The Mechanic

John Smith lay on his wheel board under the car he was fixing, unaware that three men had walked in. He had been approached weeks ago about doing dodgy MOTs and John was having none of it. "Nah, mate. Can't, I will go to prison, fella. I can't and I won't," said John.

"But we will sort you out with good money, mate," said the little fella. "Come on, think about it for a while. We will come back," the little fella said sarcastically.

John squared up to them. "Is that a threat, like? Stupid twat. I told you no, now get out of my garage. Understand?"

A couple of John's mates turned up.

"What's up, John?"

The little fella looked at John and walked out. kicking his toolset into the pit.

"A misunderstanding," said John. "Just a misunderstanding."

Turning to his car lift, this unnerved John. He had never been approached like that before and it worried him. He wasn't one for going to the police, it wasn't his style. John would sooner deal with things the man's way.

Three weeks and John had clearly forgotten about it until today. A spanner rattled as it was kicked across the floor. "Who's that?" shouted John. Suddenly the car lowered, pinning John underneath. "Whoa, whoa! Who the fuck is this?"

The little fella started to speak. "We said we would be back!"

"You fucking little wanker!" shouted John. "You little bastard, I will rip your head off!" he shouted louder.

The little fella poured petrol over the engine where John was lying. "Shut up," he said.

A sharp pain seared through John's body. The little fella's goons started to break his legs.

"You won't fucking help us. We offer you money, you tell us to leave and now we resort to this, you stubborn prick," said the little fella. "My name's Simon. You never even asked me my name. Well, Simon says you are fucked." Laughing a sinister laugh, "Drag him out," he ordered his goons. "Now pour oil down his throat and smash him up." The little guy watched as John was beaten to a pulp and left for dead. The little fella flicked his cigarette at John. "Change your mind, you stupid twat. Change your mind."

John rolled over onto his back, beaten and bloodied, spitting blood, before he passed out.

"What is your name?" said the paramedic. "Can you hear me?" The sound of the radios and siren echoed. "You have been in a very bad accident. We are taking you to the hospital." Cutting the boiler suit off, they told him, "John, your wife is here."

John's wife held his hand, crying. "You will be alright, darling. Jesus, Jesus."

As the ambulance bounced over the speed hump, almost there, John drifted back to sleep.

"Wake up, you lazy twat." A big lump stood next to the hospital bed.

John farted a sulphurous fart.

"Jesus." Opening the window, Jay stood holding a bunch of grapes.

"My nose is itchy," said John through his wired jaw.

"There you gan." Jay scratched it. "Have the coppers interviewed you?" said Jay.

"Yeshhh (yes), they've been," said John.

"I found you, mate," said Jay. "They done a number on you," he said, switching on the telly. "I am here every day. By the way, bud, your lass is fine, and the kids. Listen," said Jay, checking the room for any listening devices or ears that shouldn't be listening. "We know the fuckers that done this to you. The big fella's been kicking doors; he's been gan off it. You better get healed fast, John. Those clowns will be in here very soon." He indicated that the BFG was on the case.

John grunted in pain. "Mosher fuchhers (mother fuckers)," said John.

"The little fella is a car thief from the West End." Jay showed John a piece of paper with his name on (Alan Smith). John's eyes were filled with rage.

"Fucking little twat. The other two come from Byker." He showed the second piece of paper (Ian Jackson and Jerry Dunn). The papers were set on fire and thrown out of the window. "Just being careful," said Jay. "It's getting sorted, don't worry." John farted again. "You can cut that right out," said Jay. "A'm not scratching yer nose if you keep farting."

As Jay started to eat the grapes like a big gorilla, John watched in total amusement. *Of all the people to nursemaid me, this big bastard had to be the one,* he thought.

*

Davy's phone rang. *BFG, wonder what he wants,* thought Davy, answering.

"I need you to visit," said the big fella.

"Yeah, where?"

"My house."

Davy said, "Ok."

"Now," said the BFG, in an angry, unnerving voice.

Davy drove to the BFG's home. He was called. Something's rattled his cage.

Davy arrived at the BFG's home. Driving around the back, he parked the car and used the back gate.

"Come in, Davy." A friendlier voice. "You want a cup of tea?"

"Why not?" A look of bewilderment in Davy's eyes. "What can I do you for?" said Davy.

"You heard about the mechanic?" said BFG.

"Yeah, I heard," said Davy.

"I have names. I want 'em done badly," said the BFG. The microwave was put on full power as the men spoke; radiation messes with any listening devices. "You can't be too careful," said BFG. Pulling out a plate, he poured gravy on it and wrote the names down using the spatula. BFG rubbed the words out and Davy asked in writing, 'Where are they?'

The men relayed messages back and forth in this manner for a good twenty minutes. The last words written were by Davy: 'Ok.' With that, Davy sat back and drank his tea. Now they talked.

"How's you?"

"I am fine, buddy. Hand healed?" said the BFG as Davy lifted his hand, stretching his fingers.

The men sat chatting for most of the afternoon about family, friends, and the weather. They had a good talk. Getting up, Davy looked at his watch. "It is getting done," he said, indicating with his fingers, "in two days."

Ian Jackson and terry Dunn watched TV in Terry's flat based within Byker Wall. A parcel slip had come through the door that morning with the words 'missed delivery, will be back at 4 pm'.

"Wonder what it is, Terry."

"A fink it's a phone," said Terry, stoned from the bong he had just been doing in the kitchen.

Ian took a draw of the joint he was sharing.

Knock, knock!! The door went. It was 4 p.m.

"Parcel," said the voice on the other side. Terry opened the door with the chain on. "Parcel, mate. You need to sign for it," said the man dressed in the delivery t-shirt and baseball cap. "It's bulky."

Terry grumbled, "Fuck's sake!"

Taking the chain off, a Taser went straight into his neck. *Zap.* He lay on the floor and four burly men stormed the flat. Ian didn't even have time to shout when he was Tasered as well. Both men were quickly taped up, cable tied, and placed kneeling onto the floor. The TV was turned up enough to drown out noise. The four men stood in the living room.

"Now," said the delivery man, masked and now wearing a boiler suit. "You like beating people up?" said the delivery man, showing the men a photo of John.

They went white, mumbling under the gaffer tape over their mouths.

Delivery Man walked over to the cabinet with his wrapped-up parcel. Opening it out, a selection of knives and snips were revealed. "Now for some fun."

Delivery Man walked over, snipping off Ian's pinky finger. Crying in pain, Ian's muffled scream couldn't be heard. Delivery Man's surgical-gloved hands placed the snips down. A swift smack in the face of Ian silenced his crying. Then the meat cleaver. Delivery Man swung it into Terry's arm. Delivery Man stuck knives in their legs and arms, then he started with the snips, snipping off both the men's thumbs. Delivery Man started to go to work on their ears, snipping them off with shears, putting them on the floor. He slowly sliced off their noses using a razor-sharp filleting knife, slowly sweeping the knife across their faces.

Both men were mumbling wrecks. Kneeling them upright, the men held them. When Delivery Man pulled out the lemon juice, pouring it over their heads, muffled screams drowned out by the TVs noise went undetected. Ian shit himself, terror in his eyes as he frantically tried to breathe through the gaping hole in his face. A small hole was placed in each piece of tape covering their mouths. Terry was equally terrified.

Their ordeal lasted for half an hour. The four men packed up and quickly knocked the pair unconscious before taking their mouth tape off. Exiting the flat, the men quietly left undetected and slipped into the side alley towards their parked van.

Driving off to the waste ground, the van was torched along with the boiler suits and masks and gloves they wore.

Davy sat in his car; the phone rang. "What you wearing, baby?" said the BFG.

Davy laughed. "Fine, fine," said Davy. "I am finishing early. My hedges need pruning so I am in the garden all day," said Davy, "but apart from that it's all good."

BFG said, "Davy, guess who is wanting to meet up with me? He thinks it's North Shields lads that are after him," said the BFG.

"Let me guess – A, first name. S, second," said Davy.

"Precisely," said the BFG. "Do you wanna or shall I?"

Davy laughed. "I will let you do that one. Perhaps it would be more insulting coming from his own as he seems to believe he is protected. Ooh, tell him Simon said you're fucked, buddy. He apparently goes by the name Simon, stupid little parasite."

BFG laughed. "Will do, big fella. Will do. Talk tomorrow."

30

The Curry House

Sitting in Tynemouth front street, JJ and Jack Thompson had enjoyed a few pints. The football had been playing in the Salutation and the boys were in good spirits – Newcastle won. Jack had given JJ 200 quid that day to enjoy the day out and not feel he was worthless. JJ was a bit down on luck; he had been laid off and hadn't had a job for a couple of months. JJ sat and slowly drank his pint, ogling the women as they walked past their table.

"So, any news on work, JJ?" said Jack.

"Nothing, mate."

"Something will turn up," said JJ.

"Well I fancy buying an ice cream van myself," said Jack. "Distribution, if you know what I mean." JJ knew exactly what Jack was meaning. "Perhaps we could come to some arrangement. Money's good, you work for me, we get shot of the shit. However, the big fella needs to know of my plans," said Jack. "Loyalty comes without saying, JJ," said Jack.

"Davy likes me," said JJ.

"Yeah, I wouldn't be sitting with you if he didn't," said Jack. "Anyway, we can talk later about this. Now, what's the time?"

Time was getting on. The boys had been drinking all afternoon and they were getting a bit peckish.

"Fancy a curry?" said JJ. The Gate of India was situated next to the Turk's Head.

"Yeah, why not?" said Jack. "We can get a taxi later."

"Yeah, why not leave the car in Tynemouth?" said JJ.

Both men downed their pints and walked across the road to the curry house.

"Welcome, sir," as the men walked in. "Table for two?"

Jack received the menu. JJ ordered two pints, as the men discussed business.

"Jack, just one thing, mate," said JJ. "If I get to do this I won't let you down."

Jack looked into JJ's eyes. "Mate, this is why I am asking you, but it has to be run by Davy and Jimmy."

JJ looked at Jack. "Do you think they will go for this?" said JJ.

A young couple came into the restaurant; the couple were seated next to Jack and JJ. The men stopped talking as they sat down. "Let's phone for a taxi," said JJ.

Jack phoned Davy as the men walked out.

JJ said, "Is the taxi going to be long, Jack?"

"Ten minutes," said Jack.

It wasn't long until Davy's car pulled up. "Oy-oy, lads," said Davy.

"How's it gan?" said Jack.

"So you lads been in there?" said Davy.

"Yeah," said Jack.

Davy looked at them. "That place is owned by the former proprietor of the Bombay on Prudhoe Street. They found half an Alsatian in his freezer. When I was a kid we used to set his rubbish on fire. Maggots and rats, the restaurant was fucking lifting (dirty). Bastard. I wouldn't eat anything that dirty twat puts down," said Davy.

"I find his food alreet," said JJ.

"Each to their own. I certainly wouldn't eat his scran (food)," said Davy as they pulled off onto Tynemouth Road. Davy told Jack to open the glove box and grab a CD case. He handed Jack a bag of coke. "Do the honours," said Davy. "Three thick, healthy ones, if you please, Jacky lad!"

As Davy pulled into the Knots flats car park, "Right," he said, directed at JJ. "You want to make some money?"

As the men surveyed the area to do their lines, JJ took the rolled twenty and CD case, listening as Davy spoke.

"You will be given a Henry to start with. I want to see how you roll. The ice cream van is being bought next week, in your name mind, JJ. I will get the gear and only provide you with enough you could class as personal. Understand this – you get lifted with a shitload, you do fifteen years. A small amount, you get a slap on the wrist. You do not, however, stay in the same area on any one given day. It's got to be random. Our guys drop the punters, they ring your basher phone, drive to the area where they are. You sell the shit in the bottom of an ice cream cone and never, never mention the product by name. Use code like a JJ special with monkey blood. That's coke. A chocolate special is acid or E. Speed is a special. Don't ever mention the product in its name, do you understand?"

"Yeah!" said JJ.

"Also," said Davy, "You carry coffee a jar of it for your tea breaks. The gear – now listen, this is important – the gear goes into the coffee jar and it gets buried. Sniffer dogs can find gear but in coffee it's very hard to detect. You start next week. From now on, though, you deal only with me. Relay it through Jack. You have my word nobody, nobody in our circle grasses or tries to rip each other off," said Davy.

JJ thanked Jack and Davy, eager to get started.

"Your end, you get ten quid for every G you sell, so you bash the gear, use teething powder and Pro Plus. Plus, you can sell ice cream," said Jack.

The men sat for a while, talking.

Davy said, "Do another three of them, Jack, and I will drop you home."

Jack agreed saying to JJ, "You want dropped in Shields or Howdon?"

JJ said, "Either, mate," as he snorted his nostrils, ready to sniff another line.

31

Ohh, It's Only My Son. Go and Play.

Jimmy, Davy, Steve, Micky, and Mark were down on the fish quay. The year was 1983. The boys were climbing on board fishing vessels, trying to steal whatever they could; fishing hooks, knives, anything the boys could find useful in their active lives.

It was a Norwegian long liner sitting on the west quay on a summer's evening when the boys climbed on board. Davy remembered well, the lads climbed over the gunwales and were trying to steal bobbins of cat gut and hooks, which were used in the method of fishing that particular boat was doing. It was Steve who whispered, "Lads, look at this."

They all came to investigate through a porthole. They looked at a party going in full swing; drink. drugs, and naked prostitutes played cards. The party listened to the Black is Black song on the stereo, when it was noticed a woman was sat with her bra off playing cards.

"Give me a look," said Mark.

"No," said Jimmy. "You don't want to, mate. The party's over." He tried to prevent Mark from seeing.

Mark was having none of this, he wanted his cheap thrill, pushing and shoving the lads out of the way. "You're sly cunts. I want a look." He got more than a cheap thrill as he peered through the porthole. The naked woman walked over, as plain as day, saying, "Ohh, it's only my son. Go play."

Davy recalled the way Mark walked home, wounded emotionally, seeing his own mother in that situation. Davy sat in his car thinking of that evening. *Life's hard,* he said to himself. *Life's unfair sometimes.*

Another incident remembered well was the time in the gut (the fishing harbour) of North Shields, when Jimmy, Davy, and Steve were climbing on board the boats. One in particular was owned by two brothers. The boys were, as usual, looking for items of use, when they heard screaming. Angry, very angry screaming – the language was choice. The two brothers had only invited a well-known woman on board for a drink. The boys looked through the window on the forward cabin. The woman was tied to the table; the brothers were pissed, lopping about in the cabin. They were cutting her hair with gutting knives and they painted her arse green with gloss paint, and the crown Jewel was a lit cigar stuck up her arse. Davy laughed, remembering that sight, and what really stuck in the lads' minds that day, it was the mother of another one of their mates.

You grew up fast in the 1970s. Perhaps the drive and determination instilled, and the witnessing of a kid growing up in that era made them the people they are today. But Davy knew one thing – he never forgot the painted arse of that woman all those years ago.

The distinctive buzz of the plotter started off a job – High Farm. Davy started his engine and proceeded towards his fare.

32

The Allotment

Jimmy and Davy were driving to Whitley Bay. It was a crisp October day; the boys were away down to the allotment.

"Has that steroid boy been in contact anymore?" said Jimmy.

"Nah, he hasn't rang for a few days," said Davy, pulling into the parking bay just outside the allotment gate.

"Well he had better," said Jimmy. "One of my grows almost got stolen because of him and his fucking mouth," said Jimmy.

"Stupidity springs to mind," said Davy.

"He apparently opened his mouth at the gym he goes to. Been talking to a juice head (steroid abuser) he considers a friend. Since he has been on the juice his brains turned to mush," said Jimmy, getting angrier and more frustrated every second he talked about it. "Well, I want something done about this now. Steroid freak is going to get it (beaten). His stupidity almost cost me big."

Davy shook his head. "Stupid, stupid man. Invite him down, make it civil. It's a nice day, get my sparring gloves out the shed," said Davy.

Jimmy grinned viciously. "Why not?" Jimmy got straight on the phone. "How's it gan? A've got a surprise for you," said Jimmy.

"Ok," said Keith.

"Come down to the Seahorse pub in Whitley, next to the allotments."

"Alright," said Keith.

"It's a nice day, isn't it?" said Jimmy, keeping things civil. Keith asked if he should bring his girlfriend down. Jimmy said, "No, I have something here for you, Keith. I don't like doing business this way."

Keith agreed. "Ok, Jimmy," he said, under the illusion that he was going to get his end of the crop that was pulled down. Putting down his phone, Keith smiled. *I get six grand today, yippee!*

The events that took place at his flat in Forrest Hall were still vivid in his mind. *That fucking Eric,* he thought, *fucking tried to squirt me at my own door.* "Some friend, that one," said Keith, knowing his stupidity in trusting his so-called mate almost landed him in a whole heap of bother. *I knew Jimmy would understand,* thought Keith, checking out his bulging muscles as he jumped in his A3 Audi. Phoning his girlfriend, Keith started the car. "Won't be long, babes," said Keith. "Just have a small errand to do." She grumbled on the other end of the phone, unaware his fate was to be sealed.

On arrival at Whitley, Davy waited, stripped to the waist. His natural eighteen-stone frame glistened with sweat as he pounded the three-hundred-pound bag. "A light warmup gets the heart pumping," said Davy to Jimmy. "Bring him here to get his surprise," said Davy.

Vicious eyes stared back at his brother. "The eyes of a killer," said Jimmy.

Keith pulled into the side road of the Seahorse. Seeing Jimmy smiling gave him reassurance.

"How's it gan?" said Jimmy.

"Fine. Told my lass I was going on an errand, didn't tell her I was meeting you," said Keith.

"Good, good. The less people know, the better." Jimmy started talking, getting Keith relaxed. "So now you get paid, buddy. Good score on that last lot. Come over to my office."

The cats and dogs from the shelter barked and barked as the men walked to the allotment. Music played loudly, drowning out the football match playing at Whitley FC. Directing Keith to the shed, Jimmy allowed Keith in first then quickly slammed the door behind him. The screams started; the walls started shaking. A momentous battle was taking place in the shed, the music played loudly to drown out the noise.

An allotment neighbour shouted to turn the music down. Jimmy just held his hand to his ear, saying, "What did you say?"

The shed went still. Jimmy felt the vibration in his pocket; it was Davy sending a text. "Turn the music down and get the car." Jimmy did as instructed.

Opening the door, Keith lay on the floor, beaten to a pulp, groaning. Davy wrapped him up in a blanket like a carpet roll and started wiping the blood off his hands and chest. He quickly drew some water and washed his face clean of the speckles of blood splatter. "Get the cunt's keys for his car," said Davy, putting on his shirt. Then he started carrying Keith out of the shed like a carpet fitter. Davy threw him in the boot. "Reet, get his car and follow me."

The men drove off after locking the allotment. Keith lay in the boot, groaning.

As Davy pulled up in east Howdon, opening the boot, he grabbed Keith. "You fucking asked for that, you stupid cunt." Keith's car was parked next to Davy. "Now here's your money."

True to Davy and Jimmy's word, they gave him the six grand. "You're a fucking liability, Keith. Don't ever contact, look at, or speak to me ever again," said Jimmy.

"You fucked yourself with us," said Davy as the men jumped in their car and drove off.

Keith, still badly beaten, climbed into his car, wincing from broken ribs and covered in blood. He started the car and drove home.

Davy drove with Jimmy back to the allotment.

"Reet, find this Eric. He gets a fucking slap as well," said Davy, fuelled up with adrenalin. "Go in my glove box, Jimmy," said Davy.

Jimmy pulled out a Henry of coke. "We will have some when we get back to the allotment."

The men drove slowly to Whitley.

"I wonder if the match is finished," said Jimmy.

"Burn that blanket," said Davy.

"The brazen takes two minutes to light," said Jimmy.

Both the men arrived back at the allotment and started to turn the beds and weed. The brazen roared; the shed was cleaned and washed with disinfectant.

Davy and Jimmy sat that evening drinking a cold beer in the garden section.

"Can't wait to clip that steg-head (steroid abuser) Eric. I heard he thinks himself a tough cunt."

Jimmy laughed. "So did Keith. I think he shit himself," he said, laughing out loud. "Come on, let's do a livener (pick-me-up)," said Jimmy, putting the Henry on the tray.

*

Eric Cumberland heard what happened to Keith. *Fuck,* he thought. *Fuck.* Asking questions among his gym circle, Eric asked the name, Dangerous Dave. Faces went white.

"You stupid bastard," said one of the lads doing weights. "You realise, mate, you signed your own death warrant with that nasty piece of work."

The others started distancing themselves from Eric.

"What? How was I supposed to know? I didn't know it was his operation." He put his towel down on the bench. "Look, if you guys know him, please tell him I do not want any trouble, ok? Please. It was Keith, he never told me. Honest."

The guys looked at Eric.

"Look, mate," said one, "don't tell us your problems and especially do not talk about anything to do with Dangerous Dave. Don't. I can't be implicated in anything you get yourself into. Please." The guy said that and turned his back.

"Ok, ok."

Eric felt like a fart in a space suit. He created an atmosphere and just created himself problems. Eric finished his gym class and drove home. Locking his door, he put weapons all over his house, switching the lights off, watching through the blinds at every single car light and noise he heard. Eric was well and truly spooked. Eric decided, *That's it.* He packed his clothes and put them in his car. He left that night and with no intention of returning, he drove past Keith's, looking at the window before he drove off towards the tunnel and the south.

"Fuck!" he shouted out loud as he drove through the tunnel, thinking of the screw-up he created himself. "Fuck."

33

The Trip to Scotland

Lanty filled up the Lexus. He picked his trusted team, in particular, a sadistic specialist torturer, Big Freddy, to come on a little trip to Scotland. The car was big enough for the individuals he had chosen to sit in comfort.

Steve came back from the garage, his hands full of crisps and energy drinks. Climbing in the back seat, he put the items down. "No smoking with me in this car," he pointed out to Freddy. "I hate the smell."

Freddy laughed. "We can stop for a fag break, can't we?" said Freddy as Lanty jumped in, wired from the fat line of cocaine he had just taken in the toilet.

"I can facilitate that," said Lanty. "You should pack those things in," said Lanty, putting the chip of chewing gum in his mouth. "Reet, let's gan. The fella wants me to view his car at three p.m."

"Where is it we are going to?" said Freddy.

"Aberdeen – the granite city," said Lanty. "Like I said, guys," as Lanty joined the A19, "he thinks I am interested in his car. I get to deal with this fella personally; he has something I want."

Freddy checked the bag of tools in the footwell – knives, a cordless drill (fully charged), a Taser, snips, and gaffer tape.

"Put them under the seat," said Lanty as he drove up to the A1 northbound turn-off. "So for all intents and purposes, he thinks I am buying his car and you guys come along as a driver and mechanic to bring the Lexus back once we meet him. If it's clear, he gets Tasered and taped up. I have a location to take him." Lanty put the basher phone on the dash. "I want this done fast and silently. The little rat is at my mate's garage where he thinks he is safe. Little does he know the friend of mine has his own personal grievances with him."

Freddy listened.

"What is it all about?" said Steve.

"It's about a wedding present and a movie," said Lanty.

The men started driving to Edinburgh.

"You can have a smoke in Berwick," said Lanty.

Steve laughed.

"You pair of twats," said Freddy, as the men both laughed at his expense, chewing his chewing gum at a hundred miles an hour.

Tom looked at his watch – 13.00, time to take the car to be sold at Harry's garage in Bridge of Don. He knew at time of day traffic wasn't bad; rush hour, however, was at 1600hrs and onwards, right up to seven at night. *Fuck that*, he thought. His Vectra was parked outside his flat and it was almost time for him to go. *Hope the English bastards brought the money, it's a cash sale.* He was down a bit on luck lately. Most of his friends had been arrested and faced long terms in jail. Being caught with heroin, plus he owed certain criminals from Glasgow money, Tom wasn't fairing right at all.

It had been a year since Gillian's wedding and Tom had clearly forgotten about it his stash of porno videos in his floor safe which was almost empty of money, so the sale of his car was important, especially today. He had debts to pay and they were not going to wait much longer. However, those certain debts were already in the hands of a far more dangerous individual who had full gratis on Tom's head, and nobody was to intervene (Luke). Unknowingly, Tom's fate was travelling up the Aberdeen Road at seventy miles per hour. He was getting payment alright, just not the payment he was expecting.

The minutes ticked by.

The phone rang. Answering, Tom said, "Hello!"

The voice on the other end said, "Hello there, mate. I shouldn't be long, just entering Aberdeen." It was Lanty using his phone voice – a very posh Monkseaton accent.

Putting down the phone, Freddy mimicked Lanty's sophisticated voice, taking the piss. Steve laughed. All three men had been taking the piss out of each other for the full four-hour journey.

Lanty pulled up towards the garage. Harry sat in his garage waiting for Lanty to arrive.

As the Lexus pulled up, Lanty, Freddy, and Steve climbed out and walked into the garage. Harry walked out to greet them, "How's it going, boys?" in his thick Scottish accent. "The fucker's coming," said Harry.

Lanty said, "Good, good. Steve, be a good fellow and do some lines in Uncle Harry's office."

Harry laughed. "A wee celebration, Lanty boy," said Harry.

"Yes, something like that," said Lanty. He told Steve to wait in the office out of sight, giving him the Taser. Steve agreed.

Freddy stood having a fag. "How we doing this?" he said.

"I will ask daft lad to bring the car in. No more customers this afternoon," said Harry. "Then we grab the wee twat. He knows to bring the car to the gate. I will let him drive in," said Harry.

"Fool proof," said Lanty.

Lanty's phone rang.

"Hello?" he answered in his phone voice. "Yes, I am here. Now what? You will be five minutes. Oh good, see you then," said Lanty. "He's around the corner."

Tom approached the gate. Harry stood there, opening them. Tom drove into the forecourt.

"Drive it to the ramp inside," instructed Harry.

A shined and freshly washed Vectra entered the garage. Harry closed the gates and put the chain on. Tom didn't even notice.

"How's it going?" said Lanty as Tom climbed out of the car.

"Fine, mate. Fine. So you want to look at the car?" he asked, as Harry entered the garage, closing the main door.

"A wee bit cold," said Harry. "I will put the heaters on."

Tom said, "It's only got twenty-two thousand on the clock," unaware he was now the prey.

"Really? May we look under the hood?"

"Yeah," said Tom. Harry popped the bonnet.

"So is that new?" said Lanty, pointing to the air filter.

"Ohh, is that an oil leak?" said Freddy.

Tom looked to investigate. As he bent down, Steve, who swiftly came from the office, zapped him. Tom lay on the floor as the men beat him over the head with a mallet.

"Tape the cunt," said Lanty, "and his fucking mouth," as Tom lay unconscious on the garage floor. "Now I think I can do with a piss and a line." Looking savagely at the excuse of a human now taped and gagged on the floor, he started to come around, bewildered, with terror in his eyes. "You're coming with me for a little chat, Tom. Remember Gillian?" said Lanty.

Tom looked even more scared than before.

"Here, listen. There's someone who wants to talk to you about your 130 grand debt you owe the Glasgow firms." Lanty put the phone to his ear.

Luke spoke softly and calmly. "Your lap dancing club is mine. Your car, money, everything belongs to me, you stupid little shit, and the debt you owe is mine. You owe me the wedding present you gave Gillian, remember?" Tom started to cry. "Well my present to Gillian is you. You stupid boy." Luke asked for Lanty. Lanty put the phone back to his own ear. "Do the honours, Lanty. Get the videos and anything else," said Luke.

"Will do," said Lanty in his Geordie accent. "Will do."

Harry looked down at Tom. "Remember her?" he asked, showing a picture of a beautiful blonde lass. "She was my niece. You pushed smack into her, you wee bastard." He kicked Tom cleanly in the face.

Lanty stopped Harry. "Harry, not yet. He's going to the lab up by Peter Culter, remember?" said Lanty.

Harry looked at Lanty. "Is he going to suffer?" said Harry.

"Ohh yes, he is going to suffer, believe me. You have to get the videos off this shitbag and I am going to make him give me them and anything else." Lanty told Freddy, "Get the Lexus. The boot's been lined out."

Freddy went out through the door and started the car. The main door was opened and the car was reversed in.

"Wait until it's dark," said Lanty.

The boot was opened and Tom was searched and shoved in. His keys, phone, money, everything was taken off him. The boot was left open.

"I have a fucking sedative for this cunt," said Lanty, holding a hypodermic needle. "He gets this soon." He put it on the table next to the car.

Tom started whimpering uncontrollably.

"Shut the fuck up," said Freddy, smacking him in the face. "You can cry tonight, you little rat."

The men sat next to the open boot and played cards, occasionally giving Tom a slap. Lanty knocked up big lines. Harry didn't do coke but he didn't mind. The boys had a different feel around them; their natures were wired.

"This motherfucker gets tortured badly tonight," said Freddy.

The guys laughed. "Look at his eyes," said Lanty.

"Killer look," said Harry, rather nervous of the man he just met and had now seen in true evil form.

It was 9 p.m. "Time to go inject Tom with the needle," said Lanty. "Pee-pee time," as he rolled him onto his back. Crying, Tom's eyes started getting heavy. "Good boy," said Lanty with a sinister grin. "Reet, let's gan."

As the men opened the garage door, Lanty drove the Lexus. Freddy jumped in. "Steve, you take the Vectra to the scrapyard, get it crushed." Harry knew of these instructions. "It's worth fuck all to us."

Driving up to Harry's lab, Lanty talked to Freddy. "So mate, how's you these days?"

The music played softly on the radio.

"Ok, Lanty. Taking the kids to Disneyland Paris next month. The wife's better, had her operation. All is good," said Freddy.

Somebody looking in would have thought these two men were

just ordinary fellas on a night out. You wouldn't ever suspect the pair were transporting a man in the boot. Lanty politely stopped the car and flashed the police car through. The policeman waved cheerfully as he drove past them.

It took half an hour for Lanty to get to his lab, a container in the middle of a builders' yard in a remote part of Aberdeenshire. The high fences hid the men from view.

Dragging Tom out of the boot effortlessly, Freddy told Lanty, "Grab my instruments."

Lanty grabbed the bag then parked the car in the far corner of the yard. Freddy slammed Tom in the seat prepared by Harry the night before; plastic sheeting draped the sides and the floor. Putting his white paper suit on, Freddy pulled on the long gauntlet gloves and donned the wellingtons. "Dressed to go to work," he said to Lanty. "Keep toot."

Freddy opened his bag. Pulling out the tape, he secured Tom to the chair.

"There now," said Freddy as Tom started to wake up. "Had a nice sleep? Now I am going to ask you, where are the movies?"

The dim light shone with the red bulb glowing as Tom started trying to apologise. "Please, I will give you them. Let me go, please," Tom sobbed to Freddy.

"Where are the video tapes?" said Freddy. "I won't ask you again. All of them." Tom looked at Freddy in terror. "Ok," said Freddy. "Hard play, then. Hard play it is." He pulled out the drill, Tom looked in terror before he was gagged quickly. Freddy took long screws and drove one into Tom's foot, doing the same on the other. Tom screamed in agony under his muffled gag.

Freddy asked him again, "Where are the films?" smiling in Tom's face. "Scream and I do even worse," said Freddy, removing his gag.

Tom panted, "It's, it, itt-ttt's, in my flat, in the floor safe, I swear. Please, pleeeease."

"Has it a combination?" said Lanty.

"Yeah, it's 4321 4321. Please, please, pleeeassse," Tom begged.

"Where's the floor safe?" said Lanty.

"In my bedroom," Tom panted.

Lanty left the container. Closing the door, he told Freddy, "Watch him," as he phoned Harry.

"It's done," said Harry. "His car's crushed."

"Good," said Lanty. "You got his flat keys," said Lanty. "Go there." He relayed the information Tom gave him. "Phone me when it's done."

Lanty walked back into the container and checked his phone for a signal.

"Gag him," said Lanty. Freddy did just that. "Fancy a line, Freddy?" said Lanty.

"Why not?"

"So how much did that holiday cost?" asked Lanty.

"Ohh, a couple of grand," said Freddy. "Is it ok to smoke?"

"Yeah, why not?"

As the men sat at the table waiting for the phone to ring, two fat lines were made and the men sniffed them down. Lanty crumpled the rock for two more healthy ones. "Must feed the other nostril," said Lanty.

Freddy laughed. "You're class, you, like," he said.

Tom, in agony, looked, breathing heavily, at these two men talking like normal. In terror, he knew deep down his dirty lowlife practices landed him in a very dangerous situation. Gillian went through his mind over and over again, his whole life passing in front of him; his whole miserable existence flashing before his eyes.

"Poo, is that you, Tom?" said Lanty. "You just shit yourself, you dirty boy." He laughed at Tom in his misery.

"Need a gas mask to torture this one," said Freddy. Lanty laughed.

Half an hour passed. The men were sat talking when Lanty's phone rang. "Yeah, you got it all plus eight grand. Ahh, that's good, and anything else you got?"

"Gold rings and chains."

"Anything more?"

"Yeah, half a kilo of coke."

"Great news," said Lanty. "Now torch his fucking flat once you get everything."

Harry sniggered with pleasure. Lanty spoke down the phone. "See you here soon."

The men sat back down and talked. Tom watched in bewilderment, sitting in his own shit, his feet pouring with blood.

Freddy stood up. "Ahh, let's just finish this." Freddy grabbed his knife and approached Tom. Slicing his face, he slowly took off his ears, then slashed Tom's legs. "Get the snips."

He started to cut his toes off, then his fingers, leaving two and a thumb on his left hand.

"He needs to feed his fucking addiction after tonight," said Freddy, laughing.

Tom screamed in agony and eventually passed out. Freddy started singing Whistle While You Work, to the amusement of Lanty, who almost did a double take at the sight of his mate carving up Tom.

"Where's the gear?" said Freddy, putting Tom's big toe in his jacket pocket.

"Here," said Lanty.

"Good. Harry can get this arsehole smacked up."

Harry arrived after about forty minutes.

"Ohh, great work," said Harry, looking at Tom. The items were all in the bag Harry handed to Lanty. Lanty handed Harry the smack (heroin).

"Your play, my son," said Lanty.

Harry walked over to Tom, who was awake now, breathing through his nose, covered in blood. "Look at you now, you wee bastard," said Harry, holding up the needle. "This is for Maria, you dirty little fucking parasite." Harry injected Tom with the heroin. "Wait till it takes effect, you rat. Now you have a habit and you have nothing. Now you're fucking homeless. Sell your fucking arse, you worthless wee shite."

Freddy removed the screws and picked Tom up out of the seat, blindfolded. A van was used to dump his worthless carcass on the outskirts of Aberdeen.

"Bye-bye," said Lanty, as they drove back to the yard which had been cleaned. All the sheeting and boiler suits and the cordless drill were but in a burner, and the inside of the container was disinfected.

Lanty handed Harry three grand. "Good job."

"Cheers, Lanty boy," said Harry.

The men climbed into the car and drove back to Shields.

"Freddy, no smoking," said Steven, laughing.

Lanty said, "Wind the window down, he deserves it. He's away on holiday next month, you know." Lanty laughed. "How can you just change like that?" he said. "Jekyll and Hyde."

The men started laughing as Harry locked up and waved goodbye. Lanty phoned Luke. "Done, bud. Gillian got her wedding present." Putting down the phone, he put the radio on. The song played on an advert – Whistle While You Work. The men laughed their heads off as they drove down the road.

26

Today's the Day

···§··——————————··§··

Travelling up the motorway towards Sunderland, Davy listened to his radio. Traffic jam on the Tunnel, half an hour delay. *Shit,* thought Davy, as he noticed the sign to Durham. *Bugger it,* thought Davy. *Unfinished business.* He drove towards Horton, driving to a business that once ripped him off. Parking the car around the corner, Davy took off his jacket and placed it in the back of his car. Removing his glasses and watch, putting them in the glove box, Davy walked to the business by foot.

"Hello, sir." A smarmy little salesman approached.

"Hello," replied Davy, in a Yorkshire accent. He was good at accents; he loved playing in character. "Ey up, lad. Am after a new car," said Davy.

"Well you come to the right place."

Davy surveyed the plot for cameras. *Only one next to the dickhead's prefab. Brilliant,* thought Davy. "So A'm actually interested in the one outside the fence, the Land Rover."

"Ahh, beautiful car, sir. Beautiful. One lady owner for the past five years."

"Yes," said Davy, looking at it more closely. "So you have your card? I presume you get commission on the sales."

"Ohh no, sir. I own this lot. My name's Rick, Rick Draker. Here's my card."

Bingo, thought Davy. *Just what I wanted to hear.* Looking around, Davy surveyed the area. "So, my friend, I think today's the day."

34

Pissing Out the Bedroom Window

—◦◦◦———————————◦◦◦—

Jimmy and Davy's bedroom was on the top floor of the Gable End house in Stanley Street West. The era was the early 1970s; the bars and clubs of Shields were heaving. It was a Saturday night, their parents were working the Cresta Club and the boys' babysitter was downstairs watching the black and white TV, unaware the little shits were pissing out the side window on the Gable End.

They were woken by a couple up against the side of their house. Jimmy laughed as he remembered the couple – a prostitute and her punter, a Nigerian seaman getting a knee-trembler in the back lane.

The boys heard the commotion and decided to piss out the window. It cascaded like rain on top of the couple. She protested, saying she was soaking and she couldn't go any further with the business she had agreed to. The babysitter answered the door to a furious prostitute knocking. Luckily, Davy's mother and father came around the corner and heard the commotion.

"Your little bastards pissed on me," said the prostitute. The Nigerian was nowhere to be seen. He disappeared, leaving a whore without payment. Jimmy laughed, remembering how his father started laughing at the woman, saying, "What are you on about? My kids are three and four years old."

The woman stormed off towards the taxi rank, cursing and swearing and stinking of piss. Jimmy and Davy were smacked by their father for that, but the memory Jimmy had was priceless. He tossed the dog a piece of chicken meat. "Golden showers," he mumbled to himself as he laughed at the memory.

The phone rang; Jimmy picked up. "Hello?"

"I got some nice flake here if you want to try it," said Davy.

35

A Phone Call

Luke picked up the phone and dialled Gillian.

"How's you?" said Luke. "How's married life?"

"Fine, fine," said Gillian.

"Good news, sweetheart. It's done and Blockbusters no longer have those films."

Gillian slumped in the chair and started to cry uncontrollably.

"You ok?" said Luke.

"Yes, yes, I am just so happy. I am absolutely over the moon. Thank you, thank you so much."

"Now no more worrying about this," said Luke. "You just look after Mal and yourself."

"Yes, yes. Thank you," said Gillian, perked up and happy once again.

"Look, I am hanging up. No more talk of this ever again. It's no longer your concern. It never happened, ok sweetheart?"

With that, Luke hung up.

36

Dutch Fishing

—◆◆◆————————◆◆◆—

The year was 1988. North Shields fishing fleet was a fleet consisting of over 100 boats. Back then, fishing vessels had daily markets; hundreds of boxes filled the quay. Buyers and merchants bought the fish through auctioneers, a busy place for many who worked in the industry.

Thousands of people were in work on North Shields fish quay, and thousands of pounds were often exchanged within that very community. Some of the buyers became millionaires as a result of that.

Davy sat, as a young lad, waiting for his mate who had been fishing in the Dutch sector. He knew the boat had been landing in Ijmuiden and his friend had been on the purchase of slate hashish, kilos of the shit. It was often brought in by fishermen and hiding the stuff was a doddle. Sometimes a box filled and buried among the hundreds of boxes of fish was the best way of getting the shit into the country. It was easy money but it carried risks; a tip-off or loose lip often saw a boat impounded and searched. Luckily Davy had never encountered any problems; his operation was between his mate and himself.

Davy had a little business going for himself, a nice little earner. He would obtain the gear and distribute it within a couple of days. He never had much to do with the stuff, just selling the stuff on to the dealers was his priority. Once it was gone he would count up his green and get some more whenever the boat sailed to Holland – generally every couple of months.

Sometimes Davy's father could smell the pungent odour whenever Davy had been handling the stuff; it clings to your clothing like shit to a stick. Davy liked working with speed and cocaine, far more profitable substances.

"Don't bring a kilo through – post it," said Davy to Richard the fisherman.

"How the fuck do you do that?" said Richard.

"Simple," said Davy. Pulling a gram out his pocket, he placed the gram on the table and spread it out on a plate. He then added water, creating a paste solution. "Now watch," said Davy as he picked up a clean one-inch brush. He started to apply the paste in thin, watery swirls. He painted the piece of paper like a kid's picture. "Good, innit?" Davy said.

He also demonstrated on a birthday card, the same principle, putting it into the envelope which he also coated – only the inside. Now the outside was coated in a paste – coffee. "The trick is," said Davy, "you get it so it spreads easy and evenly, put the envelope into a slightly bigger envelope, and post it. But you must hang it up to dry." Davy hung the pages up and the envelope. They waited an hour and drank a few beers, catching up, then Davy picked all the dry pages off the clothes horse and sealed it all together in the envelope.

Richard watched as Davy put the stamp on ready for posting.

"It's going to London, to my cousin. He will get it. Watch, in the next few days he will post it back to me. We just get the product to an empty flat. We have keys to watch. Even post it to a mail box, it's fucking easy, buddy."

Richard said, "Surely the coppers can trace that."

"Ok," said Davy. "Let's make a bet. Tenner?"

Richard agreed and the men came to the agreement.

"If this works I am posting loads," said Richard.

Davy and Richard both clashed beer bottles. "So it's a business agreement," said Davy.

This was the start of what would become the makings of Davy; he was a fast learner and adapted to changing situations. Only back in 1988 he was being constantly watched by his mentors and they provided valuable advice on his criminal activity, even adapting to stuffing fish with gear.

The letters came through.

"Fucking hell," said Richard, as Davy scraped the cocaine off the cards. Two kilo mounds. Then Davy dampened it again and placed it in a press, turning it back into a cube.

"What the fuck?" said Richard. "Jesus fucking H. Christ."

Davy started shifting gear, sending it to Grimsby. He also had fishermen acting on his behalf. From Grimsby to Bridlington, money started filtering into his little business ideas. It was a beautiful time to make money, until the implementation of quotas and decommissioning of fishing boats resulted in an avenue of the business being shut down. The fact that British fishermen were being replaced with cheap labour with less fish being caught and restrictions on catches, meant only a handful of boats were left eventually, and most importantly none were landing in Holland anymore. But the late 80s and early 1990s had served Davy well in business.

Davy was a nineteen-year-old lad and was still a skinny calf; it was only until the early 1990s. The weight started coming on and the calf became the bull, and his introduction to one of the nastiest men on Tyneside, becoming his friend, created initiation time for Davy to prove his worth. This individual who sought Davy out brought out the bull, so to speak. Davy started fighting and it started turning heads. A one-hit specialist who punched on the back foot outside of nightclubs, in nightclubs, bars, getting pretty handy. He actually enjoyed inflicting pain on those who dared step within his zone. Davy hit so hard his fists became dangerous weapons. A rugby team got the biggest shock of their lives outside the Royal. A heart of a lion is what was described. Davy made his debut and earned his place in those ranks.

The foolish believed in getting at him whilst he was young. Their biggest mistake was that they actually believed he would stay that way. Davy thrived on this and he knew what his life would turn into if he chose the path of the known villain. Advice came from his father's friend, a man who Davy grew up around all his life. You're either bad, good, or clever. Davy chose the clever, to become unknown to the authorities, so staying away from the limelight was his choice. With good reason as well. This served him a clean passport, an unsigned police label, a model citizen status. Far better than the idiot who spends most his life in a jail wing.

Davy enjoyed holidays and cocktails by the Mediterranean Sea.

37

Mr Whipped Cream

JJ sat in his ice cream van. Business was going well; he was selling weight and ice creams, reading his paper. His phone rang.

"Hello?" It was Jack.

"Two customers coming your way," said Jack.

Jack was now getting involved in flake (cocaine) and he was hungry, pushing punters to his business to feed their habit.

"Sunrise specials, coming up," said JJ, going into his little utility bench, pulling the string buried in his coffee.

The two men approached the van. JJ knew they had to ask for the specific ice cream and was in no way going to give anything until they asked for the item that wasn't on his menu.

"How may I help you, gentlemen?" said JJ.

"Two sunrise specials, please."

JJ served the lads the ice cream, putting the gear at the bottom of the cone. The men handed over the 100 quid and walked away.

JJ was clearing good money; he also was involved in money drops. Davy used him often to carry numbers back and forth. Fellas would come to JJ's van, buy an ice lolly and slip JJ a parcel of cash or a load of dodgy credit cards, a few hundred E or a hundred pages of acid tabs. He was being paid as a drop by the people JJ had been meeting, especially the people who worked for Luke or the BFG. His little business was off the map. JJ was becoming known even to the point that punters referred to him as Mr Whipped Cream or Whippy. JJ enjoyed the celebrity status; he now had enough money to buy the things he wanted and pay all his debts off.

Good teachers were never too far away. If he had trouble with a punter it was immediately dealt with (Chucky). Arguments were dealt with, problems with wannabe dealers were dealt with. JJ rapidly realised the people he was involved with were certainly not the kind of people you messed with. The punishment administered to those who crossed the line, although JJ never witnessed any of the violence that came with the territory, he certainly heard and knew about it. Jokingly, he referred to them as Violence Incorporated, like a scene from an American gangster flick. The men he was in cahoots with fitted the profile very well. His Al Capone, his Capo, were ordinary British guys who resorted to a brutal enforcement method with anyone who dared step on their toes. Similar to the Glasgow ice cream wars, except this wasn't Glasgow, it was Tyneside and operations like that were ran far differently and without disputes. A sit down and a truce would be formed most of the time. After all, it was always good business to keep harmony within the criminal community.

Above all, JJ started to get to know Davy and now he realised the qualities Davy possessed. A negotiator and a very good one at that. Having qualities like that in their world was far more valuable than any street thug's reputation.

38

The Tropical Forest

Sitting in the silver foil loft, Tommy sat looking at the plants.

"They're ready for coming down soon," he said quietly.

The buds were huge, a record bumper crop – at least fifteen ounces a plant here. The nursery was showing some impressive signs as well; second generation strain, a brand new batch. The carbon filter and flood and drain system really was the way forward, Tommy thought to himself. This was the fourth crop and each time it was getting better and better; easier to produce the harvest. Tommy's hydroponics skills certainly paid off. That is why Davy chose to work with him.

Numerous systems were all over the region and Tommy was left in charge of them all. Making money was no object. Tommy was a green-fingered wizard who could bring a twig back to life with a little sunlight and some H2O. A fully qualified chemist with a degree in medicine also was an advantage. Davy often used Tommy to make M-CAT, also commonly known as bubbles, a very powerful plant food that if snorted like cocaine, the effects were mind blowing; and above all it was cheap to make. Most of Davy's trade in bubbles on Saturday night was the queer scene, as he put it. "Faggots fucking can't get enough. After one hit their appetite requires more and I can shift the cunt at an alarming rate, thirty quid a fucking gram," said Davy.

It only stood Davy three quid a gram. *How much was that big lump making?* thought Tommy.

Tommy was well rewarded, however. Davy made sure of that. So really Tommy had a very good relationship working with the big fella, and business as usual was always top of Davy's priority list. Tommy wasn't a smoker of fags, nor a drinker; he enjoyed sitting in the house getting stoned. He bred exotic cats with his wife and played video games. In Davy's eyes he was a perfect candidate. Nobody knew him and nobody needed to know the man. Davy's cute cunning made sure of that as well.

Time to phone Davy, thought Tommy. The crop would be pulled down and stripped; all the stems and leaves would be blended and put in bags. Davy boiled them and made space cakes, another little hobby of his, apart from taxi driving. Davy considered himself the Gordon Ramsey of the drug world, making scones and cakes which had potent effects. Chocolate cake and angel delight. The likes of which many would never experience, were on Davy's menu. Whenever he pulled a crop down Tommy laughed, picturing the big lump whisking and kneading in his kitchen.

Davy loved going to Blyth, especially when Tommy's wife made pies; the best steak and kidney he ever tasted. Davy had been talking to Tommy that morning. The crop was ready and it was to be stripped and processed over the next couple of days. "Make sure your lass cooks them pies mind, Tommy lad," said Davy cheerfully.

39

Party

Jimmy and Davy sat upstairs in their family home. The year was 1978. Downstairs, their father was hosting a party. The big fella had just come out of jail and everyone with a name or reputation converged on their mother's living room. The record player blared a 1960s hit parade. Sam Cook to Lulu, Cilla Black, Diana Ross and Boney M. The music was loud and everyone was there from the Shields criminal fraternity, congratulating the big fella's return.

His growling voice could be heard saying, "Geordie, send one of the kids for some brown ale from the corner shop," or, "Geordie, put that record on again," which the boys' mother would do. "And Geordie, tell so and so about this."

Davy remembers the brandy bowl on his mother's mantelpiece. When one of the guys in the crowd was so pissed he fell on it. It was all, "Howay, watch where you're standing," and, "Here, have another one."

The noises must have pissed off the neighbours but who would complain about this crowd? In this era there was them, meaning the police, and us, meaning the villains. This was a constant occurrence during the boys' childhood. You see, pubs and clubs and parties were their way of conducting business.

Whenever one of them came home from Durham (prison), they celebrated his return and the boys' father, being one of the villains, gladly facilitated a party. Another excuse to get pissed, another excuse to justify a party. The boys knew the dance and boys being boys, this opened an opportunity to raid the settee once all the grown-ups had gone. The amount of money that fell out the pockets of their father's friends was a small fortune. Jimmy and Davy actually welcomed the parties because the next day the boys could go to the shop and buy sweets with the money they found from raiding the settee and armchairs. Whenever a party took place the kids had chocolate the next day.

Davy smiled at the memory as he sat in his car, holding the birthday card. These days a party involves cakes and balloons; he wasn't one for allowing drinkers in his home, especially criminals. His criminal activities were behind closed doors, low profile, the less people knew the less people talked. It's not 1970s Britain anymore. These days they have cameras on street corners and drinking near kids invites the authorities. Kids these days can't just go to the shop and buy drink. It was accepted back in the 1970s; it certainly isn't accepted these days.

Davy wrote in the card, 'happy birthday, love Dad xxxxx'. Putting 100 quid in the card, he sealed it. *That's ready for tomorrow.* Davy pulled off, testing his meter.

40

The Drive Through

Alan sparked up his second cigarette. Sitting in the McDonald's drive through, he had been instructed to wait there and someone would contact him. The bag full of ecstasy he had brought sat in his passenger's well. Ten thousand tablets, all wrapped and ready to go. He was waiting for a blue Audi to pull up as instructed, and the two guys will drive out to the sticks. He was instructed to follow them.

"How will I recognise them?" Alan said on a prior phone call.

"You will recognise them. They will phone. They're both little faggots, just follow them and do the drop where they take you. You just need to follow, ok?" said Davy. Alan agreed. "Remember, low fucking profile." Davy stressed this. "Not like last time. No driving like a daft lad, Alan. It attracts attention," said Davy.

Gary and Karl jumped in the car. They had both been in the shower that evening after partying hard in Rock Shots the night before.

"You have the envelope, Gary?" said Karl in a feminine voice.

"Yes Karl." Gary leaned over and pecked his cheek. "What would I do without you?" said Gary.

Both the men drove off, heading for McDonald's. Karl picked up the basher phone and dialled Alan's number. The Middlesbrough accent answered the phone. "We're five minutes away," said Karl.

"Ok. I am in the car park, just drive past me and I will follow."

Karl knew the script; he was well informed by Davy. The car drove up to the McDonald's, entering the car park. Karl rang the phone. Alan acknowledged and started the car. Driving slowly, following them, he pulled out of the car park and headed for the coast towards Seaton Sluice. The transfer was to take place on the Beehive Road.

Gary and Karl listened to the radio. "Ooooh, Wham!" said Karl, clapping his hands like a girl.

"Stop it," said Gary. "If we mess this up we will get a bitch slap," said Gary.

"Ooooooh," said Karl. "Whoooo's Mr Grumpyyyyy?"

Gary stressed once again, "Look, Karl, this is serious. Please, let's stay focused."

As both the men drove into the Beehive Road, "Right, the turning into the cow field," said Gary.

As instructed, Alan was behind them. Both cars entered, switching off their lights. Gary climbed out and approached Alan's car, handed him an envelope and took the bag. The transfer was done. Alan reversed and drove off whilst Gary jumped back in the driver's seat and did the same. Both cars went in opposite directions.

"Right, I have to go past the Haven Beach in Tynemouth and put this in the bin in the car park next to the scout hut," said Gary as he headed towards Tynemouth.

Karl, still upset with Gary's attitude, grumbled.

Gary phoned Davy when he had done what was instructed. "It's in the statue (Collingwood Monument)," said Gary.

"Ok," said Davy as he walked over towards the car park. Davy had parked his car in Knots Flats car park. "Nice and dark," said Davy as he approached. He could see the car lights of Gary's Audi; he even heard both of the men argue a little before the car pulled off. Checking the area, Davy obtained the bag and slowly walked back to his car.

Gary drove back home; another job done, another 300 quid off his debt. Karl, still upset in the front seat, stared out of his window.

"Mr Grumpy won't be getting any of this booty tonight," said Karl, stroking his hand through his beard and shaking his head in a tizzle.

41

South Shields

The Ferry Tavern once stood next to the old ferry landing; it's now been pulled down. A focal meeting point for lads who visited the once vibrant town of South Shields. Either the first port of call or the last, the tavern served its purpose for many reasons. Not only was it a main thoroughfare, it was also a good place to conduct business. Its dark, dingy back room with its tiny serving area at the far corner allowed many lads to sit secretively and purchase their E and speed. The strippers would perform on the stage. Bridget with the pierced vagina or Sapphire would do their performances. The lighting was always turned down during shows and the plus side, the lads who frequented this bar were mainly North Shields lads.

The nightclubs in South Shields were on par with Newcastle. Most of the doormen were Newcastle-controlled so trying to deal weight in any of these clubs was risky. If you were caught back then you were expelled, taxed, and properly done in (beaten up). Tolerance for outsiders was low. They were met with severe penalties as it was Boss (Boys of South Shields), the gang of the south side's interests and territories, you would be stepping on. Many foolish dealers had crossed in and many learned the hard way. In other words, Boss was not the gang to fuck about with.

On a few occasions, disputes between Boss and the North Shields firms were organised in a meeting – one crowd versus the other. The ferry, on those few occasions, had to be prevented from landing on the south side's ferry port. Reason being, Boss came team-handed. The police would be called to separate these disputes, which for all intents and purposes would have resulted in an all-out war between two firms (gangs). Not many people know of the Mafia-style gangs of Tyneside, but Boss for sure was one of them. Hundreds of men, all willing to cause maximum carnage and resort to extreme violence.

Davy remembered on one occasion he travelled over with his girlfriend at the time to enjoy a night out over on the south side. The bars and clubs of South Shields were in abundance back in the 1990s. He remembers the day they went on the ferry and the scenes of police dogs and riot vans positioned on the south side were literally off the map. Hundreds of Boss crew were waiting for about sixty North Shields, who were travelling on the ferry at that time. The police turned the ferry back to North Shields where an equal amount were waiting on the North Shields ferry landing, waiting to arrest every single one of them.

Davy, quick thinking, averted his arrest, because if he did get arrested that day he would have been caught with a pocket full of weight. He went to the toilet on board and hid his stash inside the cistern. Everyone was questioned. What were their intentions prior to being arrested? Davy just acted like a terrified passenger, holding his then girlfriend's hand, who acted equally terrified.

The police officers took pity on them, stating, "We will sort these bad people out and the ferry can continue back to South Shields."

Thanking the officer for removing the thugs, Davy exclaimed he just wanted to go to South Shields trouble-free. "They're hooligans, I tell you. Thugs. Because of them our night could have been ruined."

The police officer listened, concerned.

"May I use the toilet?" said Davy.

"Of course you may," said the officer cheerfully.

As Davy went in he grabbed his stash and flushed the toilet. The officers said goodbye after twenty minutes, saying, "Enjoy your night," as the ferry let go to proceed back to South Shields.

42

Arbroath

Some people are born stupid, some people act stupid, and some people are retarded. Getty sat in his council flat overlooking the sea.

"Fuck you, you fucking dick. Yer no' getting fuck all back," he said, talking down the phone in his Scottish accent.

Luke was beginning to lose it. Keeping as calm as can be, "Listen, Getty, you took a product. You owe money for that fucking product. You pay for it. You really are frustrating people here and when they get frustrated things get done. Now I will give you enough time to realise your stupidity; when you do realise, you get back on the phone and discuss what you are going to do to rectify your problem." Luke paused. "Do you fucking understand? Don't force my hand," said Luke.

Getty laughed. "Really? Well here's the deal – fuck off!!" At that, he slammed his phone down.

Luke calmly walked to the kitchen. *Really*, he thought, phoning Davy.

"Hello?" Davy was in his garden. "How can I help you?" said Davy cheerfully.

"A favour," said Luke. "Can we meet?"

"Yeah, why not?" said Davy. "Your house, biscuits and tea?"

Luke laughed.

Getty was getting agitated. He had very little of his gear left and all his other suppliers were having nothing to do with him. They knew about his business with Newcastle and his stupidity. They distanced themselves from him.

"What's the fuckin' matter?" said Getty, directed to one of his friends.

"Nothing, Getty. Just, I know what happened in Aberdeen last year. I hear things," said his mate.

"You can't be sure that happened. Tom had many enemies, coming to the conclusion it was a Geordie outfit is ludicrous." Getty took a pause and a long drag of his cigarette. "Look, A'm not paying the English bastard and that's final," said Getty.

"Ok, ok, whatever you say," said his friend.

"Now let's do a line," said Getty, "courtesy of the fucking English."

Laughing, both the men sat around the table.

"Besides, the fucker hasn't rang me anymore. Perhaps he knows, he has got the message, stupid cunt," laughed Getty as he started snorting his line.

"So what we going to do then, Getty? If they send their fucking pals," said Getty's friend.

"They won't send anybody to Scotland. Do you honestly believe they will come here when I met them on the Forth Road Bridge? The muppets were fucking shitting their pants, fucking stupid English bastards." Getty sniggered. "Let them come, they haven't the balls to come here. You! You! Wee cunt," he said, kicking his Staffy dog. "A'm fucking sick of you shitting in ma fucking house." He grabbed the dog by the collar and threw it in the kitchen. "Fucking mutt," he said as he slammed the door. "You see?" said Getty. "That's how you treat anything English."

His mate laughed his head off, prepping another line to be snorted. Time was getting on and Getty switched on his TV.

"It's getting dark now," said his mate.

"Look, don't worry. It's sorted in my book," as he sat down, opening his can of Tennent's (lager). They don't have the balls to come here; this is our town. They have no power here."

Getty's phone started ringing. "Now who is this?" He laughed as the number came up. "Withheld, yes!!" said Getty. "Hello?"

"Hello," said the voice, a thick Geordie accent. "Have you thought of our chat last week?" said Luke.

"Yeah I did," said Getty. "The answer's still fuck off, you daft English cunt. You are getting bumped (not paid). Now for the final time, fuck off." His dog started to bark. "Hold on. Shut it, you fucking mutt," said Getty.

His friend sat smiling at his mate, in awe of his telephone conversation.

"Ohh, ok," said Luke. "No problem."

Before the phone went off the front door was kicked practically off the hinges and in steamed Davy followed by three others. Getty looked in shock, his phone still in his hand. "What the fuck?" he exclaimed as Davy ran over and chased him around the living room.

Grabbing Getty, he put his head through his TV and started to literally beat the shit out of him.

"What's going on, mate?" said Getty, screaming for an answer.

Davy just started to smash his fists into his body and face, crunching every ounce of hatred towards Getty. "You won't fucking pay."

His friend stood in the corner, terrified.

"You fucking do not fucking move," said Davy as he started to stamp on Getty's head. The dog was going wild. "Now, cunt, where's the money and the fucking gear?"

Davy picked up the telly and stotted it off Getty again. "I'll give you five minutes or I start taking your fucking fingers."

Getty knew this man wasn't fucking around. Davy started pounding his fists into Getty's face.

"It'ssssss in the bathroooom, under the flair (floor)."

Davy dragged the sack of shit into the bathroom. "Show me," he demanded, giving him another clip (punch). Getty frantically pulled the board up; pulling the bag out, Davy quickly smacked him again, knocking Getty out. "Here," he said. "Take this."

Searching its content and anything else Getty had hidden, then dragging him back through the living room, Getty was thrown in the seat. Davy grabbed his phone and kicked the table over. "You fucking create any more problems you will get more than this," Davy said as he clipped him again. "Ok? Stupid cunt. Search that cunt," said Davy, directed towards Getty's mate. A mobile and an ounce of cocaine were confiscated.

"Right." Davy slapped Getty and stamped on his head once again, saying, "We're gan (going)."

Outside, a shiny car was parked. It was Getty's mate's. Davy tungsten punched the windscreen and with the fuckers' phones in his pocket and goods in his bag, they walked to their car hidden in the next street and drove away back to Newcastle.

Phoning Luke, Davy said one word. "Sorted."

43

A Ticket from London

Davy sat talking to his old pal Richey, talking about their time in London.

"You made some fuckin money, you, like," said Richey.

"So did you, Richey," said Davy. "Don't try and pin all this on me, I might be inclined to believe I'm being questioned," he said, laughing out loud.

"Remember the fucking scams, Davy. You had it boxed off, you sly fox. Laughing, saying you do not have to say anything which you can later rely in court," said Richey.

"You fucking cunt," said Davy in banter, casting his memory back to 1989. Filofaxes, massive mobile phones, VW convertibles, it was all happening in the Smoke. Davy was working on the steel at this time. Canary Wharf to Liverpool Street; Irish and Geordie building gangs ruled fucking London, a Thatcher Britain. Industry in the South East was fucking booming.

Davy was waiting for his wages to come and a side-line of his was to go to the West End around Soho and rob the faggots blind with fake sniff. Teething powder and Pro Plus would be crushed up the night before, then soaked, moulded, and microwaved. He sat with his little mate Richey; they were travelling back to Newcastle that day and Davy had four hours to spare.

"Reet, let's offload this crap," meaning fake coke, "down to queer land (London's gay scene)," said Davy. He would stand outside and wait for the bent (gay) cunts to approach. Often thinking they were rent boys, they sharp found out that they were certainly not.

"Ohhh, sorry," said the little faggot. "I thought you were, well, you know."

Davy would say to the faggot, "Nah, fella, but if you want carry on," meaning cocaine, "I can get some," said Davy.

Generally the faggot would say, "Really? I'm interested in a purchase," and a deal would be struck. So little homo rich boy would walk away with a numb face from teething powder and a little bit more energetic from Pro Plus.

"How much do you want?"

The homo fuckers would buy as much as they could and Davy and Richey would sharp fuck off as soon as they had sold it all. Seven hundred pounds sat in Davy's pocket all from a three pound fifty pack of teething powder and four pounds' worth of Pro Plus wrapped up in tin foil.

Travelling home from London took on a whole new meaning for Davy; he could make money by hook or by crook and had the balls to step into no man's land while doing so. London was a place of sharks; every fucker was on the take, from the peep shows to the venues, the place was filled with easy money to be made in 1989.

Davy remembered loading bandits in pubs, a skill he learned as a kid in Spanish City. A little bit like fishing, you baited the trap and waited for it to load up and be robbed. For some reason Davy recalls the amount of homeless Scottish people that loitered the streets. He had no sympathy for them; they were lowlife prey, one step from a fucking rent boy in his eyes. If you want something in life you fucking take it. Rob or be robbed, scam or be scammed. Being a shark among the shoal was Davy's policy. These were the rules of London. *All the way to the escort services that preyed on the parliamentarians, fucking scum,* thought Davy, referring to the government wankers in their own Sodom and Gomorrah.

You see, a streetwise kid can make money anywhere, let it be Paris, Rome to New York City, and with prey that bites, it was an art form reeling the fuckers in. Other dealers always prowled, watching for competition. The blacks of Covent Garden to the Maltese of the then West End. Davy knew the pitfalls, downfalls, and the players; the way they walked, the knife merchants to the dirty little opportunist. Being able to deal with these people was also paramount. Davy always carried squirt (ammonia) mixed with lemon juice in a jiffy bottle. Holding it in his fist, he would aim it at their eyes, and duster smash the cunt and run was Davy's policy. Making a weapon out of a simple magazine or newspaper was also handy if needed, and of course his job. Maintaining a job on the then building sites of boomtown London kept his criminal activities to a minimum. He had to, but the artist scammer, the bastard that made money from very cunning ideas, did make that money, and managed to keep it low profile. Davy laughed, remembering the day he made 700 quid by robbing faggots in Soho.

Someone robbed the lockup. A full investigation took place; somebody stole still saws, drills, jackhammers, and industrial power washers. And to add further insult they stole the company van using their keys. Every fucker was interviewed; the security guard sat in the prefab crying his fucking eyes out, the gaffer was questioned, the whole building site was put on a lockdown. Forensics were checking for dabs (fingerprints); you name it. Prior to all this some cheeky bastard had loaded the alarm system with spray foam. The cameras that were a new phenomenon back then had the lenses sprayed black.

"Some bastard knows something," said the big gaffer in his posh London accent.

Davy and Richey sat there, keeping schtum as usual. Say fuck all. They had made their money. Typical Tyneside lads – commercial burglars who knew the dance and especially knew how to shift stuff. Six months of planning, watching the security guard order his fucking rent boy every weekend; his sloppy approach to security caused by his drug and faggot addiction, leaving the keys in full view ready to be duplicated whilst he went and waited for his black dealer friend to get his fix of rock. It was like taking sweets from a blind kid. Davy cased the joint and the fat faggot hadn't even noticed that two Geordies were ready to rob his site blind. Materials, pallets of bricks, breeze blocks, timber, it was all being robbed. London's boomtown riches were being stripped by well-organised criminal gangs waiting to take any opportunity that showed itself.

Before the introduction of 24-hour security companies, a builder would use a one-man band firm equipped with an ageing dog and a flask of soup. Certain people in other areas up and down the country were ram-raiding, creating a crime that if caught would have landed them with a lot of jail time. Davy's attitude towards these criminals was that they want the glory, the high-profile riches, in taking the risks they do fine. *I will settle for the crumbs, low key, the clever criminal way.* The way he was taught years back.

His father worked as a security guard on the Battle Hill Project (Wallsend). Barrett and Wimpy Homes; Davy remembered it well. The Swallow Marsh back then; it's now known as the Rising Sun Country Park. For months new builds were getting bathroom suites robbed, boilers taken, building materials by the vanload. *When you give a criminal the keys to your business, what the fuck do you expect?* thought Davy. His father had no criminal record, yet he was a criminal.

Davy remembered the head of security come out to the site and do a routine inspection (plus, the amount of stealing on that site was off the map. Something was in the air and Davy's father knew it). A fat fucker, Davy always remembered that day. "Stand up straight," he barked at his father. "There's been some pilfering going on."

Davy's father, still smoking his cigarette, sat at the chair, his feet cross-legged on the table, totally bemused by this authoritarian fat fuck who just came in and barked orders. Speaking slowly, old Geordie said, "Who the fuck do you think you are barking fucking orders at me like that! You fucking mouthpiece."

The security guard looked at old Geordie. "Well I am head of security. I was in the army, you know," said the fat guy.

"Really!! What action did you fucking see, sunshine?" said Geordie.

"Well I was in the army, you know. I was, six years in the army from '73 to '78," explained the fat guy."

"Really? So you haven't seen action," Geordie said. "Well I fucking have. Korea, 1950 to '53 I saw fucking action. Bendy bayonet in Pusan. You bark orders at me, you fat, useless cunt, I should fucking smack you for that." Looking at Davy and Jimmy, Geordie told them, "Kids, come on, grab your coats. We're going. Fat boy can keep the fort free from trouble, I am going home. Come on," said Geordie.

Geordie threw the keys on the table and walked out, leaving the head of security speechless.

With that, Geordie drove home with the kids. Davy learned

something valuable that day – if you think they are on to you, walk.

Canary Wharf, London.

Walker and Halls jewellers, another scam that was so obvious it could have been written by a child.

Newcastle, Eldon Square. Davy peered through the window at a divers' watch – a chronograph Seiko. Three hundred pounds' worth. Walking into the shop, Davy made purchase.

"This is an offer we have running," said the lady. "The guarantee is if the watch is lost or stolen, you can come back in the store with a crime number and your receipt. We provide you with another watch to the value of the one you lost or was stolen," explained the saleswoman.

"Ohh," said Davy.

"For an extra ten pounds it gives you the knowledge you won't fall victim to such an event happening."

Davy agreed, "Well at least I have protection," with a very concerned look. Paying for the watch and signing the agreement, Davy left the store.

Back in Shields Davy sat in the Victoria pub.

"That's a nice watch," said Micky, playing pool.

"Yeah, Micky. It is. It's a shame I have to report it stolen," said Davy, who reported it to the police, saying he was jumped on by a gang of black males.

Micky laughed. "What the fuck?" he said as Davy produced the incident report courtesy of Northumbria Police.

Davy went to the other Walker and Halls in North Shields town centre.

"My watch was stolen," he said, acting the victim.

The saleswoman took pity, saying, "It's disgusting how you were robbed," taking Davy to the cabinet to pick another Seiko.

It's amazing how a receipt and a crime slip number can obtain another watch. Davy laughed at the memory years later.

You ever hear of a credit blacklisted address? Well this is why they earned that name. Davy recalls such activities.

Catalogues were another scam that worked a treat. You would get a mate to order a catalogue; in those days Littlewoods was the preferred one. He would get credit simply by having a catalogue. Back in the early 1990s, lenders were keen on maximising credit – a win-win for those that wished to screw them.

Normally a flat that wasn't blacklisted would be used. Televisions, clothes, shoes, fridges, watches, jewellery, you name it, would be ordered. The payments would be expected at the end of a working month. Generally one payment would be made – it showed the creditors you were viable a good payer. How fucking wrong they were. Everything would be sold half bat (half the price) and when the bailiffs did eventually come they would gain entry to an empty flat with a pile of demand notices mounting up at the fucking door. The person who rented the flat generally was going to jail or was a waste of space that just wanted a little bit of money in their pocket.

Richey laughed, twiddling the watch Davy sold him all those years ago. "Yeah mate, you certainly made me money. Any other scams you currently have in the pipeline?" said Richey, eager for Davy to respond.

"Nah, mate. I am retired these days," said Davy, smirking.

44

Newcastle

Drinking in Newcastle in the 1990s, Davy was never away from the place. Like one of his doorman mates said, "No cunt can touch you up here, Davy, and they fucking know it."

Davy scammed the bandits, sold the E and speed, and he couldn't give a fuck who was upset, who was who, or where they came from. Loners like Davy didn't respect the so-called boundary lines. If he had a problem he dealt with that problem there and then. Some win, some lose. In his eyes a hard cunt was a man who accepted defeat as much as a win, and when a man's spirit cannot be broken then that man truly was a hard motherfucker. Wise people who knew Dave knew how truly dangerous he was. His silent assassination technic, how he waited like the shark. It strikes when the prey least expects it. A punch like a mule, Davy's confidence in his ability to knock people out started creating a very, very dangerous reputation for himself. He needed to rein it in and only he could do this. If not, he would attract the wrong attention – the police, namely. So Davy started using the quayside bars and Julie's nightclub; even the Boat (a ship which was a nightclub). Party tablets sold among the posh fuckers; half the motherfuckers stood with one drink all night and pretended to have money. A dress code area where only dress trousers were worn and a nice shirt. A few times Davy broke that rule – a west end kid selling shit E encroached on his pitch and he needed knocking out. Davy went to Martha's Bar, all brass and nail-polished, snotty-nosed fucks drank in this place, the piano played like Liberace.

When Davy walked in by himself wearing a tracksuit and Sambas, a nod from his doormen mates, indicating upstairs, Davy went to the toilet. The African scent attendant turned fucking white. Davy knocked the dealer in the toilet cubicle clean out and rammed six E down his neck.

He calmly acknowledged the scent attendant and walked slowly out of the toilet and outside to his car. It wasn't long before the message was relayed back to certain ones. A football sock filled with pool balls soon sorted that problem out in the Denton pub. Davy needed to sort himself out; he was becoming far too violent and aggressive. If he didn't, he was sure to go to jail.

Newcastle's night scene.

45

The Helmet

Davy started talking to the BFG. Both their lives were more similar than they actually thought. They were both brought up in a villain's world, they were both bullied as kids, and they both had issues with certain aspects of their lives. Davy started reminiscing.

"Me and my brother once pinched a policeman's hat when we were little kids," said Davy.

BFG looked in amusement. "What the fuck?" he said, laughing.

"Yeah. I was about five years old, playing at the back of my home in Shields. The Theatre Place flats had just been built, I always remember the garages. Me and Jimmy were playing on one day. A policeman, a big tall bastard, was walking along. He took his hat off and placed it on the corner of a wall. Me and my brother swiped it. We were chased for a good half hour; climbing over walls, running down the back lanes. The chase even took us into Saville Street. That copper ran after me and my brother like a man possessed.

"We got into our street and knocked on our mate's door. Running through his house, straight back into Theatre Place. our mate Micky said the policeman knocked on his door and his mother answered. puffing and panting. He said, 'Two young kids have ran through your house.'

"Old Rosey (Micky's mother) was beside herself. 'What on earth?' she said. The policeman's hat was placed in her porch. She handed it back to the policeman, who was furious."

BFG laughed his head off. "What happened?" he asked.

"Well, our father battered us and the policeman walloped us as well."

BFG looked into Davy's eyes. *He really has led an adventurous life*, he thought, passing Davy a beer.

"Another time I stole a pack of bacon and I was chased by a butcher. For an old man, this fella was fit as fuck," said Davy. "I was down Whitley with my brother again and Steve. Walking past a butchers', I swiped a kilo of bacon. That fucking butcher chased me for about three fucking miles. Rage kept him going. I ran like Linford Christie that day," said Davy. "I just threw the bacon at the old bastard who had eventually given up at the Fox Hunter's pub. This was from Station Road, Whitley, he started chasing me. I swear that bloke was the fucking fittest old man I ever encountered in my life."

Swigging his beer, Davy talked about his childhood. Being chased by the police was a regular thing growing up back then. "Good training for commercial blaggers (robbers)," said Davy.

"You know what, Davy? Do you know how I unwind?" said the BFG. "I unwind with my hobby – fishing. It allows me to reflect, think, open my mind. It allows me to make decisions and most of the time I can make a verdict on subjects. I am not a people person, you know, Davy. Never have been. I prefer my own company and the limited friends I have are countable on one hand. The rest? The rest are people I happen to know."

Davy drank his beer. "I also hold the same attitude towards certain aspects of life," said Davy. "May I?" he asked, indicating his Henry of cocaine.

"Yeah, sure," said BFG, as Davy chopped and crushed some up on the glass coffee table – two fat lines.

"And it's time to go visit, collect on some debts. Motherfuckers owe me big, fella. I have to be mean and a complete motherfucker to certain ones. If I allow one pound to go unpaid I am allowing people to take the fucking piss. That Tommy, the one with the nose," he indicated a big appendage, "he owes me. It's been two weeks. I told him I wanted the balance, he hasn't come through. So now I am resorting to some GBH (grievous bodily harm). He's getting clipped today."

BFG laughed, saying, "You certainly aren't a people person."

Laughing, Davy just looked back with a normal response. "Well I did ask the cunt."

BFG laughed at his seriousness.

Another day, another dollar, thought Davy.

Finishing off his bottle and snorting his line, Davy said his goodbyes and went out the door.

46

Through the Window

Most taxi drivers are wide boys; their job requires them to deal with the public. They all are out for one thing – money and an easy life. Some for the flexible hours and some because the job is easy. And some, well, some liked to sell things, wheel and deal, so to speak. However, mostly, all taxi drivers were legendary criminals. Clever, cunning, and above all, streetwise. Wheeling and dealing was the reason they taxied; at least that is what they try to do. That's where the stupid make the mistake of ruining their day, and the stupid find out that the humble taxi driver certainly isn't the kind of person to intimidate, especially after a thirteen-hour shift.

It was 1989. A well-known taxi driver was dispatched to a party up in Shieldfield. All the Shields (criminal idiots) were there – an eye opener to the lads and lasses who often watched from the outskirts.

"Hello," said old Geordie, a very close friend to Davy's father and a respectable criminal with old-school values. Davy jumped in the back as a twenty-year-old lad. His cousin and his lass also climbed in to the back seat that morning, and a well-known individual who wasn't wired right (mental) jumped in the front.

"So where we going?" said old Geordie.

"New York village, then on to Shields," was the reply.

Driving back, Geordie started talking. "I was at yer fatha's (father's) last night (Jingling Geordies)." Just general chit-chat, the usual banter, when the numpty in the front started being a bit aggressive.

"Come on, calm down," said Davy's cousin.

Old Geordie was having none of it. He slammed those brakes on

143

from seventy to nought, smashing Numpty's head off the front windscreen. His fucking eye came out like a rugby ball.

"So you won't fucking pay, will you? Daft cunt," said old Geordie, straight and direct towards the idiot, who now realised he met his match. After about five minutes it was agreed that the idiot was to pay double the fare.

Dropping him off, Geordie told him, "Now you fuck off, daft cunt," taking the money off the idiot, who was left outside his home with a fat eye and a destroyed ego. A memory Davy never forgot. It doesn't matter how big you are in this world, there is always someone bigger around the corner.

Taking a spearmint out of his pocket, Davy placed the piece in his mouth. "Yep, Geordie was some boy. I could see why him and my father were good mates."

Years later, Davy heard on the grapevine that the idiot that almost went through Geordie's windscreen was acting it up again, which resulted in his face being absolutely smashed in. *Well, he obviously hasn't learned*, thought Davy as he drove past the Mariners pub.

47

The Relation

Some people think because they are a relation to someone and they share the same name, that they have a status, a halo above their head. Living off a name, trying to intimidate some people because of that fact, doesn't make them immune to a slap.

Davy went to the bar. "Rum and Coke please," he politely asked the barmaid.

It was Bank Holiday Monday. Idols, Whitley Bay, was packed with revellers. Davy reminisced.

That very day there was an incident that took place with a fellow that did fit the description. A big kid approached Davy, who was still waiting to be served (a well-known hard case's relation who didn't celebrate New Year's Day, 1994). His ego was his downfall as he approached the company Davy was with. Deliberately turning on Davy, he started to square up for a fight. Davy's adrenalin kicked in. Hitting the guy with three well-aimed, very hard, rapid jabs, Davy hit him like a speed ball, breaking his jaw. The punches were heard with a resounding smack over the music.

Savagely, Davy looked at his mates, slowly talking to them. "Listen to me carefully. I hit like that every fucking time, do you understand me?"

The group nervously answered back, "We don't want any trouble." Their mate was being carried out of the bar sparked (knocked) clean out, lying up against the fence. Ambulances were called. The guy was effectively hospitalised and it wasn't long before Davy got wind his relation was looking for him. Fortunately for

Davy, his father and his father's friends all knew about this and it was quickly defused.

Davy smiled at the memory. *Villains look after villains,* he thought to himself. Being brought up in that world had its advantages.

48

Seven and Counting

Davy remembered another incident back in Shields. The Alnwick Castle, drinking on a Thursday night. Davy and three of his mates were all celebrating his birthday. They chose the bottom road to celebrate – the Vic Stanley, Colin Camble, the Mariners, and the Ballarat had all been visited that night, and they all ended up in the Alnwick; the jukebox was good.

Back in those days, Davy reminisced of many a night he spent in there. The pool table was good as well. It was all ok at first; the lads all sat next to the pool table in the back room, when in walked a group of people – six lasses and seven lads. Ordering their drinks, they came to the back room where the pool table was situated.

Music was put on and noise started to fill the bar, when all of a sudden an argument erupted. One of the lasses started spitting and gouging Jim's face. A good-looking Roger Daltrey lookalike who just so happened to be out with Davy and the rest of the lads. What really infuriated Davy that night, was that the lass was being egged on by the men in their company. And to make matters worse they started slapping Davy's mates about. What happened next reached Durham jail, as the guys that were knocked out that evening were all connected to Newcastle's firms.

Davy stood up and knocked literally every one of them out cold. He hit them so hard some were actually unconscious on their feet.

It spilled out into the street where two of the guys were fighting Jim, who looked worse for wear; scratches on his face from being clawed by the woman. Inside, Jim was putting up a good fight but wasn't winning against the beast (big guy) he took on. Davy walked over and changed that, knocking him like a ten pin to the ground. The guy was knocked out cold.

Their girlfriends were protecting the other one, who kept saying, "Please don't hit me. Please don't," literally sobbing his heart out. The cut on his eye indicating where Davy had previously clattered (punched) him inside was visible.

Davy left, calm and composed, and went to his father's place, where the guys finished off the night. The next day a message from Newcastle was relayed back to Davy's father. The guys Davy hit, their boss wasn't happy. Davy only knocked out his dealers. *Funny thing,* thought Davy. He was still waiting for that visit – it never came.

49

The Lap Dancing Club

Sitting in a lap dancing bar in Aberdeen, the announcement had been made. Luke stood on the round stage.

"Listen up, people," Luke said loudly. "As from today, you all work for me, you all dance for me, serve drink for me, and you all do as you're told. From now on I am the owner, the proprietor."

Freddy dragged a barman from behind the bar out onto the dance floor. Blood poured from the barman's mouth.

"This piece of shit stole. He has been stealing for some time; overcharging drinks and pocketing money, so an example is being made." The barman received another well-aimed smack in the face. "No longer will this behaviour be tolerated." Luke spoke directly to the bar staff and lap dancers. "Tom no longer owns this fucking place, do we understand each other? You look after me, I will look after you. You make me money, I make you money. Is that understood?" said Luke. If you do not like what I am saying then you can leave. I can easily employ new staff."

The girls all looked at each other. "What about our money? Is the rent going up for each night we work?" said one of the girls.

Luke looked at Davy and Jimmy, who travelled up that evening. Jimmy stared at the girl. "No, sweetheart. You just do a good job and make this club money, that's all we ask."

Davy indicated to Freddy. "Throw the cunt in the back lane. Clean him up first," he said, looking savagely at the barman who stole.

"In half an hour's time our doors open. The new name gets unveiled tonight."

Big Jay stood on the door dressed in a tuxedo and dicky bow tie; he resembled a silverback gorilla as he stood in the black light.

"Try not to knock anyone out," said Davy as he walked up to the door. Luke stood outside.

"Right, switch on the lights," he instructed. The cashier at the door (Mongos) was now officially open.

Davy was having a couple of beers sitting at the bar. One of the girls approached him. "So, big fella, you wanting a dance?"

Davy looked back at her. "Not yet," he said.

She stood there dressed in suspenders and a thin, see-through top. "I just paid for these tits," she said.

Davy looked again. "Very good," he said.

The woman wasn't giving up. "I said, I paid for these titties, it cost me four grand."

Davy put down his pint and looked at her once again. Freddy started laughing and indicated to Luke to watch. The girl was one of Tom's oldest dancers and by the sounds of things didn't like the new management very much. "Really?" said Davy. "Tell me, sweetheart, have you always looked that way!" said Davy, smiling at her.

"Yeah, yeah. What sort of question is that? I have always looked this fucking way."

"No, no, not your body. It's very nice. I am talking about your headlamps (eyes)," said Davy. "I am pretty sure if I had four grand I would have paid for those to be put right first. It's pointless having the chassis looking good when the top coat looks all over the place."

The woman looked back at Davy, furious. "Fucking! Fucking! Fucking! Wanker!" she exclaimed.

Jimmy, Freddy, and Luke laughed their heads off. "What the fuck are you like?" Even some of the lap dancers joined in the laughter. "You're some boy, you, Davy."

The woman stood, red-faced, furious. He dared take the piss out of her. "Here," said Jimmy, comforting the woman, "he's only having a laugh," sniggering as he said it. "I will have a dance. How much are your services?"

"You, a tenner," she said. "Him, that cunt it's twenty!"

Jimmy laughed. "Twenty, you say. Ok." He looked at Davy. "I have paid for your private dance, Davy boy."

Davy looked in amusement. "You won't get eye contact, I fucking hate you," said the dancer as she started to perform. She gave Davy what can only be described as a hate dance.

Tom's friend Jacky just came out of jail. Walking into Mongos, he noted to his friend, "Here, you heard from Tom, Joe? Last time I heard from Tom was months ago; he was done over badly. Poor bastard's blind in one eye, he has no fucking fingers barring three. His toes were also cut off, and his ears, and he was literally carved up. And they drilled through his fuckin' feet. Ohh. Also now he's a fucking smack-head (heroin addict).

"Listen Jacky, Tom was turned over badly. I do not want any trouble with the people he fucked off. Ask anybody, mate. The people he has fucked over are bad bastards." With that, Joe went silent, Freddy looked at the two men as they approached the bar. Davy was watching also.

"Time to introduce myself, I reckon," said Luke, indicating to Davy and Jimmy to approach with him. "So how's it going?" said Luke. The strippers watched nervously.

"I am fine, mate," said Jacky. Joe looked nervous, fidgeting with his packet of cigarettes.

"Well it's nice to meet you," said Luke as he walked away.

The signal was given. Davy and Jimmy approached the two men standing at the bar.

"Hey, have you seen this?" said Davy. Holding up his right hand, Davy smashed his left into Jacky's face. "Oops," said Davy as Jacky hit the floor.

"Be a nice fellow and grab your friend for me," asked Jimmy as Davy quickly finished him off with a couple of smacks to the face.

Jacky was carried out through the back door and dumped in the lane. His friend Joe was pushed and knocked to the floor as he exited with his friend.

"Now girls," said Luke, "you get the message. You do not come back here. You show your fucking face, try do something, or even think about it, you will be dealt with. This place is ours now; respect that."

Jacky tried to pick himself up, stumbling back into the bins, still semi-conscious.

"Do we understand each other?" said Luke.

"Yes, mate. Please, we don't want any trouble," said Joe.

"Now fuck off," said Luke. Turning round, he walked back into the club.

Aberdeen – the granite city.

50

Commercial Break-ins

Back in the 1980s, before the introduction of CCTV, shops and factories were the preferred choice of the commercial burglar. For Shields kids, especially kids brought up on and around the bottom roads of North Shields, it was a way of life. You wanted something, you robbed. You needed something, you robbed. You didn't have certain things, you robbed. And a commercial burglary was the thing you did. Being brought up in that world, you learned two basic rules – don't do houses (never rob your own), and never steal on your doorstep.

At the age of twelve, Davy had robbed the Jungle nightclub, stealing crates of drinks. He went around the bars selling his ill-gotten gains, from clothing to electrical goods. Boys back then wheeled and dealt the proceeds of crime. The retail outlets; from leather jackets to Levi jeans, Wrangler to Geordie jeans. Climbing through windows, tampering with alarm boxes, cutting through basic locks, using a hacksaw through the centre of locked doors, tungsten punching a plate glass window so that a shop could be robbed – from fruiters to department stores. Keeping everything low-key, boys of that era had the golden opportunity to rob from the rich and sell to the poor.

Sometimes it would be organised to go on a shopping spree, to the bright lights of Newcastle. Fenwicks of Eldon Square, the preferred blagger's choice. Gangs of schoolkids would go on the pinch; leather jackets, jeans, new shoes, taken straight from the shelf and placed on their feet. As brazen as day, they would walk out of a shop, leaving an old pair of worn-out school shoes in their place. And of course, an army of police were there to try and stop them.

Davy remembers being chased through the busy streets of Newcastle many times; sometimes by other blaggers who did not like the competition. Many a fight was had when two gangs would meet, and with Davy being one of the big kids, he, most of the time, had to settle a dispute with a fist fight. It became so bad at one point the school organised a classroom search of pupils' bags.

Where did you get this from? How did you acquire this, that, whatever they could find...

Davy used to hide his stash outside. Sometimes he would be dragged before the deputy head. Their information-gathering techniques were varied; sometimes the softy softer approach, head fucking shrink teachers saying, "Is everything ok at home? Do you wish to talk about it?" That sort of bullshit. Then other times the hard approach; a punch, a kick, a brutal 1980s-style beating would be administered by the teacher. Never ever breaking Davy and numerous others who also received the same treatment. To open your mouth was taboo.

Davy remembers the revenge plotted for those who grassed or administered the beatings. A car window, or turning the fucker's car upside down outside their address. The intimidation and extortion rackets. Ralph Gardeners and Linskill High School were not just high schools, they were training facilities for criminal activities of future villains.

Fagan must have come from North Shields (referring to the old vagabond of Oliver Twist), thought Davy, remembering the hole under the floorboards of Stanley Street West. His father, namely. Everything that his boys blagged (stole) would be stored under the floorboards like their fathers used pubs to clinch the next heist or robbery. The boys used the street, the classroom, or the gang hideout to discuss their next blag. At one point they could hide out in over ten different locations and they recruited only the best blaggers (thieves). They planned and mock tested the next job on regular occasions. Meticulousness was the key to their success; wearing gloves and black clothing, the robbing crews of lower North Shields, from one particular gang, were the most successful, cunning crew of that era. Never being caught was their key to success. Planning careful execution and being able to spot problems before they came to fruition was a quality gained by the elders they looked up to. The stupid thief gets caught; the smart one he gets his dick sucked enjoying champagne.

51

Look Guys, I Can Fly

━━━━━━━━━━━━━━━━━━━━━━━━━━━━

It was Good Friday; the boys had all been drinking in Tynemouth. Back then, fellas dressed in suits and smart clothing, but all the suits and smart clothing didn't change the fact there was a Shields lad inside of those clothes. The boys all visited the Golden Bird, a small Chinese restaurant situated next door to the Saville's bar (Garricks Head), an upstairs establishment run by a Hong Kong citizen called Joe. Back then the bars closed at half past eleven.

There was a crowd of twenty lads, Davy remembered well. Ordering their food, the guys all sat down and started to eat. Then the fun and games began. An ashtray was poured into one of the meals and the lads laughed as the guy eating the meal still continued. Then, spitting in each other's food. *A bunch of bastards,* thought Davy. He remembered a group of lasses watching these events turn green at the sight of what was taking place, but the lads still continued to eat their meals. It was disgusting, for Davy, to see lads blowing loaded nostrils into a curry dish and mixing it up, then watching as the pissed mate ate it with relish. A person can't possibly imagine this kind of behaviour without feeling physically sick.

Darren, one of the group, dressed in his brand new suit, took matters further. He spat green snots into Davy's curry and rice. It was all too much; Davy threw the plate to one side and refused to eat it. Poor Joe looked in horror at this scene taking place and just wanted them all to leave. Eventually the group left, still fucking hammered (drunk). Old Joe sighed with relief.

Walking back from the Chinese that evening, Davy remembered the shops. They didn't have roller shutters on them back then.

Walking past Rudyard Street, Davy noticed Darren looking at the Easter egg display, saying he just fancied some chocolate. Davy and Cliff stopped next to the window as well. "I fancy some chocolate as well," said Davy, and Cliff, in agreement with that. They picked Darren up and threw him through the window. He never let Davy live that moment down for the rest of his life. He will always remember the day he went through Chip Away's window.

Davy laughed as he recalled that story, a funny event that still to this day brings a smile to his face.

52

The Dinghy and Captain Underpants

"Here, young kid, do you want this dinghy?" Captain Underpants offered a dinghy to Jimmy. A skinny little kid being offered a dinghy.

"What's the catch, mate?" said Jimmy.

"Nothing," Captain Underpants said with a grin.

"Ok, cheers mate," said Jimmy, preparing it to go out in the middle of Albert Edward Dock.

Unbeknown to Jimmy, Steve, and Davy, Captain Underpants and his friend had hidden air rifles and as the dinghy was being paddled out they started taking pot-shots at the craft, almost drowning Jimmy. Captain Underpants did help him out of the boat, however, mentally scarred Jimmy over swimming for the rest of his life due to that event. Funny, however, as Jimmy chose a life at sea.

Smirking, Jimmy looked at the inflatable dinghy he placed in his pool. The kids splashed around in the hot summer sun.

"Uncle Jimmy, can I have a glass of pop?" said the little blonde girl entering his kitchen.

Everything happens for a reason, thought Jimmy. Captain Underpants and his brother became well-known villains controlling cocaine, running extortion rackets, running Whitley and Tynemouth with an iron fist. Their entourage, every one of them, all high-profile criminals. The heat they brought upon themselves from the authorities landed them on the police radar many times, and in jail. Also, the fact that they created rifts among the ranks of Shields. Their total disrespect towards people earned them the reputations of arseholes, but the crowning achievement of ultimate stupidity was to create their nemesis — a twenty-stone psychopath who they thought they could control. Like Caesar was betrayed by his own senate, so were they. The psychopath picked out all their troops like a raging bull; he took all, seizing power, gaining ground using his size, his power, and his family to achieve that. They created him. They took the piss by trying to dominate him. Their stupidity and arrogance sealed their fate, now the white Tyson was their Frankenstein.

Hearing stories on the grapevine of squirt being used on four of their friends, jaws being stamped on, an unstoppable monster was effectively unleashed on the very gang that terrorised the coast for many years, and his team his team were equally as dangerous. Intimidation; they also didn't follow the rules. Anything deemed a threat was immediately destroyed with extreme violence; from knives to guns, they enforced their order in Tyneside. Totally disregarding Captain Underpants and his brother's authority, the psychopaths of the East End had arrived. Trouble was with the Underpants and his brother; they were too ignorant to realise they were always there. They were just too greedy and blind to take notice.

Sitting on the fence, Davy and Jimmy watched. Knowing the outcome of the event before you bought the ticket was far more valuable than walking blind, deaf, and dumb into any situation.

53

The Expensive Chinese

After a full day's drinking, the group of young lads all proceeded to the Chinese takeaway, a little place situated in Tynemouth. "What are you having?" said Tom as the boys went through the door.

"I am having spare ribs with barbecue sauce and Singapore noodles."

"And for me, I am having curry and chips."

Davy surveyed the menu, still trying to make up his mind, pissed as a fart (drunk). "Fuck, I don't know. Give me king prawn noodles with hoi sin sauce," said Davy, directing his voice at the lady serving. Speaking Cantonese, she relayed everything back to the service hatch, handing the slips of paper with the orders written on.

The boys were in good spirit; a great day had been had. They looked forward to getting home and enjoying their supper, but like all towns throughout the UK, situations can change. In walked a little shit full of drink and out to create bother. By this time the boys were getting their takeaways. Davy sat on the bench, still having banter with his friends among themselves. The little troublemaker sneered at the young lads and started prowling around that little service area, intent on creating trouble. Slapping Davy's meal in his face, it erupted instantly. The sneering troublemaker was laid clean out, banging his head on the bench as he went down.

The takeaway represented more of a Wild West punch-up. People were terrified of what was happening. The young lads started fighting. The company the sneering little cunt was with were getting their lights kicked out, all thanks to a slimy little misfit whose intention was to create bother. And bother is what he got, in very violent retribution. It spilled out onto the pavement; three people lay completely sparked (knocked out). A red mist hit Davy like never before. He was wanting blood for the scalds he received for simply being targeted by the idiot, who by this time had escaped to the front street, crying like a little coward. He ran straight to the police. *The coward created the trouble and ran straight to the police*, Davy thought as he looked back. *Sly, devious little cunt creates a situation and runs to the authorities as soon as it doesn't go his fucking way.*

A three hundred pound fine and compensation was the final outcome of all that. Davy, still raw after the verdict all those years later, still remembered that sneering little cunt later on in life. Davy remembered a man walking down Nile Street totally out of it; his unclean appearance and his alcohol addiction clearly took hold. His wife apparently left him and eventually he drank himself to death, dying of a broken heart, so Davy was told by one of his friends. But Davy also remembered pulling him (confronting him) from his taxi.

"Remember me, cunt?"

The man looked in shock.

"Remember?" said Davy.

"No, no. I can't recall," was the answer.

"It will come to you," said Davy. It clicked. The little cunt did remember. "What goes around comes around. You cost me dearly because of your devious fucking ways," said Davy.

The man looked broken, standing alongside his car stuttering, like fuck. He tried to apologise.

"I don't want your fucking apology," said Davy. "Looks like you haven't long left anyway. Looking squarely into the man's eyes, "Now fuck off," said Davy as he started his car and drove off.

It must run in that fucker's family, thought Davy as he remembered the same fucker's brother also having the trait of being a fucking troublemaking little shit, as he was also slapped on one occasion in Davy's father's pub. *There must be something in the water at Marden*, thought Davy, indicating the estate the bellends (idiots) came from. The devious individuals described deserve everything coming to them. He heard how said person also tried to set up work colleagues later on in life with video tapes, trying to harm a man's career by posting shit on social networks then threatening the persons with the police. A simple solution with a cunt like that. Davy grinned. Hit his fucking pocket hard. His car gets it, not once but fucking twice, sometimes three times. The message sinks in eventually. As the cunt would rant on his network, playing the fucking victim, his wife would be losing sleep; his family would suffer also. The psychological torment of not knowing when, how, or where the next thing comes from. Playing games with people, especially people like Davy, carried grave repercussions (you pelt shit you get shit pelted back).

Davy laughed, imagining how the stupid cunt would have reacted knowing he couldn't do fuck all to prevent any future event from reoccurring.

Another job came through. Battle Hill, return. A regular coke-head wanted his fix. Davy started his engine and proceeded to the customer. He generally likes a Henry. Checking his sock for the three grams he already had hidden there, "I will have to dig some up," muttered Davy, knowing after that job he had to drive to a secret location to obtain more from one of his caches. *At least it's fucking sunny,* thought Davy. *Still, that was the most expensive Chinese I ever fucking had.*

54

A Scary Trip to Liverpool

·⸘· ———————————— ·⸘·

Karl farted a sulphurous fart. "Oops, stinky knickers," said Gary as he walked into the kitchen. "Are you wearing that?" said Gary. Karl stood in his Freddie Mercury t-shirt and underpants.

"Yessss, I am," he replied in a feminine voice. "You bought me it, Mr Grumpy." He opened the window. "That curry has messed with my stomach, I feel awful," said Karl.

"Glad I went to sleep. You trumpeted all night, there was nooooo way I was going anywhere near that action," said Gary, wafting his hand in limp fashion.

"Mmmmm," said Karl. "You don't complain normally. Sometimes I don't knowww what you expect of me," said Karl, stirring his tea.

"Never mind," said Gary cheerfully. His basher phone started ringing. Answering, Gary said, "Hello? Yes, Liverpool, ten. Ok, yes." He wrote down the address; the phone went silent.

"What is it?" Karl said as he minced through the living room.

"Another job," said Gary. "Have to go to Liverpool this afternoon." He stole a rich tea and dunked it in Karl's cuppa. "Hey!! Youuuu," said Karl.

"Bitch!!" said Gary. "Let's get dressed."

"No Mr Fun Time today then," said Karl.

"You had better use that toilet," said Gary. "Noooo way am I going near Mr Stinky until he's completely emptyyyy," in a high pitched voice. "Let's get dressed."

Both the men started to get dressed. "We have to be there by ten o'clock," said Gary.

Karl agreed. "After I use the toilet."

Gary started the car. Liverpool, an address in Bootle, and the postcode was given.

"Put this in the TomTom." Karl stroked his beard, punching in the postcode. "Right, we're off," said Karl.

Gary revved the engine and pulled away. "I have to go to Walker before Liverpool," said Gary. The address in Walker was across the road from where Davy and Jack were parked.

"Faggots are on their way," said Jack. "Shouldn't be long. Let's do a line, nobody can see," said Jack.

"Nah, just wait for these bent cunts. Plus, they're taking this package down with them." Davy pulled out the McDonald's bag. "Once we offload this onto them two queer cunts, then we can do a line."

Jack laughed. "Remember last time, the queer cunt with the beard had a fucking dress on. What the fuck?"

Davy sniggered. "How can I fucking forget?"

"Wonder what the bent cunt is wearing today?" said Jack, laughing.

"I dread to think," said Davy.

"Fucking bent bastard," said Jack.

Gary pulled into the street; his basher phone started ringing. Karl turned off the stereo – he was listening to Wham – and answered, "Hello?"

"Back lane across the street. Drive up it, we are parked halfway up," said Davy.

Karl acknowledged and relayed to Gary the instructions, driving up the lane. Jack handed the package to Gary through the window.

"Phone me when you make the drop," said Davy.

"Ok," said Gary. Karl twiddled with his beard.

With that, the cars went in opposite directions.

"Did you see what that freak was wearing?" said Jack, laughing.

"Yeah," said Davy, laughing (a woman's hat with a flower in it). "Fucking swear to God that looks more like Kenny Everett every time I meet the little queer cunt." Laughing, Davy shook his head.

"Right, let's go to mine and get a biffta (line), and then we go and see Jimmy."

"A fucking fashion understatement," said Davy, still tickled by the sight of Karl.

"A very scary thought," said Jack, laughing.

Driving down, Gary turned down his stereo. "You know, Karl, we have been doing this for almost eight months now. I am hoping that my debt gets paid off soon after this job. By my calculations I have almost paid off all my debt. I will never put myself through this again. Never. I promise."

Karl sat smoking his cigarette; his hat wafted in the breeze. "I think that Jack fancies me. I just get a feeling, a connection, like a Wi-Fi vibe. He's totally not my type," said Karl.

Gary's fists tightened on the wheel. "You're such a bitch. Let's just get to Liverpool and get this done, you fucking drama queen."

55

Waiting for a Haircut

⸱⸱⸱⸱⸱⸱⸱⸱⸱⸱⸱⸱⸱⸱⸱⸱⸱⸱⸱⸱⸱⸱⸱⸱⸱⸱⸱⸱⸱⸱⸱⸱⸱

Karen stood cutting a customer's hair when Davy walked in. "How's you?" he said cheerfully.

"Fine, fine. How's you?" said Karen.

"Well, you know, life's hard. Same old, same old. Different day, but always seems the same," said Davy.

"You know," said Karen, directing the conversation towards one of her colleagues, "I got beaten up because of him when I was a young lass in the Jungle."

Davy laughed. "You will never forget that."

"Yeah," said Karen. "I was drinking with him and his brother and two lasses got jealous. They thought I was going to pinch their lad," pointing at Davy with a look of disgust.

"I can't help it because of my looks," said Davy as he sat down, waiting for his turn, grinning.

"They followed me to the toilet and flushed my head in the toilet bowl, the twats, saying to me, 'Keep away from him, he belongs to us.' Laughing, I told them I didn't want him, he wasn't my type, so they duffed me up (hit me)," explained Karen.

Davy looked at her. Making fun, he pulled a smooch; he called it the smoulder.

"Yer still an ugly twat," said Karen.

"What is it with barber shops and this town?" said Davy. "Remember Rudy Seiber and Alan Breeze? They were never as exciting as your shop, Karen," said Davy with a grin on his face.

"You're still an ugly twat," said Karen, smirking.

Remembering Rudy Seiber, the German barber on Borough Road, Davy cast his memory back to that little barber shop. Rudy was a gun enthusiast; his shop was packed with shotguns, to air rifles, to catapults and live ammunition for clay shooting. His photos on the wall of trophies and of course himself dressed in a German Wehrmacht uniform during the Second World War. He was a crack-shot sniper who actually served in Hitler's ranks on the eastern front. A fifty pence haircut was like having a history lesson from Rudy. All the kids went there. Rudy only had one haircut that was performed in seconds – it was the skinhead. He also singled out his favourites; blond hair, blue eyes were always front of the queue.

Davy remembered on one occasion two black kids, Davy's friends, came to his shop, and Rudy refused to cut their hair. Their father was going off it. He was going to tear Ruby's head off that day. *Yep*, thought Davy, *some rare selection of barbers in this town.*

"So what we having?" said Karen, inviting Davy to the chair.

"Short back and sides, please," said Davy.

"Like I said, you're still an ugly twat," said Karen, lifting her shears.

A well-known tramp came through the door.

"Here, Beani," said Karen, throwing a pound at him. "How's you, love?" Karen said. "Comes here every day, offers to sweep the floor, bless him."

"Bye," said the tramp.

"See you around, Anthony," said Karen.

Davy smiled. "You never give him a hard time."

Karen clipped Davy's lug, telling him to shut it.

56

Tynemouth Castle

⸻

"Where are you?" said Lanty. "I have been standing here for half a fucking hour. If I stand here any longer they will be offering me a job in this fucking place."

Lanty stood outside the entrance of Tynemouth Priory. Tourists clicked away on their cameras, photographing the keep and dungeons. A Japanese voice spoke as Lanty listened to the answer on the phone. "Won't be long, fella," said the voice on the other end.

"Well fucking hurry up," said Lanty.

The car pulled up outside the Gibraltar Rock. Jumping in, "About fucking time," said Lanty.

"I was stuck in traffic. Road works outside the top house," said Steve.

"Ok, right. Head towards Blyth. I have a package that needs to be picked up, then it's going up to Newcastle. Take the side roads, head towards Seaton Delaval."

Steve drove the car down Front Street, heading towards Manor Road. The stereo played an old classic (*Burn baby burn, disco inferno, burn baby burn*). Lanty turned it up slightly. "I always liked this song. You got a CD case?" he asked, pulling the rock of cocaine out of his pocket. "Do you want one?" said Lanty. Steve declined. Chopping and crushing it up then loading it on a fifty-pence piece, Lanty snorted it back.

Black is black, I want my baby back, started to play.

"Fuck," said Lanty, "I love your choice in music, Steve."

"It's my favourite CD," said Steve as he drove towards Hillheads.

"Where we going?" said Steve.

"To meet Mr Whippy," said Lanty.

JJ sat in the car park outside the Kings, drinking his coffee. Two McDonald's bags lay on his utility area floor; the burgers on top disguised the items underneath. His basher phone started ringing. "Five minutes away," said Lanty.

"Ok," said JJ, waiting patiently, reading his newspaper.

A family approached the van.

"Hello," said JJ. "How can I help you?"

"Two 99s please, and a screwball," said the people.

JJ grabbed the cones. "With monkey blood or chocolate sauce?"

The little girl asked for sprinkles and chocolate sauce. Serving the man, JJ said, "That's seven pounds forty, please."

"Thank you," said the man and his family.

JJ noticed the car pulling into the car park. Pulling up, Lanty greeted JJ. "How's it going?"

"Fine. What can I do you for?" said JJ.

"Two burgers," said Lanty, looking around.

JJ handed over the parcels that were quickly put into the car.

"So how's tricks?" said Lanty, buying a 99.

"Same old same. That pair of faggots you have grafting for you, the freaky one with the beard," said JJ.

"Yeah, what about him?" said Lanty.

"Well, he attracted attention today and it caused a lot of people to look at the commotion outside my van. I don't like him delivering to me," said JJ.

Another family approached; the men changed the subject. Lanty looked at JJ. "It will get sorted." As he jumped back in the car you could see he was getting angry. It wasn't the first report he'd heard on the gay fella in Manchester dressed like a woman. He attracted attention in Liverpool; he almost got the car attacked with weight (cocaine) inside. People were talking and it wasn't good. The fella was attracting way too much attention and if he was allowed to continue he could attract the law, something everyone would suffer for.

*

Steve asked, "What's up?" as the pair drove out onto the road.

"Drive to Davy. Tell him the poofs (gay guys) are out of control. Not with weight, though. Drive to the safe house where I can get this shit offloaded." Lanty clenched his fists. "Fucking little fucking faggot," he muttered to himself. He phoned Davy.

Davy sat with Jimmy in his back kitchen.

"So how's the fish?" said Davy.

"Ok. They're still alive," said Jimmy. "Fucking next door's cat keeps milling around. I swear I will shoot that little bastard when I get the chance," said Jimmy.

Davy laughed. "Just put starfish down. It kills them," said Davy.

"That's an option," said Jimmy.

"Right, Lanty is wanting to see us for something. Something to do with the puffs," explained Davy.

"Really? Is he coming here now?" said Jimmy.

"Yeah, he's coming with Steve. Apparently there's been a bit shit at Mr Whippy's van. Apparently," said Davy, "that little bearded faggot Karl. Something to do with him. You should have seen what that freak was wearing, Jimmy. A fucking dress and carrying a handbag on the last job, and the one before that he had a fucking woman's hat on with a flower in the brim."

Jimmy laughed. "No fucking way," he said.

"Yeah. Yeah fucking way. The queer twats looked like Pinky and fucking Perky coming up the lane to collect. I swear me and Jack could hardly keep a straight face when they pulled up, especially when the little bearded fella speaks. I swear I was almost crying trying to hold back laughter. And his steg-head (steroid abuser) boyfriend. What the fuck? You could see in his eyes he hates the humiliation. Fucking bent freak show!! The pair of them are fucking freaks. I think it's time to say goodbye to these two motherfuckers anyway. Their debt was paid off almost two months ago, I just made my little bit extra on those two fucking mugs. I can't go smashing them up, Jimmy, as they will expose certain business ventures and interests, namely Mr Whippy. So I think a quiet word in their ear saying they have paid off their debt and then cut ties with the fuckers. Let them live in a faggot heaven, so to speak," said Davy, sniggering. Davy reached for his tea.

"Yeah, you're right," said Jimmy.

"The door's open!" shouted Davy, hearing, "Hello?"

In walked Lanty and Steve.

"How's you?" said Jimmy.

"Been to the castle to do that thing you wanted. Learned fucking Japanese in the process. Anyway, do you guys fancy a line? Your lass isn't here, is she?" said Lanty.

"Nah, she's out shopping. Why not? Let's have a couple. You get the burgers? Everything fine, yeah?" asked Davy. "The faggots. I know, I know all about it. Don't touch them. I have a cunning plan," said Davy.

Jimmy agreed. Lanty put four Hollywoods on the bench.

"There's a nice breakfast," said Lanty, laughing. "Can I kill them?"

Davy looked at Lanty. "I told you, it's getting sorted."

Lanty looked back at Davy. "I didn't mean them, you mad bastard. I was meaning the lines."

Laughing, "Fucking hell," said Steve. "I actually thought you were meaning the puffs."

The men laughed their heads off, passing the £20 note around.

"What's the plan?" asked Lanty.

"Well I want that freaky bearded fella slapped. So do you, yes?" said Davy.

Lanty listened. "Yeah, but why can't we just beat the shit out of him?" he said.

Davy explained the conversation with Jimmy. "He knows things. How would you get someone slapped and make it so nothing comes back on you?" explained Davy.

"Ermmm, I don't know," said Lanty, looking at Steve and Jimmy.

Davy explained. "We buy flowers. Get a card written out, saying,

'To Karl, thanks for the good night we had. Love Tom xxxxxx' or John, some fella's name. Incorporate a card with a love fucking note. Place two condoms in the card and get the motherfucker delivered. I bet my bottom dollar that muscle freak boyfriend of his gets it and fucking flips, and by the looks of things the Kenny Everett motherfucker looks like the one that gets bitch slapped around the house." Davy laughed. "This will kill two birds with one stone."

Steve sniggered; Lanty looked open-mouthed. "How the fuck!!! Whoa, remind me never to cross you, please," said Lanty. "Holy shit, ingenious plan," he said.

"Get the lines on then!! Wor lass is back soon," said Davy.

Karl started taking a shower, singing cheerfully, listening to Barbra Streisand. Gary had heard news his debt was clear. "Yesssssss!" shouted Gary in a gay voice.

The night before, he celebrated in Rock Shots. Karl and Gary were in jubilation. "I get to keep the car, whoohhhoooo!" said Gary. "I wonder if they will contact us again for more runs. I could make a little money from that."

Karl shouted, "What was that, honey?" as the shower muffled what Gary was saying.

"Never mind that, chubby, you just hurry up with Mr Bubbles in that bathroom. I have a surprise for youuuuuuu," Gary said in a super gay voice.

The doorbell rang. Walking like cloud nine, Gary went to answer. "Yes?"

The Interflora man handed him flowers and a card. "Ooooh, I wonder who these are forrrrr."

The delivery man looked disgusted. "I am just a delivery boy, mate. Certainly not from me," he said as he turned on his heel and proceeded back to his van.

Gary walked upstairs, reading the card. His eyes started to well up; he could feel rage as he went silent. Karl lathered up his chest with soap, singing to himself. "*No musclebound man could take the hand of my guyyyyy, my guyyyyy.*

"What's up, honey bunny?"

Gary approached the door, throwing the love letter. "Who's Frazer Caruthers?" he directed at Karl, and lashing him with the flowers, "You dirty bitch, you fucking dirty whore!" shouted Gary, flinging himself at Karl. "You fucking bastard!" Gary grabbed Karl, punching him squarely in the face.

"What-what-what have I done, Gary?" Karl pleaded.

"You know, you fucking slag. You fucking know," said Gary, punching and scratching Karl's face. "I fucking hate you, you dirty bastard. How could you?"

Karl frantically tried to get away. running into the kitchen as Gary continued the beating. Grabbing the knife on the bench to defend himself, Karl lunged forward, repeatedly stabbing Gary. Gary went limp.

"What have I done?" said Karl, lifting his hands to his face. He started to scream a high-pitched girly scream. The neighbours downstairs had already heard and phoned the police. Gary lay in the passageway next to the kitchen door. His life slowly edged away. Karl crawled up into a ball, naked, crying, "What have I done? What have I done?" over and over again. The sounds of Barbra echoed throughout their home (*I'm coming out, I'm coming, I want the world to know*). Crying profusely, Karl crawled up next to Gary.

"What have I done?" he said over and over again until the police battered the door in.

57

Chopsticks and Cocaine

—·⋛·•——————————•·⋚·—

"Hello, welcome to the Noodle Bowl," an up-market Chinese restaurant situated in Whitley Bay. "How can I help you?" said the waiter.

The couple ordered their food.

"Would you like something to drink with that?" said the Chinese gentleman standing next to their table.

"A bottle of wine. Red, rosé, corked," was the answer.

Cheki sat in the office looking at his restaurant through the fish tank that separated his restaurant with a partition wall. His coke addiction was getting worse; he had to pay Luke money every week without fail and Luke had him ordering cases and other items using his restaurant's credit. Televisions stacked in his freezer room and other contraband were stacked up in his office area, all ready for shifting. The amount of items he had stored there was off the map, and more importantly, he had fifteen kilos of Cuban flake (cocaine) stuffed in his safe.

Just a little, thought Cheki, taking a few grams and grinding it up on his office table. The photo of his deceased father looked down on him. One could get the feeling he was staring at Cheki.

"What the fuck have you turned into?" would be his words. Cheki was a cocaine addict and a very bad one at that.

Knocking on the door, a waitress spoke in Chinese. "Boss, there are some guys in the restaurant wanting to speak to you. She opened the door.

"Send them in."

Locking the safe and placing the picture back to hide it, Cheki sat ready to greet them.

"How's it going?" said Lanty, holding a sports bag.

"Fine, fellows."

"I have come for my weight."

Cheki went to the picture and opened the safe. "Here," he said, handing Lanty two kilos.

"You been enjoying some of this again, haven't you?" said Lanty.

"Yes, I have had a couple of ounces. Is this ok?" said Cheki.

"Yeah, it's fine by me, but if Luke finds out it's for the chop-chop, Mr Wong."

"When are you guys going to take all these televisions? I can't get food in my walk-in freezer," said Cheki.

"They're going this afternoon," said Lanty, crushing up a rock on Cheki's office table. "Our money, do you have it?"

"Yes," said Cheki, handing him the brown envelope.

"This is fucking light, Mr Wong." He rolled up a twenty, offering Cheki a line. "Too much of this is turning your fucking head to mush, bonny lad."

Cheki snorted his line. Sitting back in his chair, Lanty started to snort his.

"It's light because business isn't very good. Plus, you guys have put credit on everything I am worth. I need to speak to Luke," said Cheki.

"It can be arranged," interrupted Lanty. "Besides, all the rest of that weight will be gone by tomorrow, but you have been putting thousands up your Ho Chi Minh (nose) Mr Wong," said Lanty.

"That's in Vietnam, Mr Lanty. I am fucking Hong Kongese, and the reason you are light is because I am trying to pay everything and your boss is squeezing everything from me. I lost my wife and kids since you guys came into my life," said Cheki, wanting another line.

"Well if I recall correctly it was fucking you that created your own problems by gambling and owing the big man money," said Lanty.

Cheki looked tearful. "Don't I know it? Don't I know it? I lose everything. My father-in-law won't talk to me, my brothers and sister hate me. You guys squeeze everything from me and now I become fucking addict. The only thing I have is an addiction and now you question me on this. I can't do nothing, nothing. You have my hands tied. I am going to lose my restaurant, you know this."

Lanty looked over at Cheki. "I will talk to Luke, get this straightened out, but you're going to have to address this with the coke, Cheki," he said, changing his tune to that of a sympathetic nature.

Cheki looked at Lanty. "What will I do?" said Cheki.

Lanty looked at Cheki. "Sell this place to us, full ownership, then you work for us but you go bankrupt, taking all the debt in your name. It's only six years and you will be clear again. Think about it. I will talk to Luke and you and him can discuss this possibility."

Lanty's phone rang – it was Davy. "Meet me at the lockup," said Davy. Obviously he needed the gear to bash and bury.

Lanty answered, "I won't be long, ok big fella. Do you want another one?" said Lanty.

Cheki agreed. "Yeah, why not?"

Lanty put the lines on the bench. "Here, buddy. Think about what I said," as Cheki snorted the huge line before him. "See you later on today," said Lanty as he stood up.

Steve sat in the reservation area when Lanty walked back into the restaurant. "Let's go," said Lanty.

Davy sat in the caravan. The heater was put on as the caravan needed rid of the dampness. Preparing the scales and small bags, his basher phone rang. "It's Lanty."

"Caravan's open," said Davy as Lanty came into the lock-up, entering the caravan.

Davy had made a cup of tea. "Milk, two sugars," said Lanty.

"Yep, already done," said Davy. "So Mr Killer Flora, I presume you heard about the homos," said Lanty.

Davy laughed. "Fuck, I didn't realise it would have went like that. I owed the freak shows two grand for their last little excursion." Laughing, Davy passed him the tea. "Holy shit. Murder. Some fucking flower service, that," said Davy. "Well Mr Kenny Everett certainly did get slapped and now he looks at going away for a very long time. Anyway, you got the weight?"

"Yeah," said Lanty, "and Mr Wong is he thinking about what I said, selling everything to us half bat."

"Let's hope he comes to his senses," said Davy.

"Yeah, let's hope so. He was off his nut when I seen him, mind," said Lanty. "He's always off his nut lately. His bird's fucked off, hasn't she? Poor twat," said Lanty.

"No, not a poor twat. He's a fucking mug. He can sniff coke like a degenerate so he can't fucking say he is a victim. Get the rest today, Lanty," said Davy. Davy gestured. "It gets buried. He sounds like he's out of control at the moment, Keep pushing for him to sell his share of the restaurant, the goal is to take control of it all. Next month, we become the owners. Pass me those scales."

Counting out fifty bags, Davy started to load them in one-gram packages. Gathering up some of the pure, he made four neat lines. Handing over his snorter, "Here, enjoy. Get the rest today and leave him three ounces. I need that restaurant," said Davy.

Lanty agreed and started his two generous offerings.

"I have buyers for the TVs and all the other stuff that's been credited. We get up to the lock-ups, the cases of whisky and vodka, I have a buyer for that shit straight away. I reckon he's chuckied (borrowed on credit) about one hundred grand up to now, and with his coke addiction twenty-five grand offered to him for his share, the Noodle Bowl will be ours. You watch. Luke always gets what he wants, playing smart gets us that," said Davy.

With that, Lanty stood up and said goodbye. "I will get that shit sorted today."

"Great, let's get it done quickly. Send Cheki my regards," said Davy with a smirk. Davy phoned Luke. "I have something for you. Can I see you?"

As Lanty pulled away, "Four o'clock," said Luke. "Scott's Park." Northumberland Park was the real destination, at six.

58

The Last Line

Freddy Brown started getting out of control. He was becoming more paranoid and more aggressive as a result of his paranoia. People were getting worried and people, when worried, start to talk. He started taxing the low-level dealers, taking gear money and using extreme violence to assert his growing addiction. Freddy wasn't taking cocaine in lines anymore; he was smoking cocaine, turning it into crack. His appearance, his clothes, everything bore testimony to his frame of mind. He carried a razor with him and used it at the drop of a hat pin. A psychopath if ever there was one was the only description a person could give this man.

Sitting in his living room, gone were the fine furnishings of a man who basically had it all one year prior. Lanty, Davy, Jimmy, and even Luke tried to help Freddy. There was no helping a man who couldn't be helped or basically didn't want help. Freddy was a lost cause and things were getting worse. He started getting sloppy and forgetful. A job in Middlesbrough almost ended with his arrest; he got stoned and lay in bed all day most of the time. His woman left him after he beat her up, this sent him into depression and with that, drugs, namely crack. Luke ordered no more cocaine at all for him, he was genuinely worried. Freddy being Freddy, however, just went and started stealing it and dealers were complaining to Luke and the BFG about this.

Davy's phone rang. "Yeah? How can I help you, fella?" said Davy. It was the BFG.

"Can we talk?" said the big fella.

"Yeah, what time?"

"Five o'clock, my house." With that, the BFG hung up.

Davy drove up. He had a rough idea what this was all about and whether Davy agreed or disagreed, if BFG made up his mind about someone there was very little anyone could say or do, the inevitable was going to happen. Freddy had to go. Davy took half an hour to get to BFG's house. Pulling up around the back, he used the usual entrance.

"Oy-oy," said the big fella. "You want a cuppa?"

"Yeah, why not?" said Davy.

"Come with me to my study," said BFG. His wife was sitting with friends reading kids' books. Little Red Riding Hood was being read to the little girl on the chair.

"Hello sweetheart," said Davy as he grabbed his cuppa and walked through the kitchen. Jokingly, he said to BFG, "I remember a film about that book distributed around Shields, Naughty Red Riding Hood."

Laughing, BFG said, "Pull up a chair. Right, your boy Mr Flintstone (Freddy), he's done some bad shit lately, very bad." Speaking in code, "One of our friends was carved last night at his home in Shafto (Bladen). His kids were there, plus he had weight taken, which was a friend of mine (his gear)."

"Really?" said Davy.

"Half a block to be precise (a kilo)," said BFG. "Is he working for you fellas still?"

Davy looked into BFG's eyes. "Not anymore. After this he's gone too fucking far!!" Furious, Davy took a deep breath.

BFG sat back in his chair, a big sigh. "It's a fucking mess, Davy. This is going to lead into a war, mate. I want to prevent a war, fella. Wars are bad for business," said BFG.

"Luke know about this? I think he should be kept in the loop, don't you?" said Davy.

BFG agreed. "Where is Mr Flintstone now?" said BFG.

Davy shrugged his shoulders. "Motherfucker has possibly gone to ground. He's a fucking crack-head isn't he? With any luck he's overdosed, fucking wanker. He's turned into a bad apple, mate. What can I say? I used to like him but that shit's got hold of many good lads and it changes them," said Davy.

BFG agreed. "I will phone Luke tonight. Rome wasn't built in a day. Anyway, how's you?" said the BFG.

Davy's phone rang. Indicating with his hand for silence, Davy answered. "Hello Freddy. Long time no hear."

"You alreet, Davy?" said Freddy.

"Yeah, yeah. So what you been up to?" said Davy.

"The usual, busting heads. Listen, I have some flake if you're interested. Decent gear," said Freddy. BFG listened carefully. "Really? I might be interested. You mobile? (driving)," said Davy.

"Yeah."

"Meet me at the warehouse, Ambleside, say seven o'clock," said Davy.

"Yeah, no problem," said Freddy cheerfully. With that, he hung up.

"He's all yours," said Davy.

BFG phoned Luke and told him everything that was going on. Luke agreed. "He has to disappear, mate. Let him have his last line, the stupid bastard."

Freddy sat in the disused unit looking at the clock. It was five thirty; his basher phone was fully charged. Pulling the half kilo from the sports bag, he ground some off. He already smoked some of the rock. He had previously prepared just a little line, he thought. Taking a sizeable chunk, he crushed it up. He was already wired to the maximum but once you get that hunger it's very difficult to stop. Taking the fiver from his pocket, he began to snort a monster line. His head was thrown back in a spasm. Frothing from the mouth, he bit down through his tongue. His heart started to beat faster and irregularly. A gurgling noise started coming from deep within his stomach. Like a bellowing, drowning sound, he violently flicked his head back, thrusting it into the table, smashing down with enough force to knock everything off including the half kilo. Blood trickled from his nose. Freddy sat, head on the table, stone dead.

Davy was driving up to Luke's house when he took the call.

"Fucker overdosed," said BFG.

"What?" said Davy.

BFG explained, "He's up at the lock-up, stone fucking dead. That shit was pure, Davy, uncut. Must of burst a fucking blood vessel. Can you believe it!! We got the gear back, however, and the lads took his mobile phone."

"Really?" said Davy, still trying to get his head around the events. "Is he still in the lock-up now?" said Davy.

"Yeah," said the BFG.

"Fuck," said Davy. "Get the place wiped down. Not where he is sitting, however. Leave the twat."

BFG agreed. "There's enough gear left on the table to make it look like he died from personal. His crack pipe is shattered on the floor. Also, the lads haven't touched anything around him, they have just taken the half kilo, that's all," explained the BFG.

"Search his fucking car. The police find him, we make it look less suspicious. I want that mobile phone, I need to look at it," said Davy.

BFG agreed. "I will meet you near Seghill in an hour," said BFG.

"No problem," said Davy. *Jesus, he was getting set up for a clip and ended up clipping himself. There must be a fucking angel watching over us,* thought Davy.

59

The Barbecue Among Friends

Steve Todd looked at the paper nervously. Headlines – 'Man found dead after overdose. Police furthering inquiries. There are no suspicious circumstances.'

Steve put down the paper. *If it all comes out I was in with Freddy I am fucked. Shit,* he thought to himself. He just hoped and prayed that Freddy's phone wasn't in the hands of the police. Certain messages and names were on that phone and if they delved into any of that information, a lot of jail time for certain people would be on the cards.

Luke browsed through Freddy's basher phone, drinking his rosé wine. He slowly scrolled through the messages. "Well, well," said Luke. "Looks like a certain friend's been involved in this as well."

Davy and Jimmy looked over at Luke. "Give me a look," said Jimmy. Jimmy's fist clenched. Addresses, names, contacts, everything was in there, and one address from Steve sent eight days ago really stuck in Jimmy's mind. The fact was, it was a grow and the motherfucker was getting ready to rob it. "Where is that cunt?" said Jimmy, raging.

"Calm down, calm down," said Luke. "He doesn't know we have this information, does he?" said Luke.

"Exactly," said Davy. "Let's just play the stupid cunt for what he is. I can't believe he would do this after knowing him mostly all our lives. We set him up to take a fall, the cunt gets it. Far better to smile at a victim then let him know his card's marked," said Davy.

"He doesn't even know it yet, but he will. Patience catches the fish, watch," said Luke.

"Let's phone him, see what his reaction is," said Jimmy.

Steve sat in his flat looking out of the window, contemplating, worrying. *What should I say if the police phone?* He had absolute no idea that he had been found out. His phone started ringing. Steve answered it.

"Hello," said Davy. "How's it going? Haven't seen you in a while, thought you might be ill or you stopped talking to us. Mate, the reason I am phoning you, it's bad news. Our mate died." Davy grinned as Luke and Jimmy listened intently. "It was Freddy, mate. Poor cunt died in the lock-up, Ambleside. It's a bit of a shock, I know, but far better it comes from one of us, and I know you and him were pretty close," explained Davy.

Steve paused. "I hadn't seen or heard from him for about one month, Davy. Was that who died in the lock-up? Fucking hell." Steve pretended to be shocked.

Davy grinned at Luke and Jimmy, sinister looks on the men's faces. "I know, buddy. Look, we are having a little get-together, do you want to come? We will be getting a collection for his family. I think you should be the one that gives the collection to his ex-lass. What do you say?" said Davy.

Steve responded. "I would be honoured, Davy," said Steve.

Jimmy punched the air, pretending to strangle the cunt.

"Great news. Tomorrow at the yard, a few small ones and a couple of grams," said Davy.

"Yeah," said Steve. "Barbecue as well?"

"Yeah," said Davy, looking sinister. "You bring the meat, I will provide the drink." With that, Davy said, "See you tomorrow, mate," and hung up the phone.

Luke poured a whisky in three glasses. "Here, lads."

Davy raised his glass. "What that stupid motherfucker forgot to answer was what kind of meat we wanted. It's ok, I like tenderised steak bloody and raw." Laughing viciously, his eyes glazed like a killer.

"Barbecue it is, then," said Luke.

"Yeah. I pick his fucking head," said Jimmy. "Go easy on the sauce," swigging his whisky down. "Tomorrow, he gets it."

Steve pulled into Tesco's. A barbecue pack, sausages, burgers, steak, and lamb chops. *I wonder if I should take some sauce as well.* He grabbed some just in case. Paying the checkout girl, he pushed the trolley out into the car park and headed towards his car. The sunshine was hot. *It's going to be a scorcher,* thought Steve as he loaded his boot.

Davy sat in the caravan. Jimmy and Luke were in the container getting things prepared for Steve. The meat hook and rope were readied in preparation.

"You got those sparring gloves, Davy?" said Jimmy.

"Yeah, in the bottom drawer at the front of the caravan," said Davy as he prepared a big line. "Stoke the barbecue, daft lad will be here soon," said Davy.

Steve pulled into the garage on the way. He forgot cigarettes and he needed to fuel up his car. The man was oblivious that within the next hour he was to be seriously beaten up and hospitalised. He phoned Davy.

"Hello," said Davy cheerfully. "How's it gan? Barbecue's on, we're just waiting on you to bring the meat," said Davy. The music played softly in the background (*Born, born, born... born to be alive*). "Patrick Hernandez, can't beat the classics," laughed Davy.

"Hurry up. I have beer. If you don't hurry up I will do your line," said Jimmy. Luke grinned.

"Ok guys, I have the meat and brought some more carry on as well. See you soon," said Steve, putting down the phone.

"Yeah, see you very fucking soon," said Jimmy, turning the music up. The men had a couple of lines.

"Keep that loud and lock the gates once daft lad comes in," said Luke.

"I hope he brought lamb chops," said Davy.

The other two looked at him. "What the fuck!!"

Davy looked back. "Well I do get hungry, you know. It would seem a waste not cooking off all that food he bought." The men laughed.

"You mad bastard," said Jimmy.

Steven's car approached up the narrow lane.

"Here he comes," said Luke, prodding the barbecue.

"Get the meat and sniff off the shitbag first," said Davy.

Jimmy and Luke looked like they were going to burst out laughing. "What the fuck?"

Steve climbed out of the car. "How's it gan, lads?"

"Fine, mate. You got the meat?" said Davy.

"Yeah," said Steve as he went to his boot.

"Great, get it over here, then," said Davy.

"Here," said Steve as he handed the bag. "Ohh, and here, guys." He handed over the gear he promised (cocaine).

Davy walked to the caravan door. "Here, mate," said Davy as Steve followed him as if to get a bottle. Davy Tased him straight in the neck. Steve went down like a sack of shit, shaking from the shock.

"Tape the cunt," as Jimmy came back from locking the gates. Drag him in the container and hang the cunt up by his feet," said Davy.

Jimmy put the gloves on when Steve hung, swinging like a side of beef. "You really shouldn't have worked with Freddy, Steve. Did you really think we wouldn't find out you broke the golden rule, Steve? Rob from us, you stupid wanker," said Luke. Luke turned to Jimmy. "Do the honours."

Jimmy walked over with sparring gloves on, ready for beating. Steve started trying to move the gaffer tape covering his mouth; muffled screams and shouts as Jimmy started his warm up. The beating started. Davy opened the meat and put it on the barbecue. "How do you like your steak, lads?" he asked, turning meat on the griddle.

The men took it in turns to use Steve as a boxing bag. The music played, the men spent the day up at the lock-up. "At least it's a sunny day," said Luke.

Davy turned the sausages on the grill. If a person was looking into the yard they would have actually thought it was an ordinary barbecue.

"Do you fancy a line?" said Luke as Jimmy came out, sprayed in claret.

"Yeah, why not?"

Taking the sparring gloves off and receiving a bottle of Budweiser, Davy walked over to the container. Steve was semi-conscious. "Hey Steve, I really enjoyed those sausages, mate. They were delicious," he said, laughing. "Ohh, not in the agreeing mood, mate? Ohh dear." Putting his bottle down, Davy put on the sparring gloves. "Well Steve, they always say keep the best till last," said Davy.

Steve started a muffled cry. He knew a workout from Davy was a workout.

"They were just softening you up, sunshine. Now it's my turn. I was cooking, mate. Whenever there's a barbecue I cook the meat. You do understand, don't you?" Davy set his watch. "I am ready for a five-minute workout now." Getting straight into the beating, he began rapidly punching into Steve's torso with jabs, then huge right and left hooks. Davy danced around Steve's body, hitting harder and faster, punches aiming for his face, double punching, lightning-fast jabs to the ribs and head. Sweat glistened off Davy as he took the gloves off. Steve was a bloodied mess swinging like a slaughtered pig.

Luke looked at his watch. It was late afternoon. "Shit," said Luke. "Have you seen the time already? We have been here for four hours, lads. Right, let's cut daft boy down and take him and his car an' leave them at the top of the lane," said Luke.

"Let fuck face wake up first," said Davy, spraying Steve with the garden hose.

Steve groaned as he was carried out.

"Stand him up," said Jimmy. "Right, you." Jimmy held Freddy's phone. "I know fucking everything. Everything. You no longer are our friend, you no longer can do business with us."

They cut his bonds and flung him into his car.

"Let's disinfect the unit," said Davy, after washing down and changing his shirt. "There's a shirt for you, Jimmy, in the caravan," said Davy. "Get washed up."

The men washed and wiped down the scene, swilling it with the hose. By this time Steve was awake, groaning from broken ribs and swelling, as Davy approached Steve's car.

"We will follow," said Luke, "after we lock up."

Davy looked at Steve. Steve looked at him in terror. "It wasn't me," said Steve through his smashed face. "Davy, please. It was Freddy, it had nothing to do with me!!" Crying profusely, Steve sat in the car whilst Davy, wearing leather gloves, drove the car outside the compound.

"Listen here, you little rat. If it had nothing to do with you why didn't you tell us? Why didn't you say Freddy was trying to rob us from day one? That tells me you were in with him," said Davy.

Steve looked through a puffed-out face, his eyes smashed, covered in blood. "A'm sorry."

Davy looked back. "It's a bit late for that now, sunshine," he said, wiping the fingerprints off Steven's car. Jimmy and Luke pulled up behind them. "Here's my lift." said Davy. "Don't ever show your face again. Goodbye, Steve." With that, Davy climbed out the car. Turning to face Steve, Davy pulled Steve's phone out of his pocket. "Before I go, Steve, take note," said Davy. "Here's your phone. Get a fucking ambulance. Talk about this to the authorities and you won't be so fucking fortunate next time I give our friends your name and your involvement. Us handing Freddy's phone into the right hands, sunshine, you will wish we had killed you today. Ok?"

Davy slammed the door. Steve acknowledged, groaning in pain, cursing Freddy. *It's his fucking fault, leaving all the messages on his fucking phone*, he thought to himself painfully. Grabbing one of his cigarettes, he opened the door and rolled out, stumbling and grabbing the door frame painfully. He lit the cigarette. Getting around to the driver's door, he opened up and rolled in, screaming in agony, and slowly he started the car, driving off, crashing into the side bushes.

Steve needed to get to hospital. Driving was a very stupid decision. Pulling out onto the road, he accelerated, losing control, and crashed the car into a bus stop, totalling the car. A man grabbed and dragged Steve out of the car. "Are you ok, mate? Holy hell!!"

"Mate, is he alright!!" A woman's voice could be heard.

Steve passed out.

60

The Noodle Bowl

Cheki was doing a Henry (three grams of cocaine) a day; his habit was getting totally out of control. He was also paying Luke back with increasingly light packages. Luke was getting impatient.

"That's the fourth time, Jimmy, that chink (Chinese fellow) hasn't paid me the correct amount. I am going to have to have a fucking word with my little oriental friend. He has one option – sell me the rest of his restaurant including the deeds. It's the only way. He has fuck all money left, just the collateral tied into that place. Lanty's told me he wants a word so I think it's time I had that word."

Davy walked through the door. "A stiff drink is in order. The taxi's parked up for the night now Wednesdays are always slack," said Davy. "How's you, fellas?"

Luke looked at Davy. "Faring well. Do you think Mr Wong is ready to sell his share?" said Luke.

"Yeah, he is in debt to me of thirty large. The amount of coke he's had for the past three months, he owes me big time. Big enough for us to squeeze the rest out of his worthless Chinese arse. When you giving Mr Wong a visit?" said Davy.

"Tomorrow morning," said Luke.

"Should we come along as well?" said both men.

"Nah," said Luke, "I will deal with him, Davy."

"Offer him twenty-five grand for him to sign over full ownership. Throw an ounce in, he will snap that opportunity straight from our hands," said Davy.

"He has two options; he either deals with us or the bailiffs. We best move fast to secure that property. Anyway, his loan to me has been paid off at least four times and the amount of chucky we have squeezed out of his restaurant is well over a hundred and forty grand," explained Luke.

Davy sniggered, drinking his whisky.

"Looks like our cards win yet again," said Jimmy, pouring himself a Jack Daniels.

Cheki looked at his reflection in the mirror; his eyes were sunken into his head. He couldn't remember the last time he ate a proper meal or slept a full night's sleep. His staff were talking in Chinese as he walked out of the rest room. "Boss, boss." One of his waiters came walking towards him. "Boss, the brewery they say we not getting any more drink. They will not deliver here and the butcher, he has also been back on the phone wanting money."

Cheki looked up at the waiter and said nothing. He walked straight to his office and slammed the door, cursing in Chinese.

Luke entered the car park, parking his Jaguar alongside Cheki's Toyota. Taking a long draw from his cigar, he stretched his arms out before he slowly walked over to the main doors at the front of the building. Savouring his Cuban cigar, he sat down and finished it on the tables and chairs outside. *A sizeable chunk of property, this*, thought Luke, cupping one of the flowers that were in the tubs. "Right, time for business to be conducted," Luke muttered.

As he walked through the doors, Cheki sat in his office. Two fat lines on his desk, he was ready to snort when a waitress knocked on his door. "Mr Cheki," she said as she opened the door, "a man is here to see you." She looked at the lines on Cheki's desk and wavered.

Chinese could be heard, muttering as Luke closed the door.

"Well now, Cheki my old son. Looks like you are in a spot of bother, aren't you?" said Luke.

Cheki responded. "Do not patronise me, Mr Luke. I still have my dignity."

Luke grinned. "Still fight in you yet, Mr Wong," said Luke as he sat down.

"I have no money this week. You going to kill me? I don't care anymore. You kill me, at least you can't get me from the fucking grave. What the fuck?" said Cheki.

"Hey, hey. Calm down, fella," Luke said, laughing. "I have a solution to your problems, Mr Wong, so at least allow me to propose the solution first," said Luke.

"I am listening," said Cheki.

Luke pulled out his pocket paperwork. "Sign over this place to me. You can work for me. I will own your restaurant, you will get a wage. I am willing to pay twenty-five grand for your share."

Cheki looked at him in disgust. "What you think I am, Mr Luke? Twenty-five grand? This place is worth three time as much," said Cheki in a heavy Chinese accent.

"Ok then. I want thirty-five grand for your coke debt then, Mr Cheki," said Luke. "I shall phone Davy. He won't be pleased you aren't playing the game, sunshine."

Cheki went red in the face. "You keep that brute away. He is very dangerous man. I want no trouble from Mr Dave." He was almost crying. "You bunch of horrible motherfuckers," said Cheki

Luke turned his gaze directly at Cheki. "Listen you, you're fucking paying whether you fucking like it or not. Here." Luke handed him the phone. "Listen, cunt. Just reflect on what you're saying."

Cheki's brother and sister answered the phone on the other end. "Hello? Hello Cheki, Cheki hello."

Luke switched the phone off. Cheki started crying. "Now listen," said Luke. "You sign the paper, you get twenty-five grand and I get this fucking place. Do you fucking understand?"

Cheki started to cry. Grabbing his pen, he signed the contract and paperwork. Luke confirmed it and put it into his pocket. "Good man," said Luke with a sinister grin. He pulled out of his pocket twenty-five grand. "Here, Cheki, and also your debt is clear as from today."

Cheki looked at Luke, humbled and less vocal.

"So, you can either work for me or not, Cheki. Ohh, almost forgot." Luke pulled out two ounces. Do you want some?" said Luke. Cheki nodded his head. "Listen," said Luke. This isn't a bad deal. I get the restaurant, you go bankrupt. Win-win for both of us. You work for me in capacity as an assistant manager. You speak Chinese so your workers can still work here. The only thing that changes, Cheki, is the owners and management."

Cheki looked at Luke with tears in his eyes. Luke began talking about a prosperous business. and crushed up two fat lines.

"As from today you now work fully for me, Cheki. This," indicating the cocaine, "needs to be kept in check. Let's make money."

Shaking Cheki's hand, Luke stood up as the now outright owner of the Noodle Bowl.

61

A Trip to the Cash and Carry

JJ tried starting the van. The engine laboured as he turned the key. "Fucking starter motor keeps playing up," he cursed. Eventually the engine started. "Right, Cash and Carry for some more lollipops and ice cream solution, monkey blood and cornets, sprinkles, tea and coffee, and some sugar. JJ looked at the list, allowing the engine to warm up. "Going to be a nice day today," he muttered to himself, checking his pocket for his basher phone.

JJ pulled off and headed for the Cash and Carry, almost crashing into the red Astra that came speeding past. "Fucking prick!" shouted JJ as he was forced to brake hard.

Fridays are always busy at the Cash and Carry. JJ stood in the queue waiting to be served.

"How's it going, mate?" a voice in the background directed at JJ. It was a punter JJ had served once before.

"How's it going?" said JJ as he started to pay the cashier.

"Fine, fella. You working today?" said the punter.

JJ felt a bit uncomfortable. He was getting the feeling he was being questioned. It was the way the guy positioned himself, and his loud approach. JJ felt it was odd and above all he felt he was trying to get too familiar. JJ said goodbye and walked quickly back to the ice cream van. Loading up his stuff, he was just about to shut his door.

"Hey there!" The same punter stood next to JJ.

"What the fuck?" said JJ. "Can I help you, mate?" JJ now was ultra-suspicious.

"Sorry mate, I just thought I would say hello," said the punter with a grin. "See you around," said the punter as he walked back to his car. JJ watched him pull out and drive away. It was the same red Astra that cut in front of him. JJ watched it drive through the gates of the car park.

Picking up his basher phone, he pressed the button. The battery was dead as a dodo. "Fuck," said JJ. "Of all the fucking days." He started the van. Once again it started idling. "That fucking starter motor," cursed JJ as he pulled out of the car park, heading for the coast.

He was driving up Norham Road when yet again he noticed the red Astra. "This is getting fucking too suspicious," muttered JJ. As he looked in his mirror the car pulled out and darted across to Verne Road. Thinking nothing of it, JJ continued up Norham Road, heading for New York.

JJ pulled over to the side of the road and searched for his charger for his phone. "Fuck," said JJ. There was no charger. He needed to head back or pull into the garage to obtain one. He needed the phone to take calls. He was expecting it to be a very busy day. JJ pulled off, heading towards the garage on Norham Road north. Checking his mirror, JJ noticed the red Astra yet again, four cars back. "What the fuck?" said JJ. Now he knew he was being followed.

JJ pulled into the garage alongside the petrol pump and jumped out of the van. He ran into the shop looking for a charger. Picking a multi-charger, JJ went to the counter. "Give me a packet of cigarettes also, mate," he said, pointing at the Regal.

The cashier handed JJ the change.

Looking out of the window, the red Astra was parked in the other bay.

"What the fuck?" said JJ as he approached the door. Walking out, he walked up to the van, taking a mental note of the car reg. as he briskly walked.

JJ opened the van door; he put the key into the ignition and turned. The engine laboured again. "That fucking starter motor." After couple of turns the engine turned over. "Thank fuck." JJ grabbed his pen, quickly writing down the number of the car. "Right, I am not going into work until this fucker gets sorted," said JJ.

As he pulled out of the garage he started driving down Norham Road again. The red car was behind him. "What the fuck?" said JJ. Keeping an eye on the car, JJ lit a cigarette.

Just before the traffic lights, a hand reached around JJ's neck, holding a knife. "Pull into the next left," indicating the dirt track leading to the park. "Good fucking boy," said the knifeman.

JJ did as he was instructed, saying, "Look, mate, you can have the van, ok? Just let me go."

Pulling into the dirt track's side halfway up, the red Astra pulled up behind the van. "Right, carefully pull the keys out the ignition. I swear I will carve your fucking face off, any false moves, do you understand?" said the knifeman.

Behind, the driver of the car ran up to the car. JJ looked as he was instructed, "Into the back of the van. Right, Mr Whippy, where's the gear?" said the punter.

JJ looked at him. "I have only a Henry, mate (three grams)," he said, pointing at the coffee jar. Getting a good look at his face, JJ tried making a mental note.

The knifeman quickly slashed JJ's cheek. "You have more. We want it."

JJ held his hand over his face. "Look, mate," said JJ loudly, "that's all there is. Take what you want but I beg you, I am just a monkey. I only get a small amount each day."

The punter punched JJ in the face, and smashing the coffee jar over his head, they tossed the ice cream van over, smashing everything. "Where's the fucking gear!!" said the punter, kicking JJ in the face.

The knifeman stabbed JJ in the leg and arms. "Where's the fucking gear?" Throwing cornets and sprinkle all over JJ, "Where is it? Where is it? Where is it?" shouted the punter. Getting increasingly violent, he grabbed JJ by the hair, holding up the Henry. "Where's the fucking gear! I am asking you again."

JJ looked at the punter. "I told you, I haven't got none."

The punter punched JJ in the face and stormed out of the van, smashing the door and throwing a brick through the window. The knifeman took JJ's takings bag and left as well. JJ lay on the floor covered in blood from his stab wounds. A dog walker heard the commotion and investigated. "Hello? Are you alright?"

As JJ picked himself up and stumbled to his door, falling out, the dog walker phoned the police.

"It was obviously someone that doesn't know us," said Jack as he sat next to JJ's bed.

"Yeah," said JJ, the bandages on his head giving him a comical look.

"Have the police asked you anything?" said Jack.

"Yeah," said JJ indicating he said nothing at all. "They said it was unheard of, an ice cream van being robbed in this way. They tried saying there's something you're not telling us," said JJ.

Jack adjusted JJ's blanket. "What else did they say? Are they coming back to see you? Are they going to question you any further?"

Jack looked at JJ whilst he spoke quietly. "Nah," said JJ. "They said that area wasn't covered by cameras. JJ described the car. "A red Astra. They followed me, mate. Everything yesterday was a disaster," said JJ. "The van played up in starting, my phone wasn't charged. I pulled into the garage and that's when the bastards took the opportunity to get into the van. I should have locked it," said JJ. "What a fucking mess," said JJ.

"Do you remember their faces?" said Jack. "Have you served them before?" asked Jack.

"Can't say I did but I will definitely remember their faces, the pieces of shit," said JJ.

"You just heal, I will deal with them," said Jack.

The nurse came in through the door.

"Looks like you get your bed bath, you lucky twat," said Jack, laughing.

*

"See Mr Whippy got hit," said Jimmy, lighting his cigarette.

"Yeah, lucky escape there," said Davy, messing around with his radio. "It has to be someone he served," said Davy. "Has to be. I also believe they knew he was a drop because they followed him from his house, evidently. Jack's told me, a red Astra. JJ said they had been following him all morning so obviously they had been doing some degree of homework. Whatever the case, Mr Whippy is being put into retirement, His van's been marked not just by the toe rags that robbed him, but my guess is now the coppers will be watching that van. From now on we had better tread carefully," said Davy.

"Totally agree," said Jimmy.

"Put the word around, Mr Whippy is no longer in business. Now we have to find these wannabe gangsters and torture them, the knife merchant especially," said Dave.

"Carve the twat up properly. Make a fucking example. I bet they're some opportunist kids that have seen an opportunity and acted on impulse," said Jimmy.

"Whatever be the case, their intention was to rob a dealer. Now the biggest problem for them, is the fact that dealer has people that he works for. A small cog in a very complex wheel. Find these two and destroy their stupidity," explained Davy.

"Six tonight, card game at yours?" asked Jimmy.

"Yeah, why not? Get a Henry, bring Jack. We need to discuss business. With Mr Whippy out of action we need to find a different avenue."

A police car slowly drove past the taxi, heading down the street. "They're pretty busy today," said Jimmy.

"Yeah, they are after a smack dealer that lives on the corner. Dirty junkie," said Davy. "I hate heroin dealers. They need to be executed in my book."

A certain moral code which was among the criminal world, burglars of homes and heroin dealers fitted into a category of lowlife shit. The reasons – most smack dealers prey on weak people and when weak people become hooked they become burglars. Davy reminisced back to when he had dealings with one such scumbag, forcing raw bleach down his neck at a flat in High Farm.

"Never seen that fucker again," said Davy. "That's what you get for selling to kids."

62

Slash Slash

Alfie Rider looked out of the window of his fourth-storey flat overlooking the sprawl of Walker.

"That Henry was good gear, wasn't it?" said Jason.

"Bit excessive, you slashing his cheek and stabbing him," said Alfie, laughing. "You brayed the coffee jar over his head. Could of least had an ice cream, haha. You fucking mad bastard. Did you see his face man? 'I beg you,'" he said, mimicking JJ.

The two lads were typical brainless thugs trying to make a name for themselves. The red Astra sat tucked in the corner of the walled car park. Lanty sat across the road. He knew the flat, their car, everything. It's amazing what information you can find out on the waiving of a coke debt.

"It's got to be done fast," said Lanty, checking for security cameras.

"How we going to do this?" said Smithy.

Lanty looked at the car. "We park right in front of their car, let their tyre down, then pretend ours went down as well. Blame it on glass or the neighbourhood. When they come out they ask for our help, then if the coast is clear they get it. Use the cattle prods, the twats will drop like a stone. The big fella wants the slasher carved," he said, holding the machete. "Cut the twat's hand off. Something noticeable. They will think twice before ever taking from our own ever again."

"What about the other one?"

Lanty showed the acid. "Throw this in his fucking face. Burn his eyes out."

Smithy looked at him in shock. "What?" he muttered.

"If you're not up to this, Smithy, then we call it off. I am not going into this without a loaded gun."

Smithy looked at Lanty. "I have the minerals, mate. I just, well, just think it's a bit excessive, that's all," said Smithy.

"Well that's what's happening, so you're either in with this or not," said Lanty, taking a rock out of his pocket. "Here, it's getting dark now." Crushing up some coke and sniffing it straight off the card, he offered Smithy his share.

Starting the car, Lanty drove into the car park, parking right in front of the Astra. Lanty said, "Let their tyre down. They will come asking for a brace and a hand. Watch these two stoned fools."

Alfie came out the doors leading into the car park, noticing his car slopped, indicating there was a flat tyre. "What the fuck?" said Alfie.

Jason came down shortly after him, carrying a small sports bag full of weed. "What the hell, man?" said Jason. "How the hell has this happened?"

Lanty stood next to his car with Smithy, pretending they had just changed a tyre. "I wouldn't know, mate. I got my front tyre bust by glass or something. It's a fucking rough neighbourhood. It could have been that glass just on the road there," said Smithy, holding up a broken glass bottle.

Jason walked to the Astra. "Well, we just have to change it."

Alfie came to his aid. "Trust it to be the tyre nearest the wall," said Alfie, cursing.

"You want a hand, lads?" said Lanty, walking over with Smithy.

"Yeah, mate, if you don't mind," said Jason.

"Right, you put this under the car." Lanty said, handing Jason the jack.

Smithy said, "Give me a hand, mate," to Alfie.

Before the lads knew it, they were Tasered under the armpit. Alfie as he bent in the boot, and Jason as he leaned down. Both the lads were quickly laid alongside the offside of the car near the wall.

Putting the stuff back in the boot quickly, Smithy handed Lanty the machete and he opened the acid. Alfie's face was literally saturated in acid. Jason's left hand was hacked crudely off and a slash was placed across his face. Smithy and Lanty quickly looked. Nothing was left behind and the men calmly drove off. Lanty drove towards Wallsend before he phoned Davy saying, "They're not healthy anymore."

Police and an ambulance raced along Wallsend high street as Lanty pulled onto the high street.

"The response time on that was fucking quick," said Smithy.

Lanty laughed. "Yeah, well, we have to ditch this car now. Burn it out with our jackets and these hats and gloves up at Earsdon."

The car was a ringer (stolen) from one of his friends. "It will be reported in the morning as pinched by the owner. Sharon's a lass, so if there is anyone saying they saw two fellas in the car park there will be no problem convincing the law her story of it being stolen. So there is absolutely no chance of it being traced back to anyone. Once we get there I have a quiet spot. We pour petrol all over it inside and out, and light a match. Davy's going to pick us up. No mistakes, ok? Just make sure everything gets saturated. We don't want to have any trace coming back to us," said Lanty.

Smithy agreed as the car went up the A19, heading for Backworth.

Lanty parked the car and broke the key housing (keep), and ripped out the wires, making it look like it was hotwired. Putting the keys in his pocket, Lanty positioned the car along a dirt track not far from the scrap yard. Emptying the petrol cans all over the vehicle, the empty plastic cans were also thrown into the car. Everything was well and truly soaked in petrol.

"Now pour a line about five meters from the car."

Throwing the can into the open door, Lanty stood back. Lighting a match, the men ran away quickly. Behind them, the car went up like a Roman candle. Davy sat in the bay just off the dirt track. Both men jumped in Davy's car. Good job, lads," said Davy. "Let's gan back to Jimmy's. A nice stiff drink and a Henry is waiting for you courtesy of Mr Whippy. He's at Jimmy's now."

Lanty laughed. "So Scarface got out of hospital early," he said, making fun.

63

Space Cakes

The pan boiled away on the stove; the leaves and stalks bubbled, extracting every bit of goodness, leaving a dark, rich fluid. Davy whisked and stirred the solution ready to make cakes, mixing the water in with the dough. A bumper crop – ninety plants each producing eight ounces of skunk packaged and shipped; an operation that Davy considered money growing on trees.

"They're going to taste delicious," said Davy. "I don't touch the stuff, it stays in your system for fucking weeks," said Davy, "But I do not like wasting any of this, so a hobby of mine is to be the Gordon Ramsey of narcotics," he said, jokingly.

JJ laughed. His wounds had healed; now the new avenue Davy had him doing was the back seat distribution of Davy's ever-increasing skunk enterprise. And at £160 an ounce, JJ could see the potential of making money.

"So who eats these cakes, Davy?" said JJ.

"Me and my friends."

JJ laughed. "Fucking hell, talk about baked cakes. With this pile we will be baked for a year."

"The dog eats them as well. Little fucker can't get enough of them, the fucking little stoner," said Davy, grinning. "Anyway, I have something to show you today."

Davy put down the oven gloves. Going into the cupboard, he pulled out a glass jar with a golden brown oil as its contents.

"What is it?" said JJ.

"It's cannabis oil, buddy, and it's potent shit." Davy pulled out a contraption.

"What the fuck is that?" said JJ.

"It's a vape, buddy. This is the future. I want to straighten you out selling this shit with vapes, JJ. I think we could make money on this."

Davy knew JJ smoked. Pouring the oil into the glass, he switched on the Subox vape. "Watch." Davy turned it up to half power, directing JJ to the back door. "Now take a suck of that."

The plume of vape streamed out. JJ was amazed.

"What the fuck?" said JJ.

"No, not 'what the fuck', buddy. It's the future," said Davy.

JJ hinted about the ice cream business. Davy looked at JJ. "Look mate, it made money, I totally agree, but the police will be watching any business, especially ice cream related with you behind the wheel. Work it by all means but I am telling you now, no drops. Our gear will never be used or distributed from any ice cream van ever again. Those two knob heads and their stupidity, by robbing you, effectively they have closed that avenue down. The coppers will be watching you very closely," said Davy.

Davy walked over to the oven and checked his cakes.

"So, Mr Whippy. New business opportunities. Selling ice cream without the gear is one of them. I can justify where our money comes from with a legitimate business. Ohhh," said Davy. "The van's been fixed by the way, Mr Whippy. At least you will be working, buddy," said Davy, laughing. "I put it back in my name now, also, so now Mr Whippy, you really do work for me," said Davy, smiling.

64

The Runner

Jimmy stood in the chip shop on Verne Road; the queue was a mile long. Waiting his turn to get served, he cast his memory back to when he and a few others all had been drinking in Whitley Bay one night. It was about three in the morning; himself, Davy, Dean, and Richey all left the Sands club which used to stand on Park Road. The lads decided to walk home that evening – it was, after all, summertime. Heading for the long sands, the guys walked along Whitley Road.

Across the road from the Station Hotel was a chip shop restaurant, and at three in the morning they were open. Plus, the other good thing was they also served drink.

"Let's go here," said Jimmy to his three pissed companions.

"Yeah, why not?" said Davy.

The guys went inside and sat at a table. Jimmy remembered the waiter took some stick (was made fun of) from Davy as he had a hairstyle that needed drastic attention. "What we having?" said the weightlifter chef. The guys placed their order and a round of drinks. "We can't serve you those drinks," said the weightlifter, "but you can order wine."

"Really?" said Jimmy, looking at the list. *Seventy fucking quid for one bottle,* he remembered thinking to himself. "I will order two bottles," said Jimmy, flashing a wad of cash.

"It's ok. Pay after," said the waiter, indicating the house rules.

"Ok, that's fine by me," said Davy as he started talking to a group of birds (women) on the next table. Jimmy laughed at the memory of

Davy feeding these birds wine and the bastard even ordered cream cakes for dessert. What a lad. He thought the bill for all four of them must have easily been £250 pounds.

With his stomach full, Jimmy stood up and approached the bandit as if to play, then Jimmy walked out of the restaurant. Next thing, Jimmy recalled shouts. "They're doing a fucking runner!"

Dean was second, Davy was third, after pitching the table at the staff, and Richey was last. They ran like the clappers (fast) down towards Cullercoats Metro. Davy and Richey ran onto the Metro lines whilst Dean and Jimmy hid in separate back yards.

"What you having, sir?" broke Jimmy's concentration.

"Ohh, sorry. Fish and chips three times," said Jimmy.

The woman looked at Jimmy. "Salt and vinegar, sir?" she said.

"Yeah, plenty," said Jimmy as he reached in his pocket for his money.

"Where the fuck is Jimmy?" said Davy. "Is he catching the bastards?" Meaning the fish. "He said he was going to be five minutes; he's been half a fucking hour."

JJ laughed at Davy, who was still dressed in his apron.

65

New Boots

Davy picked up the fare – a doorman, one of the new breed, council approved. A skinny college kid who couldn't fight his way out of a paper bag. "Where to, fella?" said Davy cheerfully.

"The Toon," said the fare.

"Another night on the door, I take it," said Davy.

"Yeah," said the doorman.

As Davy drove to Newcastle, he remembered the days when he participated as a door supervisor – a far different experience back then, when criminals ruled. Casting his memory back to The Traveller's pub in Cramlington, it was a rough house. Every drug dealer and wannabe villain frequented that bar back in the day. Davy remembered the days a certain group of villains tried testing the group of North Shields lads who worked that door, constantly trying to test their defences and trying to probe for weakness. Like the time a certain imbecile came with his mate, mentioning names.

"Do you know Charles? Do you know him?" Constantly opening their mouths. "We are well known around here."

The name-dropping became ridiculous to the point that Davy directly told them, "Yeah, I know you."

"How do you know me?" said the main mouthpiece.

"Pizza Corner, Whitley," said Davy.

The mouthpiece looked inquisitive.

"It will fucking come to you," said Davy. "Think deep and hard if you have half a fucking brain cell, which I very much doubt," said Davy.

The idiot's friend kept retorting, "Charles, you know him. He's our friend."

Davy stepped forward. "If I hear you mention that daft prick's name again I will strangle you. Now, brains of Britain, you have some fucking thinking to do. Pizza Corner. Surely you remember the pizza shop, the one with the big window," said Davy.

The idiot turned white. "Yes, yes. Now it's flooding back."

"You must have fucking strained a fart to activate those brain cells. You're remembering. Good boy," said Davy.

The idiot started stuttering. "How youuuuuuu doing? Fuck," said the clown.

"I am fine now," said Davy. The last time," he quickly slapped his mate's lug, "we met, I threw you through a fucking window, didn't I, gob shite? And if memory serves me correct you were a mouthy little shit then. And what name did you use then, stupid boy?" said Davy.

"Looook, we don't want any trouble," said the idiot, trying to look for an exit.

"So you have an option this time. Either you can leave on your fucking feet or you can leave on your back. The choice is entirely yours," said Davy.

The other doormen started laughing.

"The clock's ticking. Tick, tick, tick."

The idiot ran for his health. His mate was quickly slapped and thrown out the door, running across the road, flagging a taxi down.

Numerous times Davy came across idiots like that. Another time, a certain two brothers well known from the area came to the bar. They were both barred but they tested constantly, using the fire exit to gain entry. A clip and choke hold around the pool table dealt with that.

Another time he was slapped again. This time he was thrown out of the front door.

"Here, daft lad," said Davy. The stupid idiot looked at Davy as he was thrown to the ground. Davy smiled. "Do you like my new boots, bonny lad? They're brand new steel toe caps. Here, let me show you," grinned Davy, kicking his knee caps. The stupid fool looked at him in terror.

Davy often wondered what the imbecile was thinking, what was going through his head. Here's a door supervisor kicking the fuck out of his knees with steel toe cap boots on, actually laughing at him whilst he performed it. You see, Davy wasn't an ordinary doorman; he was a cunning, nasty bastard who fought like a villain. And putting cunning and nasty in a door role was what was needed in Cramlington at that time. Unleashing cats among the pigeons in Cramlington was exactly what the owner wanted and needed.

Cramlington received more than what they bargained for. The owner's business suffered because of the idiots Cramlington produced, and if it were to continue the place would have closed down. It actually got to the point where word was put round: if you go to the Traveller's to cause trouble, trouble is what you received. Also, this opened the opportunity for Davy to sell speed and ecstasy. He was making a tidy sum selling and taxing the other drug dealers.

Like lions feed in pecking order, Davy took prime position and he fed first. Any fucker that dared try and take a bite without permission was quickly taken around the back and seriously beaten.

The job lasted for eight months. Davy had other activities that needed attention, plus he always watched an old saying. Familiarity, people become short-sighted. They become complacent and with that they attract attention, and eventually the authorities. You have to learn to say, "Enough is enough." Make it whilst it's good.

Davy's suspicions served him well. His training throughout life taught him tell-tale signs, as four weeks after Davy left, the pub was raided and the door staff were searched. It turned out one of the local dealers copped a plea and provided information to the police. He was dealt with severely as it all came out, but because of him opening his cake hole (mouth), activities ceased.

Davy's suspicions were right once again. Davy laughed as he looked at the new breed of doormen, standing with their badges plastered on their arms. In his day, to be a doorman you had to be a criminal. Villains with a badge. These days you get vetted by the Council.

Davy ate his sandwich as he waited for the next job to come through on his plotter as he watched the skinny kid and fat lesbian stand on the door. *What the fuck?* Davy thought, whilst he reminisced his youth. Davy remembered the days well.

Robbing bandits up the town (Newcastle) and the coast, loading pay-out chutes, and scamming domino cards. It was all part and parcel of working doors. Davy always made money using numerous scams and when you have thousands of punters and hundreds of bars, each bar having at least three bandits, each bar having numerous themes, it was a very lucrative time to commit crimes. Door charging being one. You charged five pound for entry. It sharp mounted up. A free door carried a charge to a pissed punter; it went unnoticed.

Then there was the charity scam. A bucket at the door; you held it out and people threw change into it. Under a false pretence, making it look like a charity and starting the bucket scam at 7 p.m. through to 12 a.m., the sharp money mounted up. Sometimes four buckets would be full of silver and pounds; shared out at the end of the night, a five-way split.

How much money was coming into the doorman's hands? Fucking hundreds of pounds every weekend. Then there was the dealing. Davy would have a muppet (a wannabe villain) hold the gear and a signal would be made. The dealer would turn up and serve the punter, then pass Davy his cash for this. The dealer would get a couple of grams for himself for being the mule. He was allowed to sell or sniff in the pub discreetly. His choice. The dealer was given free passage. After all, he was selling for Davy and numerous other doormen.

Doors were territory. To control a door meant you controlled the drug trade. Turf wars were part and parcel of the vibrant night scene of Tyneside during the 80s, 90s, and early 2000s. Hard cases ruled this era and none were more infamous than the ones who controlled Newcastle. Davy grew up around these people; he fitted in like comfortable slippers. It's as if he was designed to be part of the wheel. Criminals keep criminals close, and especially smart criminals. Davy and his associates were the smart ones and the powers that be knew this. It was also a curse in more ways than one. Being well-known attracted the police and Davy literally hated the police (them and us).

In this world you have two kinds of people – police and criminals – but when you are faced with a villain there is no difference which side that villain was on. It was something you learned in Villain Land.

Villains were ruthless and so were the Old Bill. In some cases, some of the police used to throw about the gear as well. Davy actually witnessed off-duty police sniffing cocaine on numerous occasions.

Fucking hypocrites, thought Davy as he drove towards his next fare.

66

A Very Taxing Time

Davy sat in the house watching the news. The night before had been pretty lucrative and also very educational. There was an individual running around taxing people, taking their gear and money, and the individual was very well equipped in using extreme violence in order to obtain his quarry.

Davy's phone rang.

"Hello?" said Davy.

"Can we meet?" said the voice on the other end.

"Yeah, what time?" said Davy.

"Three thirty at the RVI (six thirty at the back of Rake Lane Hospital)."

"Ok," said Davy. "I will be there."

Luke sat back in his chair. Taking a deep draw of his Cuban, he blew the plume of blue smoke into the air. *What the fuck am I going to have to do here?* he thought as he sat back in his Chesterfield, deep in thought.

Jimmy sat in the house as well that day. As Davy walked in, "How's it gan?" said Jimmy.

"Yeah, fine," said Davy.

"I hear there's been some taxing going on. Word on the street," said Jimmy.

"Ohh yeah, there's been some fucking taxing, Jimmy. Some pretty hardcore shit going down. The word on the street is saying some fucker's going to get clipped sooner than later. He's behaving like a one-man army, Jimmy. Well, the old saying goes, one-man armies don't win wars."

Davy poured himself a Jack Daniels.

"Remember the Toon."

"Remember?" said Jimmy. "How can we forget? A hard man that once controlled all the doors, a one-man army, remember. Didn't he try and control the drug scene, calling everyone up to the Queen's at set times, telling them he was now in charge?"

"A .357 took care of that in a side street in Wallsend. Somebody just had enough," said Davy.

"Yeah, same thing will happen with this scenario. Someone somewhere will say, 'enough is enough', and bam, it hits headline news. But in the meantime we keep our wits about ourselves. I hear he is luring dealers using knives and guns. The man is a walking psychopath. He will come a-cropper, but let's hope he doesn't take out some poor bastard in the process," said Jimmy.

"Anyway, I am meeting Luke today. You coming along?" said Davy.

Jimmy agreed. "I will pick you up. Perhaps it's best you come along. The way I see things, you're being kept in the loop on what needs to be done. Or more importantly, how we can prevent certain things escalating into an all-out war."

The men both sat around the kitchen table, both in agreement that the best solution was to basically do nothing. The smart criminal is the one that is ahead of the game in any situation. The idiot criminal will make the move, not knowing the situation he has walked into. A trap will be set. Watch, it's only a matter of time," said Jimmy.

Davy poured another drink. "Nice whisky, this is, like," he said, adding the cola.

Luke walked slowly, strolling on the grass at the back of Rake Lane. The hospital sprawls right around, buffering up to the housing estate of Preston Grange. Davy drove up and parked the taxi. Both Jimmy and Davy climbed ou.t Luke acknowledged both the men as they approached.

"How's it going, fella?" said Jimmy. All three men held their hands over their mouths and spoke in code.

"Motherfucker wants thirty grand or he cuts up my family," said Luke.

"So Alfie likes to play games involving families now," said Jimmy.

"He's been fucking taxing everyone, phoning threatening dealers' families. The fat little twat has absolutely no morals or common sense," said Luke.

"How do you catch a rabbit?" said Davy. The two men listened as Davy explained. "You use a trap. Leave a little money as bait and play patiently. The rabbit comes out its hole and goes to feed. Fight fire with fire, that's my policy."

"True," said Jimmy and Luke as the men strolled.

"So how's you apart from our little problem?" said Jimmy, directing his conversation towards Luke.

"Fine, Jimmy. Fine, fella. You're not taxing me on my fish if that's your line of questioning."

Jimmy laughed. "Well you can't blame me, your koi carp are a welcome addition to any man's fish pond," said Jimmy.

Luke looked at Jimmy. "I may have to have you taken care of if you tax me on my fish," Luke said jokingly.

Davy just ambled along, playing no part in their banter.

"It will get sorted one way or the other. The smart criminal way. There is far too much police involvement at the moment. Whilst Alfie boy has all this heat and emphasis on the street, he basically has cocooned himself with protection. Tell him to fuck off on the thirty grand," said Davy.

"I already have," said Luke, laughing. "He fucking started stuttering down the line, saying he was going to do this and do that. I just basically told the idiot, I can also play games. You go pop pop, I go pop pop."

"Really?" said Jimmy.

"Yeah, really," said Luke. "And guess what happened next. I go driving out of my street, four hours later and rapid response are sitting across the road. Can you fucking believe that?" said Luke.

Jimmy and Davy looked into Luke's eyes.

"Some fucker's been squealing. I smell police informant," said Jimmy.

"Told you," said Davy. "Like I said, sit down play safe and don't do anything. The more I hear, the more this picture I am building makes sense. Alfie is either working with the police or is too stupid to realise he is being watched. Either way, he is fucking toxic to everybody. Time will tell. He can only play this game for so long then it will all come crashing down. Watch," said Davy.

The men all walked back and jumped in their cars.

"I will come see you next week," said Davy.

"I will bring a net and bucket," said Jimmy, laughing.

Davy sat in the car, reading his newspaper. The radio reported in the background, 'Weather today is going to be sunny – a risk of showers.' Davy looked up into the sky; some of the rain clouds started gathering. *A busy day*, thought Davy. *When it rains, I make money*.

Davy didn't notice at first but he spotted a car parked behind him four back, and the figures in the car had the visors down so he couldn't see their faces. A deliberate ploy used by criminals and the police. He gripped his mag light, looking in the mirror at the two people sitting waiting. They looked to Davy as if they were watching him, and the tell-tale sign was their posture. The way they moved was way too unnerving for Davy. He looked in the rear-view mirror, trying not to make it obvious that he'd spotted them.

A job came through. Davy accepted it. Pulling out, he kept checking his rear-view mirror all the time. Sure as hell, the car indicated and started to shadow Davy as he drove, joining the Coast Road, driving up to the A19 turn-off. Davy indicated for the Silverlink. The car, sure as hell, followed as Davy turned into the car park leading to Halfords. Now he started getting nervous. He quickly dialled on his phone.

Jimmy answered. "Hello?"

"Hello Jimmy," said Davy. "I am being followed, bud. I have no weight on me. I am in the Silverlink," explained Davy.

Jimmy responded. "I am coming up with a team. Do they look like coppers?" said Jimmy.

"Nah, I recognise one of the cunts from the Ridges. Their car's a shitty-looking Micra. I think it's something to do with Alfie, two of his daft cunts trying it on," said Davy. "Whoever it is, stay behind a good distance and I will lead them to a secluded place, give the fuckers a hiding. Set the trap, as they say."

Davy cancelled the job and proceeded to the place, talking to Jimmy on his loudspeaker, guiding them to the place. The car followed, unaware of the trap that was being set. Davy drove towards the disused scrap yard down the old dirt track, looking in his mirror all the time as the Micra followed, winding down the dirt track towards the dead end. Davy stopped the car and quickly got out, hiding behind his car as the Micra came around the corner.

Armed with a Browning, he peered underneath his car, ready to blow their feet off. The men climbed out.

"Where the fuck did he go?" said a voice. It was Alfie and two others.

"So there are three of them," said Davy as he aimed the pistol at their legs from underneath his car. Davy's phone was set on vibrate, as Jimmy and three others were only fifty feet from the bend leading into the dead end.

'There's three of them careful' texted Davy as he offloaded a salvo towards their legs. The two men dropped like flies. Davy shot at Alfie and missed. Alfie started running up the dirt track, leaving his henchmen screaming, holding their legs. Alfie puffed and panted as he ran straight into Jimmy and the three others, who quickly Tasered him, sending his body into spasm. Fifty thousand volts caused him to piss and shit himself.

Dragging Alfie back around, Davy opened the big gate leading into the disused scrap yard. The heavy door was pushed open as the three men were dragged inside the yard. The Micra was quickly driven into the yard as well, along with Davy's taxi. The men were all pulled into the motor pool and systematically beaten with baseball bats. Alfie tried to crawl out of the motor pool, smashed and bleeding. As Davy and two others dragged him back in, he screamed as the men started the beating, more savage than the other two holding Alfie's arms.

Davy started kicking Alfie in the face and torturing him. "This is what you get for fucking taxing people," said Davy in a vicious tone. "You're going to be administered the biggest kicking of your life," said Davy, smashing his fists with kicks into Alfie with absolute hatred. "You're a fucking excuse of a human," said Davy.

The beating continued for hours.

"Take their car and dump the bastards up the dirt track," said Jimmy. All three men were dragged to their car and driven up the country lane.

"Alfie," said Davy, "you show yourself in our area ever again, if I hear you are taxing or trying to tax any of our friends ever again, you will be seriously dealt with. Do you fucking understand?"

Alfie groaned in agreement, acknowledging Davy's words.

With that, Davy drove off.

67

Paying for Your Own Windows

Alan Henderson was sick as a chip. Every night noise came through from next door – loud music and shouting – most of the time leading right through into the early hours of the morning. Alan sat up, listening. *Fucking wankers, fucking dickheads.* Banging on the wall, Alan was furious.

Sharon came through with a cup of tea. "Calm down," she said. "We will deal with them tomorrow."

"Tomorrow!!" said Alan. "Fucking tomorrow. The bastards have been pulled how many fucking times? Tomorrow, the next day and the next day. We will still be sitting here this time next week, drinking a cup of tea at three in the morning. Ohh, I will have a word alright, except I won't be approaching these cunts tomorrow, asking. I will be telling the bastards." He banged on the wall again and shouted, "Shut the fuck up!!"

Laughter came from next door.

"Motherfuckers!!" said Alan, seething, switching on his television.

Alan phoned Jimmy the next day. "How's you, fella? said Jimmy.

"Fine, fine, Jimmy. Apart from the smack-head neighbours partying all hours next fucking door. I am sick to death of the cunts," explained Alan.

"Have you had a word, then?" asked Jimmy.

"Yeah, three times. The cunts are taking the piss. That's it; they're getting dealt with. Their fucking windows are getting put in. It's being arranged," said Alan.

Jimmy sighed. "Well let's just hope they get the message. Let me know what happens, buddy," said Jimmy.

"I will."

With that, both men hung up their phones. Jimmy walked out through his kitchen door, his hot pot of coffee and cigarette in his hand. The dog playfully jumped around his garden as he looked at his watch.

Alan approached the street; his black BMW X5 glistened in the sunlight as he pulled up outside Terry Jackson's house, a young lad who did work for the firms. An up and coming street thug who was making good money doing the dirty work of the known villains.

"How can I help you?" said Terry as he approached Alan's car.

"I need some window replacing done," said Alan. Alan handed over the address on a piece of paper. "All of them," he indicating. "The windows, usual payment. Anything else costs extra, agreed?"

Terry agreed and went off with the address in his hand. "It gets done tomorrow."

As he turned, Alan drove off, satisfied that something was getting sorted.

"A cuppa?" said Sharon.

"Yeah, darling," said Alan. In pretty good spirits, the old villain felt at ease as he stretched his legs out as he tried relaxing on his sofa. A smile came across his lips as he looked at the wall. *Very soon,* he thought to himself. *Very fucking soon.* "I think an early night is in order, sweetheart," said Alan. "An early-morning rise and a good day's graft tomorrow."

Sharon passed him his cuppa, switching on his television, catching the start of East Enders. Sharon cuddled up beside him. With a sinister smile across his lips, Alan settled down to watch the telly.

Lads approached the street in the early hours of the morning, dressed in black. The lads cycled through the park. The catapults and the chips of car spark plugs were all made ready. Gloved and hooded, the lads approached the address given. Aiming at the windows, the thud and spray sounds filled the air. Watching the double-glazed windows shatter in the distinct diamond shard display, front and back, all the windows were done in the same fashion. Darting off, the lads picked up their bikes and silently rode through the pitch-black park.

"A job done," said the biggest lad on his mountain bike, satisfied with the result.

Alan heard the thud and shatter of the windows. As he lay in bed hearing the glass fall like rain, a smile came across his face. He cuddled back into Sharon, who was sleeping heavily. Little did Alan know, but the windows that had just been put in were his own.

The next morning as Sharon arose out of bed, she opened the curtains. "What the fuck!!" said Sharon as Alan started to stir. "Alan!!" she shouted. "Our fucking window, it's been smashed!"

Alan shot out of bed like a bolt of lightning. "What the fuck?" said Alan. "What the fuck!!"

Sharon opened the living room curtains, the spare bedroom and the kitchen blinds. What the fuck?" Sharon started sobbing. "The whole fucking house is the same!!" she bawled.

Alan was furious. He effectively paid for his own windows to be done. Putting on his clothes, he angrily grabbed his car keys. "Fucking wankers!" he shouted, skidding down the stairs. "The dirty, stupid motherfuckers." He was in red mist. Grabbing the machete at the front door, he climbed into his car in full red rage, heading for Terry's home, speeding out of the street like a bat out of hell with absolutely no concern for pedestrians. Alan was seething and baiting for blood, cursing and swearing all the way to the Ridges.

Alan pulled up at Terry's house, beating on the door. Terry looked out the window.

"What's up, Alan?" said Terry, still half asleep.

Alan asked him to come downstairs.

"Only if you calm down, mate. I would like to know what this is about, fella," said Terry. "I will let you in. I want no kick-offs. I haven't a fucking clue what is going on, I am just out of bed. I want your promise, no kick-offs at my house," said Terry, alarmed by the very angry man standing at his door.

"Ok, no kick-offs," said Alan. "We talk."

Terry came down the stairs and let him in.

"What's up? I am not doing that thing until tonight, mate. Too many coppers about yesterday," said Terry.

"So it wasn't you?" said Alan.

"Wasn't me, what?" said Terry.

Alan sat down in Terry's kitchen.

"Do you want a cuppa?" said a concerned Terry.

"Yeah," said Alan. "Some fuckers put my windows in last night. All of them," said Alan, trying to calm down.

Terry passed him the cuppa. "Fuck!!" said Terry. "Well it wasn't me, mate!" explained Terry.

Again, Alan looked at Terry savagely. "For your sake, I hope not. I dig something up, some fucker gets a bullet. I am telling you."

Terry looked back at Alan, terrified. "Look, Alan, I swear it wasn't me. I swear on my mother it wasn't me, fella. You got this wrong," pleaded Terry.

Alan drank his cuppa and stood up. "Ok, I will check my CCTV and get to the bottom of this." Walking out the door, he turned his head to a terrified Terry. "I will be in touch," he said as he walked to his car

Alan headed back to his home, still furious but more controlled, rattling through his brain. Who should he pay a visit to? Who could the people be? Everything was playing in his mind. Someone was going to get clipped. Alan's bad side, his days as the trigger man all too vivid, all too real, coming back like it never left him. Hidden in his darkest corner for so many years, just waiting to be unleashed once again. His dark side, he remembers well. His sadistic nature, its ugliness back with a vengeance. He remembers the days when he dragged victims across a field holding a sawn-off at the back of their head, doing the bidding for the twenty-stone psychopath. How his victims pissed and shit themselves, their last gasps of air, the crude way their eyes bulged as their final breath would be drawn before he twisted the wire around their neck. How some of his victims pleaded for mercy before his knife slit their throat or the shotgun blew their head off. Their faces gazing into the hole prepared crudely; their final resting place. No ceremonies, no last farewells. An unknown grave with a cold-hearted killer that showed no remorse. Their executioner and their gravedigger, who only wanted to get it over and done with so he could go home.

This was Alan. This was who Alan was and people who knew Alan knew of his reputation. If you fucked with Alan, the Grim Reaper himself paid a visit. Your days were numbered.

Alan certainly wasn't the man people toyed with and certainly was not the kind of person you wronged. Somebody was going to get done, clipped, dealt with. Question was – who, where, and when?

Alan drove into his street. Looking at his windows, he started getting angry again. Looking at his neighbour's upstairs flat, tightening his grip on the steering wheel, Alan calmly exited his vehicle and walked upstairs into his home. Seething, he comforted his wife, Sharon, sat in the living room, eyes puffed out through crying.

Alan walked into the kitchen and put the kettle on. Picking up the phone, he dialled his cousin, a glazier, to come and replace the windows. He then phoned some of his mates as well.

"A simple twenty minutes. Yeah, and see you then with that."

Alan sat down and spoke to his wife softly. "Darling, I am going to do something soon. Our house will not get touched ever again. I guarantee, after today, whoever it was that done this will be either on the run or dead. I love you, Sharon." Alan grabbed her hands and kissed her, looking into her eyes. Alan walked back into the kitchen and made a cup of tea for himself and Sharon. "Once I finish this I am going kicking doors in."

He could hear the sniggering coming from next door; the steam started to build up around his neck. "And that's first port of fucking call," said Alan

The car honked its horn outside. Alan kissed Sharon, telling her Albert was coming to replace the windows. Walking down the stairs, he pointed at the driver. "Stay there." Two others climbed out of the car and walked towards the neighbours' door. A swift kick and their door caved in.

Alan ran up the stairs, full adrenalin mode. Seeing pots of paint, he grabbed them. Entering their living room, the neighbours turned white at the maniac now inside their home.

"Now, you cunts! Now you find out just what I am."

Throwing paint all over their living room, Alan was on full form, slapping them around, smashing their home to pieces. "You're not laughing now, are you? You stupid cunts." Grabbing the male of the house, he started to gouge and punch his face in. "Got anything to say, have you? Have you?" said Alan, getting increasingly sadistic as the minutes rolled on. "Now! Today, you are moving, getting out of this street. Understand?" said Alan.

One of Alan's mates threw a chair at their window as the three scumbags curled up, terrified.

"You go to the fucking law and I swear you and your friends will be tortured." Alan kicked the main instigator in the face a couple of times. His girlfriend started opening her mouth and was quickly smacked in the face. "Understand this. If I find out it was you that put out or had anything to do with my windows, you better emigrate. Do you fucking understand?" stated Alan, swiftly kicking the main instigator in the face. "Do! You! Understand!!" shouted Alan.

"Yes, yessss. Please, pleeeaaase," pleaded the mouthpiece.

*

Davy sat in his car, laughing to himself. He had just received a phone call from Jimmy about Alan's window situation. Terry was running around Shields like a headless chicken, explaining to everyone it wasn't anything to do with him. Davy laughed his head off at how Alan had actually paid for his own windows and the paint thrown around the neighbours' living room topped it off completely. *What the hell?* thought Davy, in uncontrolled laughter. *Why didn't Alan just do the paint thing in the first place?* thought Davy, bursting out in fits of laughter.

Once again, another story, another day in Tyneside.

68

Greed and Stupidity

Jack and JJ sat in Jack's living room. A Henry of cocaine lay on the table; two huge lines had been made. JJ snorted back; he had been on one (partying) all night. "A much-needed pick-me-up," said JJ as the coke took effect. "You know, I could start flogging this again," said JJ. "From the ice cream van. I made money the last time."

"JJ, yeah, but if we do it this time it's our operation, nobody else's," said Jack, rolling up his twenty ready to snort his line. "We have the contacts from Liverpool and Manchester, and all the money comes to us. Cut out the middle men as they say." Jack slugged back his vodka and orange and continued. "But we do not tell Davy or any of the others, otherwise they will want a percentage."

JJ raised his glass. "To our business deal, then," stroking his bank card on the table top, making a couple more lines.

JJ sat in Mr Whippy (the van), the same old set-up as before; a Henry in his van and a couple of wraps ready to sell to punters. Word soon got around he was back in business; their little enterprise was starting off on a good footing. Jack, true to his word was making regular runs to Liverpool and Manchester and not before long they were making a small fortune.

JJ would use his basher phone and get gear dropped off when he ran short of supply. JJ wasn't taking any chances this time around, however, remembering the last time he was carved up. He was more interested in regulars, people he knew, and was suspicious of those he didn't know. But what JJ didn't know and didn't realise was that he was being watched, just as Davy predicted the year before. The coppers had marked Mr Whippy and just as Davy advised JJ, it was a lame duck.

All the time JJ was dealing, photographs were being taken. Pictures of Jack, pictures of the punters, pictures of JJ. The police were gathering evidence and unbeknown to JJ, he was about to get busted. And the reality of it all was, they had enough evidence to put JJ and Jack away for a very long time.

It was a Saturday afternoon. JJ sat in the car park of Seaton Sluice. Mr Whippy was selling ice cream and gear to the punters. Pulling up, asking for a special cone, an unmarked van sat fifty yards from him. He was unaware there was a sting operation taking place.

A man and woman sat in the front seat dressed in plain clothes, reading a newspaper. The man spoke into his radio to the other two unmarked cars parked not too far away. A traffic copper sat on the Blyth roundabout and another on the Holywell Dene roundabout.

Jacks VW roared up the Beehive Road, unaware of the sting. He slowed down as he saw the traffic copper parked near the pub. Indicating left, he headed towards JJ who was waiting for a drop. Two punters climbed out of their car and approached Mr Whippy, also unaware that they too, were on the police radar. Regular coke-heads, JJ knew their faces.

As Jack pulled into the car park, he climbed out. Approaching, he walked to the side door and opened it, handing JJ the package. JJ wore surgical gloves as he handled the package before he placed it on the bench inside the ice cream van.

"Two specials," said a punter.

JJ grabbed two cones. He placed the plastic bags containing a gram in each of their hands. As he handed the ice creams to the two punters, the police screamed in. The van's doors burst open and police raced out, pinning Jack to the ground. The two punters were quickly arrested.

Before JJ knew it, he was being read his rights as the copper arrogantly stormed inside JJ's van, finding the drop, cocaine and money. "Ohh, you're not going to talk your way out of this one, Mr Whippy," said the policeman, sneering at JJ.

JJ put his head to the floor, turning away, saying nothing.

It wasn't long until the word on the street got around. Jack and JJ had been busted. Davy sat in his house, disappointed and annoyed that JJ and Jack could do something so stupid. He phoned Jimmy and Luke, asking for a meeting. *If this goes down the wrong way everyone is going to be put in the spotlight, and people could be going to jail if certain evidence can be linked back to them or any other activities,* thought Davy. "Fuck!! Fuck!!" cursed Davy.

What was more worrying for Davy – what if the police do have enough evidence on Jack and JJ? They might offer them a deal, play one against the other to extract more information. "The coppers are devious bastards," said Davy, as he thought out loud. "Whatever the case, all operations cease as from today. All gear and other items get buried; money as well." Davy was fully expecting his door to get caved in and wasn't taking any chances if that event should happen. Butterflies in his stomach began – a clear indication his nerves were shot to shit.

JJ sat in the police holding cell awaiting questioning when the duty officer opened the door. "Come with me," she indicated as JJ was led to the interview room.

Two CID sat at the table along with the duty solicitor. As he was led into the room the fat copper that sneered at him sat at the table. Items lay on the table; the cocaine, the basher phone, and the money in evidence bags.

"Looks like you have been a busy boy."

JJ looked at the coppers and said, "No comment."

"Ok, this interview starts." Clicking the tape recorder, reading out the charge, stating their names and the prisoner's name, the interview began.

All the way through the interview JJ replied, "No comment."

The officers showed JJ the photos, the dates, the times, everything and all JJ said was, "No comment."

The fat policeman started getting agitated. Smiling at JJ, he looked directly at him. "You can 'no comment' this as much as you like. Evidence is here right in front of you. You're looking at time, sunshine," said the policeman.

"What!! All I see is a bloke selling ice cream from an ice cream van," said JJ. "And all you got was three grams – a Henry – my personal shit. So there's not much evidence, as I see... So no comment," said JJ to two sneering policemen.

The policeman looked at JJ. "Yes, three grams, I agree, was found in your van," explained the policeman. Then he pulled out two wraps. "These were on both punters." The officer described the items shown. "And guess what? We have photos of you selling these ice creams."

JJ sat, silent.

"So from where I sit with this evidence it looks like I have caught you red-handed," said the policeman.

"Prove it. They both bought ice creams. Did you see me handing the pair of them coke? No!! So no comment," said JJ.

The police looked at each other, agitated. Their interrogation techniques were futile against JJ. They called the interview to an end and switched off the machine.

JJ was taken to the desk sergeant, where his bail conditions were set. "Do you plead guilty or not guilty to the following charges?" The charge was read out. "Intent to supply a class A drug to supply the North East."

JJ looked at the sergeant. "Not guilty," was his answer.

"Bail has been set and you will answer bail in four weeks' time, and you will be set to stand before the magistrate."

With that, JJ was given his personal belongings and let out of the station. JJ ordered a taxi to take him home; he didn't know whether Jack or the other two were out of the police station as well. JJ's taxi arrived – it was Davy. stone-faced.

"Get in," said Davy, driving off. "Right, what the fuck did I tell you?" said Davy.

JJ feared Davy's wrath more than the police. "Sorry, mate. I messed up," said JJ.

"I just picked Jack up an hour ago. Funny thing, he said the fucking same," said Davy.

"They got my phone. I said nothing, honest," said JJ.

"Well you can't be trusted, that's for sure. In my book you messed up big time. I told you not to sell from the van. I am expecting a visit now, thanks to this. The van was in my fucking name. Cheers, mate. You certainly opened a can of worms on this one," explained Davy.

JJ looked at Davy. "Sorry, mate. I really did mess up this time and I fully expect to take whatever punishment they give me like a man. Look, for what it's worth nobody's names were mentioned," said JJ.

Davy looked at JJ. "I now have to straighten this out before a real can of worms gets opened."

Pulling up outside JJ's house, "I will be in contact once your solicitor sends your depths. I will be curious what was said. Until then, say nothing to anyone," said Davy. "Just keep working the van once you get it back. Only, I repeat, only ice creams," said Davy.

JJ exited the vehicle as Davy drove off. JJ walked up his path, thinking hard. "Shit!" he muttered to himself as he went through his door.

Jack sat in his flat. He was to answer bail in six weeks; released on bail, suspicion of supplying a class A drug. The police couldn't find anything on him at the time of his arrest, nor did they have any photographic evidence of him handling cocaine. They did, however, have photos of him visiting Mr Whippy on numerous occasions. His reply to that was, "I like ice cream and he's my mate."

They could only presume Jack was supplying Mr Whippy. They took his basher phone; that was all they had. JJ's number minus the name was on there. Jack needed to see JJ. He needed to know what was said. As for the other two punters, Jack didn't have a clue what line of questioning they had been asked. They wouldn't know anyway. Jack was adamant the police didn't have enough evidence to make a conviction, but that still didn't change the fact JJ was caught supplying. It all hung in the balance. If they get to JJ, would JJ squeal to cop? A plea? Jack became very suspicious of that very possibility. He was very sure that others would want to have a word about what happened, and he was also well aware of the punishment the very individuals would administer if any of them were to be linked with the events that took place. He only could presume JJ said absolutely nothing. Otherwise, he and many more would be charged.

"What a fucking mess," said Jack, putting his head in his hands.

Davy went to see Jimmy. The warm evening provided perfect garden lounging.

"How's it gan?" said Jimmy.

"Fine. Fine, buddy."

Davy popped the top of his beer bottle and walked over to Jimmy's fish pond.

"I have seen the both of them," said Davy, indicating Jack and JJ. "What a mess." Speaking in code, Davy explained, "All the gear's underground (hidden)."

"We had better watch now," said Jimmy. "There might be surveillance teams watching us all now."

"Exactly," said Davy, taking a swig of his bottle. "Do you want some?" said Davy, indicating his Henry (three grams of cocaine) on the kitchen bench.

"Yeah."

Davy went in and prepared two lines as Jimmy walked in. Five minutes after, Davy handed him the note. "So Mr Whippy's been pinched (arrested) good and proper," said Jimmy.

"Something doesn't fucking add up here," said Davy. "He was two days in the slammer and he's now out on fucking bail. I remember when he was arrested they threw him on remand straight away. Someone's opening their mouth. Has to be," said Davy.

"Or the police are using him as bait," said Jimmy.

"Or, and you might think this is crazy, has Nancy boy (slang for gay) been opening his mouth?" said Davy, referring to Karl, the queer who murdered his boyfriend. "He went to London, Liverpool, and Manchester. He also dropped at JJ's van, remember? It's been a year since he was carted off," said Davy.

"You know what? Maybe you're right on this," said Jimmy. "If this is true the police will know more than what we are presuming, but then it might not be. We don't know. It could be a number of things. The facts are, JJ shouldn't have started dealing again from that van, especially when he was told the van was no longer viable," said Davy.

"Well everything stops now until this shit-storm draws to an end," said Jimmy, meaning all activities related to their line of business. Davy nodded in full agreement.

JJ contacted Davy. His depths (police statement) came through and he wanted to clear things up. Next week he was due up in court – a not guilty plea was his course of action. However, he was being advised by his solicitor to switch to guilty. But after talking to Jack he was told go not guilty. "The wankers are in the coppers' pockets. A guilty plea would mean you actually are admitting to supplying the North East. Be careful."

JJ wasn't stupid. He knew the dance. After telling the solicitor to basically fuck off – "It's a not guilty plea, understand?" – he felt pretty confident he would have the charge reduced to mere possession and personal use. It wasn't as if he was caught with twenty wraps.

Davy arranged for JJ to be picked up as a fare. He was still pretty suspicious that he could be being watched and was taking absolutely no chances. JJ heard Davy honk his horn outside. Putting his depths (police statement) into his jacket, he headed off out to Davy's car.

As he boarded, Davy switched on his meter and pulled off. Two men sat in a blue car just up JJ's street, Davy noticed them as he came in. Coppers. Their body warmers and radios were distinctly visible. "You see, they're watching us," said Davy.

JJ asked if he could spark up a cigarette.

"Yeah, why not?" said Davy, pulling out of Ridley Avenue, heading towards the A19. "We're going to Alnwick North so I can get to read these depths. They're all there, aren't they?" said Davy.

JJ confirmed.

Davy handed him a rock. "Get a CD case and do the honours," said Davy.

JJ crushed the rock and put it on a fifty pence piece, and snorted it, doing one for Davy, who snorted his, watching in the rear-view mirror, making sure he wasn't being tailed.

"We're going to my caravan. We can do some more there," said Davy, turning on the radio.

"Luke's collar's been felt and Jack was dragged back into the station," said Davy. "Some fucker's been opening their cake hole," said Davy. "The flat in Percy Main was raided also. Something tells me that the people getting targeted are all to do with the gambling den that used to be set up there."

JJ looked in surprise. "That Golf Jack won; the police were particularly interested in that cunt. The ice cream van and Luke sealed it for me. I think the faggot's been talking," said Davy.

"The one that done in his boyfriend?" said JJ.

"Yeah, that fucking one," said Davy.

"But if that be the case, why haven't the police come to you?" said JJ.

"Because I was good to them. They got a car and money off me. I treated them with a little respect. That's all I can think. Who knows? I might be fucking next. Who knows? But I am surmising this be the case," explained Davy. "He was sentenced to twenty-five years, what's he got to lose?" said Davy.

JJ looked out of the window. "You know what?" he muttered. "You could be right."

The men drove to Davy's caravan on the outskirts of Warkworth – a secluded campsite.

Davy drove across the ford in order to get to it. Parking up the taxi, the men went into the caravan. Davy scrutinised the depths (police statement), reading carefully all the words that were said. He told JJ to knock a couple of big lines up and grab two beers from the fridge.

"So you're going not guilty," said Davy.

"Yep," said JJ, handing Davy his beer.

"They will possibly drop to a less serious charge," said Davy, snorting his line. "I mean this, JJ. No more dealing from that van. A lot of people are worried and when they get worried things happen," said Davy.

"I won't. I promise you that, from now on," said JJ.

Davy looked at JJ. "Second chances in my world are rare. You both got greedy and stupid at the same time. It doesn't fucking happen ever again," said Davy. "Now we have to be more alert. If the gay fella is opening his mouth in the nick (jail), we could all be under surveillance, including our business interests, and that little homo bastard always had a way of sticking his fucking nose in places he shouldn't have," explained Davy, making another line.

Lights filled the field's entrance. Davy told JJ, "Get another two beers for Jimmy and Jack."

Their car pulled up outside and the doors slammed shut. JJ hadn't seen Jack since the arrest.

"It will be good. You two get to talk, get your stories straight. Just as Jimmy entered the caravan, followed by Jack, "Coppers were in his street," said Jimmy. "Unmarked car."

"Snap!!" said JJ. "There was an unmarked copper car in his street as well."

"Somebody is definitely squawking (talking)," said Jimmy.

"It's the queer, I am telling you," said Davy.

Jack and JJ looked at Davy and Jimmy. "Look, fellas, we fucked up. We feel a bit shit for not cutting you in on our little enterprise," said Jack. "I have half a block (half a kilo) stashed. Do you want in? It's our way of saying we are fucking sorry, like," said Jack, apologising and offering an olive branch.

Davy looked at Jimmy. "Well it takes a man in my book to offer such a lucrative deal and to come out with honesty. That deserves another fat line and a thank you." He raised his beer bottle. Jimmy agreed to let the past be buried.

"What did they do with your car?" said JJ, directing the conversation towards Jack.

"Fuck all. They asked me how I obtained it. I showed them the papers and told them to fuck off. I won the car fair and square. Then they questioned me on my flat. I told them winnings as well. I have all the fucking slips, receipts, everything in my life is legit. They crawled into my arsehole, the wankers," said Jack. "I am answering bail. They haven't charged me but they have you, JJ. Remember that, bud," said Jack.

Davy reminisced about the time he was in the Compass Club and the police raided the place. The Compass Club was a nightclub at the top of South Parade, Whitley Bay. One night Davy was drinking in the place along with half the Ridges when the police raided the place. He remembers the policeman lining everyone up at the bar and telling them to empty their pockets. Davy must have had about three grand on him and the lining inside his hat was stuffed with gear (E and speed). The policeman ordered Davy to remove his hat. As instructed, Davy did so, cool as a cucumber. He lay it on the bar. The policeman searched Davy from top to toe but he forgot to check the hat. He remembered the policeman questioned him, "That's a lot of money for a young lad to have."

Davy replied, "That's a lot of money because I work hard, mate."

The police officer, frustrated as he found nothing, cursed as he left the club.

Davy put his hat back on, picked up his money and started selling again.

"The art's in how you respond," Davy said to JJ.

69

A Bitter Fruit

—————————————————

Karl Pell lay on his bed, his one-bedroom Hilton, sitting in Durham Jail. Given twenty-five years to life, being used as a toilet by every lag (prisoner) on his wing. Brutal, rough, forced penetration; his arsehole bled many nights. He cried, dreading the next day. He was in prison for the wrong reasons, set up by some sick bastards. Gary was constantly on his mind. Revenge, hatred towards the men he believed put him there.

Karl was a bitter fruit. The card game, the trips to London, Liverpool, and Manchester. The laughing and jokes made at his expense and the most hated of all, Mr Whippy; how he felt humiliated and tormented by the men that he met all because the love of his life got himself in debt to a loan shark. A cruel, sadistic, evil individual who forced his man to take trips and become a mule in order to pay off his debt.

Karl lay in his bed, ignoring the shouts and abuse directed at him from the other cells on his wing. Thinking of Gary, Karl wept.

Someone shouted, "Grass! You fucking little faggot grass!"

Karl curled up in a ball, aware he was going to be a target for many in the prison. He had been talking to the authorities; a cardinal sin among the criminal fraternity. Karl was a marked man. His days were numbered. He needed to speak to someone and get segregated or he was going to get hurt or even worse, killed. His only protection in jail at the moment was a bull queer lifer who passed him around like a piece of meat.

How the fuck did they find out I opened my mouth about them? Karl thought.

231

Luke knew. Luke knew everything. A phone call and an ounce of cocaine promised Luke could reach into any jail. It was even easier to get someone taken care of in jail than outside in the world. Karl didn't take into account he was dealing with criminals, and one thing prison is full of, is criminals. Many knew the villains that Karl was so eager to blab about.

"Grass! Grass!! Grass!! Grass!!" The noise was getting louder. Karl buried his head in his pillow and sobbed.

Big Darren Duck shouted from his cell, "Don't you take any notice of them. As long as I am in here, you're my bitch. See you tomorrow."

70

The Fruit and Veg Heist

Way back in 1987, when Jingling Geordies was in full flight, Davy recalls the day two known toe rags used Jinglers as a watering hole. Two of the most stupid criminals that North Shields ever produced – Edd and Paul. They stole a lorry; not full of televisions, clothes, nor anything else worth any value. They stole a lorry full of fruit and veg.

Davy laughed at the memory. Of all the fucking things to steal. Pinky and Perky (referring to two comical pigs) he fondly nicknamed Edd and Paul, they stole a fucking fruit and veg lorry. How fucking fantastically stupid was that?

Davy peeled his banana as he sat in his taxi. Many times Davy encountered similar stupidity, like the time he came across two burglars who had just got out of jail. They broke into a shop using a sky light to actually find they were locked in. The police simply opened the door and arrested the stupid fuckers. They both got six months to reflect on that error.

Or the time the policeman walked past a shop on Bedford Street to see a commercial burglar standing in the window pretending to be a fucking mannequin. Stupidity at its highest level.

Davy gazed at the sky, reflecting on his memories. The door opened – it was JJ. "Two hundred hours' community service and a two hundred pound fine. "The magistrate said it was possession, and because it was an ice cream fucking van they made an example of me as I served kids. She gave me a stern telling off, saying if that had somehow dropped in a cornet and it was given to a kid, I would be in Durham. Bastards. The health and safety at work fucking act. Fucking wankers," said JJ.

Davy started the car and drove back to Jimmy's. "Never mind, lesson learned," said Davy, laughing. "So you will be cutting grass for the next few months? At least you get to go to the meadows on set days," laughed Davy as he drove. "Anyway, get these done," said Davy, pulling a gram from his pocket. He handed it to JJ. "At least you don't get put on my stupidity wall of fame."

JJ looked puzzled. Davy looked back. "It was just something I was thinking before you came out," explained Davy with a smirk.

"It all has to come to an end," said Jimmy.

Jack took a swig from his bottle.

"It was a close shave, you know. Fortunately they could only get JJ on a possession, but it could have been far worse," said Jimmy.

Just then, the door opened.

"Hello," echoed in the passageway of the old Edwardian house. It was Davy and JJ.

"How's it going?" said Jimmy. "Well?" he asked with a smirk. Jimmy looked at JJ. "Well, what was the verdict?"

Jack smirked as well.

JJ explained he was going on community service. He broke health and safety laws. Jimmy was trying to keep a straight face. "You're serving the public whilst you have an illegal substance in your van which could have contaminated the products you sold," said Jimmy in amusement.

"Having an addiction like that should have been kept well away from dairy products," said Davy, bursting out laughing. Jimmy handed Davy and JJ a bottle each.

"Funny though," said Jack, laughing.

71

A Breakdown of Morals

Arthur Smith dabbled in the drug world. He wasn't a mainstream dealer shifting copious amounts, but he was a dealer all said and done. Others thought differently. A small amount was enough to allow him to keep his head above water. He used his ill-gotten gains to enhance his life. Starting up his small gardening business, wheeling and dealing in second-hand cars; he was always looking for legitimate business opportunities. His idea of selling cocaine was a pathway to providing a legitimate life. He never thought he would attract the attention of those that didn't see his interests beneficial to theirs.

Making a cup of coffee, he could hear the pitter patter of small feet upstairs. Two small bowls were readied on the kitchen bench and a selection of cereal with the quart of milk stood in the usual place. A morning ritual for Arthur. Breakfast, wash, then the school run – a daily occurrence on weekdays in Arthur's household.

Arthur didn't know it yet but the events that were to take place that day, were to send shockwaves throughout the criminal world and attract mainstream media coverage.

A power vacuum was taking place in Tyneside. Scrupulous individuals were plotting and a turf war was beginning to unfold. Controlling the drug world and controlling the dealers was top of their agenda, and the morals and respecting of certain boundaries were not the qualities these individuals respected. Tyneside and Tyneside's criminals were changing. The gentleman gangster was a thing of the past. No longer was the victim approached and beaten up in a secluded place; no longer was the victim given the opportunity to face his would-be opponents like a real man. Their idea of squeezing a man was to threaten his family, holding a gun to a man's head whilst his baby sucked its dummy in his arms. Respect? Anyone saying they have respect and morals whilst they participate in activities like what has been described was in complete denial, and were no more decent than the house burglar or smack-head (drug addict). At the bottom of the pile in many people's eyes.

Arthur was a tough cookie (hard man). He had been approached two weeks beforehand by the very people who were plotting his demise. They wanted eight grand (taxation) and complete control of his business interests. One had walked past one of his cars he was selling and deliberately keyed it, which ended with Arthur battering two of the men. They ran down the street near his parking lot, leaving their car still running. Arthur phoned their mates and told them, "Come and get this piece of shit away from my car lot."

He keyed their car letting, them know he was no muppet. They eventually sent a woman to collect the car. "Fucking cowards!!" said Arthur as she collected their car.

Arthur waited for his little daughters to finish their breakfast. "Now go upstairs, get washed, and your uniform is hanging in the closet," said Arthur. The girls quietly went up the stairs.

Arthur's phone buzzed – another text. He picked up the phone. Another anonymous threat; he had been receiving threats on a daily basis.

'You're going to get it', 'your house is getting it', 'your bairns aren't going to have a father'. The same old bullshit. Arthur read out the newest addition – 'fucking prick watch what happens!!!!!'

"Ohh dear," said Arthur. As he turned around, a little girl stood in the doorway dressed for school. Her little sister followed shortly after her. "Right, you two. Let's go," said Arthur, walking towards the coat hanger. He grabbed their coats.

The doorbell rang as the girls started putting on their coats. Arthur went to answer it. The silhouette looked like the postman. "Must be a parcel," said Arthur as he opened the door, and then it happened. The man on the other side, at point blank range, shot Arthur's knees. The shotgun blast echoed through Arthur's house twice.

His wife shot out of bed, frantically running down the stairs. Arthur lay in the doorway as the girls screamed. A piece of shot had hit the youngest girl's arm. Blood soaked her coat. Arthur lay on the floor, shouting as the motorbike roared off in the distance.

The little girl collapsed from shock, being scooped up by her mother, stemming the blood that oozed from her arm. As for Arthur, he started shouting in pain, "Are my girls OK! Are my girls OK!" over and over again.

There was a media frenzy the police. Forensics were all over Arthur's house. A very bad situation for everyone. Davy was disgusted by the events that took place. "They shot him and hurt a child. Fucking disgusting!" said Davy.

"Apparently the kid could lose her fucking arm," said Jimmy.

"If this is the new I feel our days of doing this business will soon be over. A man's home, on his fucking doorstep, and his kids get hurt in the process," said Luke.

"What was their response?" said Davy, talking to Luke about the perpetrators.

"They just said he had it coming," said Luke.

"I am sorry. I do not wish to know them daft cunts anymore," said Davy.

"They chose the coward's way. Why not go to his fucking car lot and do him there?" said Jimmy.

"Nah!! They have categorically gone right down in my book. Fuck them; sly, horrible cunts. Any one of us could fall victim to these muppets now they have opened a can of worms." Davy paused. "I hope to fucking God that little girl doesn't lose her arm, for their sake. If I was Arthur I would be plotting right now and he's not the fucking only one that will be plotting a revenge attack. If I were you, Luke, I would distance myself from the likes of them," said Davy.

Luke looked at Davy. "I have, mate. I have."

"So what are we going to do?" said Jimmy, pouring three whiskies.

Dave blew a sigh. "For a start we have to go and see Arthur and hold out our olive branch. Secondly, we are going to have to seriously stop selling this shit. This world's getting too fucking violent for me. Going to a man's home certainly has made me think about a total recalculation on my business activities. That's just my opinion. Feel free to add anything I left out," said Davy.

The weeks that followed became worse. People were being dragged in by the police and questioned. The little girl didn't lose her arm, thankfully, but Arthur was wanting revenge. His car lot was fire bombed and his stock was destroyed. The criminal gang responsible were becoming relentless. A tit-for-tat policy was adopted with people turning up at A&E covered in blood, either by foot or by ambulance.

A car was blown up on a drive of one of the known dealers, shots were heard in Wallsend, a shop was burned out in Whitley, and this was just the tip of the iceberg.

If things keep going on like this some poor fucker's going to wind up dead, thought Davy.

Davy had ceased all activities. He didn't want to attract attention of any kind. With a feud going on the last thing he needed was to be fingered as a suspect in any of the shit that was taking place, especially with weight on him. Plus, he was seriously considering wrapping in villainy. He had made his money and the new crews emerging throughout Tyneside were the kind of people Davy considered untrustworthy. He certainly had no intention of having any dealing with people who hurt kids. The old-school rules were truly dead.

Davy looked at his plotter. Accepting the job, he drove off, heading up the street, effectively heading out of a life that once consumed him.

THE END

Cocaine/coke/Charlie

The root of all evil. Men kill for it, homes are destroyed by it, and villains get rich from it.

Well, we come to the end of this book; the scams, racketeering, theft, wheeling and dealing, the criminality, the betrayal, the greed, and the corruption. North Shields certainly had a rich history of all of the above. A community of vagabonds, cut-throats, and thieves. A town unique in every sense.

Everybody has a story to tell; everybody has a tale to yarn. It doesn't matter what town you come from in the United Kingdom, there's always a villain somewhere. But some towns have more than one villain, and North Shields had plenty of characters who deserved the title of villain.

I have watched my hometown transform over the past twenty years; public houses, nightclubs, social clubs, all started to disappear, with the loss of industries and a smoking ban in public houses introduced by a Labour government in the 00s. You walk along Saville Street or up Bedford Street these days and you're confronted with second-hand shops, cafes, and charity shops. The days of vibrant pubs have well and truly disappeared. The people who frequented those establishments all worked in our factories on Norham Road, the textile factories on Lawson Street, the ship repair yards, the fishing industry, and the engineering yards dotted all over our towns.

The north-east of Britain was once alive. Going out on a Saturday night was religion to many socialites. You made friends, sorted disagreements, dated your girlfriends, found love from socially interacting. With the bars, clubs, and pubs, our seaside towns catered for all generations, from bingo halls to fun fairs. Growing up in Tyneside during this era had its advantages; kids were tough then, and most importantly they were workers. Being workers and earning a wage was instilled into them from an early age. Our parents disciplined us, along with our teachers and the police. I dread to see Britain fifty years from now. I just pray Britain will heal itself and recover our values – respect, being the main value.

The drugs trade and the criminal entrepreneurs also did no favours for the vibrant club and pub industry. The idiots and their friends made it virtually impossible for trade to flourish in the already struggling 1990s and early 00s. People started to fear going out, afraid of the aggro and thugs that destroyed business through stupidity and arrogance within North Shields. Especially waiting for a taxi. For instance, in the once bustling Tynemouth people actually feared standing in the queue. The author recalls a few occasions where innocent revellers were deliberately targeted and beaten up by the mob. They kicked and beat people on a regular basis. Always a crowd of them, never one-on-one. The coward's way was always their preferred method.

The author meets some of them today on the street. They have nothing to show for a life of crime. Fresh out of jail, an addiction, not a pot to piss in, homeless and hated by those who remember them.

There's an old saying in this world: what goes around comes around.

The author's verdict: crime doesn't pay, because in the long run you eventually lose something. Freedom, family, friendship, and respect. But the old-school villains, they will always have respect. They did things in an organised manner and were respected for doing so.

You see we're born, born, born to be alive. Born to be alive.

Born to be alive.

Picture of the author with his baby daughter, Lexi.

Printed in Great Britain
by Amazon